Angus

Colin Edwards

For Chrissie, Angus and Duma

ISBN 978-1-0685281-0-1

Chapter 1

Mary

The Carpathian Mountains. Famed as the shadowy cradle of Stoker's Dracula, they arc north from Romania into Ukraine before plotting their spiralling form into Poland and Slovakia. The range casts a protective arm around Hungary, the gateway to Western Europe, as if God had pre-empted the political discord of His creation and expressed his concern five thousand feet high and some misty millions of years in advance.

Mary panted at the apex of her own mountain. It was barely fifty feet above the rickety timber home that she'd reclaimed from dereliction with months of drudging sweat. The calluses which twisted her fingers stood as high in testament to her as the mountains beyond stood to God Himself. The ache in her joints felt righteous as the squealing shriek advanced upon her. She grinned through the pain and waited until the breathless gaggle was almost upon her, before launching herself down the grassy slope with the giggling monsters at her back.

Mary tanked down the field. Her legs spewed widely on the uneven ground as she added her laughter to the pack. Zina was twelve and matched her pace with an easy grace. Hardly surprising - she had outgrown Mary by a full foot in the last year. The youngest, Hannah, was not so quick, and Mary scooped the six-year-old into her arms as they barrelled forward.

Hers was an eclectic brood. It had been fashioned from the remnants of Ceausescu's rancid state, and extracted from the orphanage which sat alongside Crisul River, just south of Oradea in north-west Romania. She'd been a child herself, when the doors had shut – a stout, dirty, frightened child. But she'd been the eldest.

Her straining lungs turned her face scarlet, and she coughed spit across Zina's face as she gasped for breath. 'Jesus Ma!'

Twenty feet from home, Mary's legs lost the race with her body. She tumbled gracelessly - a dumpy Laura Ingolls spinning down the hill toward that Little House. She heard the air plunge from her lungs - 'FOOF' - as the first of her followers slumped across her frame. Another followed, and another, until limbs and heads formed a cascade of screaming playmates. The clunky human softball took two rotations to stop, and each part gasped for breath as it separated, kneeling, sitting and finally lounging onto the soft grass.

Mary spat hay and plucked at her dress. A yellow stain stuck the fabric to her skin. 'Oh, shit!' she bellowed accurately, grinning at her children as they laughed.

It has been well documented that babies in Romanian orphanages did not cry. Each learned in its own time that no one would come. The sheer volume of inmates had become unmanageable due to Ceausescu's ban on contraception and abortion - and an austerity so severe that families were forced to abandon their children to the institutions or see them starve.

Orphanage employees who didn't hit the children were considered weak. Corporal punishment was encouraged to maintain control. The older children hit the younger ones. The staff hit everybody. Virtually all workers stole from the children's rations to supplement their own. The misbegotten suffered. Neglect was rife. Children were ignored, tied to their beds with their own clothing. Those who soiled their bedding were washed with their sheets, if they were washed at all.

Mary could not fight the system - that would take decades of education and reform. After Ceausescu's death, there'd been no system to fight. She hadn't been taught the arts of comfort and love. They were just within her. A year later she was known as 'Mother Mary'. Her name was given, and carried, without irony.

Mary contorted as she rose, protecting her hands from the stink on her dress while turning to each child to expose her disgust. 'Gross' she coughed through the smell and exaggerated her countenance with comedic intent, before priming to chase them home with the whiffing drapery held before her.

She didn't see the stranger emerge from the trees behind her. She didn't feel the pain from his blow, or see the stain on her dress turn red. Neither did she hear the laughter of her children die. She just wasn't.

He didn't even pause to hear their lament. It wasn't for them you see, but for God himself.

Chapter 2

Records

The Catholic Church has maintained records for over two thousand years, if you consider Saint Peter to be the first pope and his gospel the first record.

In pagan times, a Roman necropolis stood on Vatican Hill. When a great fire levelled much of Rome in AD 64, Emperor Nero took time off his fiddling to blame the new Christians for starting the blaze. He executed them by burning them at the stake, tearing them apart with wild beasts and crucifying them. Among those crucified was St. Peter, disciple of Jesus, leader of the apostles and the first bishop of Rome, who was supposedly buried in a shallow grave where the necropolis once stood.

By the fourth century and official recognition of the Christian religion in Rome, Emperor Constantine began construction of the original basilica - an early Christian church - atop the ancient burial ground. What was believed to be the tomb of St. Peter was at its centre. The present basilica was built a thousand years later at the same site, crowning St. Peter's suspected grave. If he is actually there, looking down upon the state of the world beneath the bluster of history, he must be turning in it.

The libraries of the Vatican have been in place in a form which would be recognisable to modern scholars since the 14th century, following the papacy's return to Rome after a brief sojourn to France orchestrated by their King Philip IV. As with any library, there are elements which are available to the general public, and elements which are reserved for more 'deserving' eyes.

I shall assume at this point that none of us wish to visit the complicated management structure of the Catholic Church and say instead that only the Pope himself has access to the whole of the library. Each of the two dozen or so leaders of the congregations, tribunals, secretariats and councils which make up the Curia are offered access to those pieces which are felt to be historically relevant to their roles. On rare occasions information can be shared with Cardinals or relevant others who are sworn to secrecy under threat of excommunication and eternal damnation.

After two millennia of collecting, the Vatican library is as extensive as one would expect. It has collected all manner of information, artifact and curio. Mostly, relics are bequeathed or offered voluntarily. But sometimes acquisition is deemed a necessity.

At many churches around the world there are relics celebrated for containing the blood of Jesus Christ - a thorn which bleeds on Good Friday is kept in a cathedral at Andria, Italy. There are often secular causes to explain away the miracles associated with such items. Where there are not, and public access is not sufficiently controlled to satisfy the demands of the hierarchy, the relics are inclined to disappear. A few such relics are considered overtly dangerous, 'though the rationale behind their threat is rarely discussed, even within the Curia itself. Whether this threat is to Catholicism, its followers, or to heaven itself, such items - whether they are books, or thorns, or cups, or sometimes even people – the church may deem it necessary to remove them from the world at large.

In these times of darkness, however - at least for one individual who seeks a shard of light within the shadows - such items may yet offer more than just a line in a Vatican inventory.

***

There are some days when the rain falls peacefully and gently, nourishing the Earth. On *this* day, the clouds burst open. God's creation could have washed away in the flood.

A handful of uniforms giggled as they splashed through El Retiro Park, just East of central Madrid. Underdressed for the monsoon, the schoolgirls raced for the warmth of the Sucre Tearoom.

One uniform paused, just for a moment, to glance at him, and watched as the drops recoiled from his form. He stood alone, frozen in the downpour. The blue of his coat had turned dark, and a thick, heavy load sagged at his shoulders. His head turned toward her, and she hurried after her companions, blinking the gathering raindrops from her eyes as she escaped his gaze.

Beneath the blue, his garb was black. All bar the white band at his throat. A canvas shoulder bag dragged at his collar. Lifetimes and fortunes jangled as he shifted his weight, and he knew that the damp would permeate, to cause irreparable damage. It didn't matter. They had all been tested and found wanting, and now swung at his side in heavy confirmation of his fears.

He stared up toward the monument – the Fuente del Angel Daido, or Fountain of the Fallen Angel. The monolith soared seven metres high, the figure at its apex depicting a winged angel restrained by serpents, denying even the hope of ascension. It is described within

UNESCO world heritage guides as the only prominent statue on the planet dedicated to the devil.

The torrent beat at the earth in tangible disdain - enough to send the world scurrying. The figure didn't scurry. He merely looked on, beyond the sculpture, and shrugged his coat to the floor in provocation of the rain.

If you are a follower of sixties pop culture, you may have seen a particular episode of the original Star Trek. Its premise is the guilt of a powerful alien who destroys a whole species with a thought. Imagine owning that level of might and the responsibility that sits alongside it. The unrelenting concentration needed to avoid the devastation that could be caused in an instant of anger, or frustration, or even imagination. Perhaps that's how God feels.

Conversely, imagine the level of rage it must take to consciously wipe out a whole civilisation - the anger that must be felt in the instant of the act. Now try to imagine feeling like that all the time. Maybe you'd stand out in the rain too, hoping that it would wash you away.

Of course, no amount of water can cleanse such hatred.

His thoughts were his own. Why would he even try to project them further? The world was already screaming its pain to the heavens to no avail, and he had learnt long ago that his words meant nothing to God. It needed something else, something bigger, to steal His attention.

In these days of worldwide discontent, the FBI will tell you that hate itself is not a crime. It is merely an 'added element' to an offence. It can, on occasion, motivate the courts to add time to a sentence. When this happens, the crime is referred to as a 'hate crime'. It is what motivates a man to kill two Muslims on a Portland train after shouting anti-Islamic slurs, and what prompts a bigot to spray 'nigger' on an NBA star's home.

The FBI don't feel that 'hate' is a sufficiently descriptive moniker, and seek to categorise such motivations, as if the depravity itself could be rationalised.

'Thrill seeking' hate is often driven by a childlike itch for excitement. Think bored or drunken young men marauding through neighbourhoods, mayhem on their minds. Often there is no real reason for their actions other than the thrill of the damage itself. Still, almost three quarters of thrill-seeking victims are hospitalised as a result of their attacker's random animosity.

Then there are 'defensive' hate crimes, where the attackers see themselves as defending their 'turf'. This turf can be a neighbourhood, workplace, religion or country. Whichever, aggressors justify their behaviour as necessary to protect their way of life against such heinous acts as a foreign family moving onto their street.

Retaliatory crimes are seen by their perpetrators as justifiable acts of revenge in response to crimes against themselves or their families. These 'avengers' target members of the racial, ethnic or religious group who they believe committed the original act, irrespective of whether their victims were personally involved. After 9/11, hate crimes against Arabs and Muslims in the US rose by one thousand six hundred percent.

Finally, 'mission' offenders are considered the rarest but deadliest of all. These crimes are committed by people who consider themselves 'crusaders', intent on total war against members of a rival race or religion. These individuals may write lengthy manifestos explaining their views, revel in websites steeped in hate speech, and target symbolically significant venues to seek maximum carnage. They are likely to believe that the systems of society are rigged against them and that this justifies their excessive violence against total innocents.

There is a fifth category, not recognised by the FBI. One where hate exists without reference to the trivialities of society. Such motivations sit beyond groups, individuals or even the realities of this world. This hatred is aimed directly at the heart of God.

He sought out a memory. One to warm him as his clothes grew heavy. So many of his wrongs had grown old, forgotten even by the victims, but he would keep trying. They, and the world, deserved that at least. The sky beat upon him, and the narrowing of his eyes betrayed his contempt.

'Mary.' he whispered, his lips curling.

He hoped that his act had wounded the Heavens, compelling them to notice. To notice him. Maybe even to notice the world again, and to reconsider its abandonment.

He picked up his coat, glancing once more at the monument, before turning to trudge through the rain, throwing up mud and filth with his footsteps.

Chapter 3

The Train

A fast train from Madrid to Rome takes around twenty-four hours, with a minimum of four changes.

Father Janus found his seat in the final carriage, centred as far from the doors as possible, and tossed his wet clothing into the space beside him. The damp drained from his coat, staining the upholstery. The rows of empty seats stood grey and black around him, guards for his isolation. There was no earthly reason for anyone to disturb him, or even to choose to seat themselves in his vicinity.

'Could I sit with you Father? I have some questions, if you wouldn't mind?' The Spanish was broken and clumsy – typically 'English' – and the question came from an adolescent, spotty and enthusiastic and still totally devoid of the world-weary sag that sits across the backs of the old. The phrase 'God botherer' could have been written for him.

Janus held the boy's eye, drawing him uncomfortably into his stare. Company was not on his agenda.

'God is a cunt. And an unadulterated liar. Now, does that answer your questions?'

'What ... sorry. *What*?'

Janus sat forward, his knees jutting toward the boy. They were thin and wiry through his cassock and fenced the route to further conversation. The damp from his coat continued to drip unapologetically across the seat next to him.

'Ever watched a Parliamentary debate, child? The constant spin, name calling and sheer refusal to actually *debate* the issues at hand? It's little wonder then that the popular press feels comfortable feeding the same bullshit to an apathetic public. And the point is, *they fall for it*. No-one *wants* an elitist government hell bent on re-creating the era of 'old money', or a cabinet with a casual disregard for everyone but themselves, but they still keep voting for it because their mighty red top tells them they should. The facts - including that their morning paper is owned and edited by the old money they blindly support - are irrelevant.

Now consider the nature of God. Omnipotent yet absent. Unchanging yet changed. Overflowing with the love and kindness of the ages but still happy to create evil, torment and misery as a test. And a test of what exactly? To see whether we're good enough for what? To receive His love? To spend eternity bowing and scraping at His feet? Well, I didn't buy that particular newspaper, and neither should you.'

The two stared. Janus won. The youth dropped his eyes and retreated, leaving the priest to fidget in his bag, contemplating the effects that his words would have for the shortest of instants, until his fingers found the leather binding and he placed his bible on the table in front of him.

The book was an original King James version 'with apocrypha', dated sixteen eleven. It was worth thousands but had been lifted from the Vatican archives by Janus as his 'everyday' companion. The 'old man' could spare him that, at least.

The apocrypha is a series of books which once sat between the Old and New testaments. It had been accepted into Catholicism as God's word until the sixteenth century, when Martin Luther translated the Latin text into German, stating that since the books were not found within Hebrew texts that they could not be considered canonical. For

Janus it was one more reminder that the unchanging, unquestionable version of God thrown down the throats of the uneducated was not to be trusted.

The smell from the pages was pungent, a heady mix of age and mildew – the aroma of degeneration from the fabric of the testaments. The spores invaded his nostrils, and he slammed the book shut as he sneezed, opening a tiny split in the fragile binding. He cursed, then smiled scornfully at his own reflex.

'Still can't get snot on the old man's words, Janus? Well, shame on you.'

The world outside barrelled past, drawing a moment's attention from the virgin crack. He exhaled, steamed the window, and considered re-reading *that* report. Its pages had crumpled as he'd punched it down to the base of the bag, screwing it into the fabric with such force that he'd heard the cotton binding pop. It hadn't changed the words within, and neither would reading them again. No. It could stay where it was, muggy and crushed under the haul of priceless artifacts.

He'd been curator of the Vatican archives for two decades now. It should have been an honour – a sacred trust bestowed by the Church of Rome. But it wasn't, at least not for him. They just didn't trust him with the public. You can't minister to the people without faith you see. Yes, he still had *belief*. In fact, he believed in God's existence more than he ever had. He just didn't trust Him anymore. He certainly didn't like Him, sitting nonchalantly in His Heaven as pointlessly narcissistic as the politicians he'd berated to the naïve little boy who'd invaded his peace. As for His son? Jesus Christ - sent by God to renew His father's relationship with humanity? Not according to *that* report.

He watched the world outside. Cameos of creation speeding by. Scene after scene of humanity's take on the world. Not a forest or plain or even an unadulterated mountain left to muddle the concrete vista. Barely even a field he thought, as the conductor disturbed his contemplations. 'Next stop Palermo,' he announced, and a distant memory wormed its way into Janus's thoughts.

Saint Rosalia. Janus had read about her in some seminary magazine. Saint Rosalia was a young girl who, in the eyes of the faithful, devoted herself wholly to God and lived as a hermit in a cave until her death in the year eleven sixty. Rosalia's body remained undisturbed until a plague struck Palermo in sixteen twenty-four, and residents began having visions of 'the little saint' buried somewhere within their community. Believing that God had identified the means for their salvation, they sent a tracker to find her bones, which were subsequently venerated through the streets of the town causing the plague to subside. Rosalia was granted her sainthood. Her cave became a place of worship and Sicilians prayed over her bones whenever hardship threatened. To this day they are considered relics of holy significance, and retained in a church nestled against the stony face of Mount Pellegrino despite the inconvenient report of William Buckland, a British geologist who in eighteen twenty-five was given permission to examine them, and determined that they derived from a goat.

'All goats' thought Janus as he patted his bag, but still opened his bible and began to read, until the motion and monotony enabled the exhaustion which follows rage to be followed by sleep.

Chapter 4
The Curia

On a warm but otherwise anonymous Wednesday morning in the Spring of nineteen ninety-four, the Curia of the Roman Catholic Church called an impromptu meeting of the church's highest representatives. The big wigs of Congregations, Tribunals and Secretariats - in fact all departments of the Curia. It was as terrifying as it was exhilarating for a young priest, freshly out of seminary school and bursting at the thought of the world. Janus. *Father* Janus, no less, was genuinely worried that he may pee himself.

Centuries of cardinals shuffled through the enormity of the Vatican meeting hall, ridiculously oversized for the event. Its volume reverberated with the snorts and groans of strained mobility, as if the air itself complained at this archetypal showing of church hierarchy. Eventually, the people settled, and the noise settled with them.

Viewed from above, the layout of Vatican Hall has been compared in design to the head of a snake. Completed in the nineteen seventies, it was constructed on land donated by the Knights of Columbus and straddles the boundary limits between Rome and Vatican City.

All eyes turned toward a single cardinal as he entered quietly and sat opposite the congregation of old men. Contrary to protocol, he was alone - granted unprecedented freedom of expression by the Pope himself - perhaps in hope, rather than expectation. He sat silently for several moments, greeting each corner of the room with a genuine smile before raising a hand to call for attention. No preliminary agenda had been circulated and several of the old men shifted uneasily at this lack of organisation. A handful, perhaps older in spirit, welcomed the informality.

As the room settled once more, he spoke. He could have been forgiven for hesitancy - an anticipation of the outfall to come - but instead spoke clearly and directly.

'We are going to join the World Council of Churches'.

Silence. The fractious opinions of thirty odd cassocks had nothing to say. Not yet anyway. To smile at this point would have been grossly inappropriate. Instead, someone laughed.

'Thank God himself,' came the voice 'I thought you were serious'.

The Cardinal did not respond. His restraint would reinforce his intent, staying his words while the weight of his statement took hold.

The World Council of Churches is a worldwide inter-church organisation founded shortly after the second world war. It's aim - to work for the cause of ecumenism. For that likely majority of people who don't know, 'ecumenism' is the concept and principle that Christians who belong to different denominations should work together to develop closer relationships among their communities. It has as its basis the statement that:

'It is a community of churches on the way to visible unity in one faith and one eucharistic fellowship, expressed in worship and in common life in Christ. It seeks to advance towards this unity, as Jesus prayed for his followers, "so that the world may believe". (John 17:21)'

It was not enough to tempt the Catholic church. They abstained from the group, indicating that the Roman Catholic Church was already 'a great ecumenical instrument'. A statement of extreme self-aggrandizement that had for fifty years remained largely unchanged.

Within Vatican Hall, the voices of dissension began, as if paraphrasing from this decades old sentiment.

'Father, in case you have forgotten, we are the *Roman Catholic Church'* - as if the name itself were sufficient to demonstrate hierarchical privilege. And so, the arguments began.

Convoluted intellectual debate is exhausting for most individuals, even those without egotistical leanings. It's surprising that several hours of argument, resistance and the endless citing of scripture didn't kill off at least one old clergyman - each a protagonist for his own beliefs. Centuries wouldn't have been enough.

The only consensus was to pause and reflect, and it was left to the cardinal to close the meeting.

Before he spoke, he focussed - inwardly reaffirming the reasons to proceed. Power, wealth, tradition, all of these excuses - indefensible 'justifications' for the organisation's steadfast determination to set itself apart from the world that God had intended it to serve. He viewed the faces in a narrow circle. It's ongoing obstinacy in maintaining a misogynistic hierarchy was a body of evidence in itself that the church had failed. Failed to realise that it's superiority and bias was no longer tolerable. There would be further discussion, arguments, meetings, but no-one present was left in doubt of his intent.

'We are going to join the World Council of Churches. If they will have us. That is not all. As we begin this journey, we will pave the way for the ordination of women into our clergy. These are just two of the changes that the church will make. Our wealth shall be disseminated to those in need. We shall become guardians for our Lord's creation where the world is threatened by the actions of humanity. We will speak truth within the turmoil of conflict and take our place once more as apostles of Christ in this world, as God intended.' It was as if John the apostle himself had returned from the grave.

Silence returned, to be broken by a gummily viscous snort. All eyes looked toward the sound. Father Filippo Russo was sobbing. In truth, he shouldn't even have been there. Only his proximity to the event as local priest had engendered an invitation, but here he was. He certainly shouldn't have taken Janus with him – but the boy was new to the city, and it would have been rude to leave him alone. For a moment, it wasn't clear whether his countenance was one of despair, but the hope in his voice, despite its words, was evident.

'You flying fucker,' he exclaimed at the astonished speaker. 'I haven't cried since Rosa Valentina dumped me in front of half the population of Castelluccio when I was sixteen years old. And then I was pissed!'

***

The World Council of Churches was still absent a member.

The proposals had been deemed radical and threatening, the pope had gotten older and the commission for change had been, well, *de-*commissioned. The cardinal, so inspiring to a young priest had been absorbed by a grateful Jesuit community in some far away corner of existence and so far as Janus knew, he may still be there. Maybe God was there with him.

Janus sat at his desk and peered over Rome's skyline, pausing for moments at St. Peter's Basilica before positioning the paper in front of him and writing his letter to Filippo.

Chapter 5
The Rain

Due South from Vatican City, lying between the constellations of Gemini in the West and Leo in the East, is the faint and rather undistinguished constellation of Cancer. Rather like the triskelion, the symbol for the Isle of Man, it has three legs radiating from the centre, where there is an open cluster 'Praesepe' or 'The Manger'. On a clear night this cluster, known since antiquity, is just a hazy spot to the naked eye, but appears in binoculars as a group of dozens of individual stars. Tonight, the skies were not clear.

As a young man, Father Janus had loved the rain. Perhaps it was the way in which it concealed the world, bringing hope of it's cleansing through an opaque blanket of renewal. He sat to one side of the bench, 'though there was no-one else with him to share it. He stared at the stars as the downpour cleared, hesitating before lowering his gaze. The world sat heavy in the darkness, unchanged.

The tree he had chosen was threadbare now, but he had seen times when it's leaves would bob in the wind, glistening bluish green above a carpet of pink at its base. Those times, at least, would come again.

He heard the ticking of his life within him, but it failed to obscure his pain.

The things he had done – those *things*. It would be easy to blame his rage – to plead illness or insanity, or even justice in its own perverted way. But that wouldn't be true. It had all been his *choice*. The tempting of God to intervene. To *see*. And perhaps in the seeing, to act, not just at Janus' actions but at the actions of humanity itself. His own damnation would have been a small price to pay for that.

He had worn his hate like a veil. A sad pretence to shroud himself – to hide his hurt from his maker. Hatred had been his shield, and his actions his sword. He knew that he was beyond forgiveness, but what did that matter now?

There was nothing. No God to intervene. No Son to save. Maybe He existed somewhere, but it wasn't here, and he didn't want to live in a world without God. Without hope.

He heard the patter begin again and waited to feel the moisture on his face before reaching for the rope at his side.

The deluge mourned upon him, sorrow from the eyes of He who made him - for the loss of his life, and for the loss of him.

Two thousand years on the world reveres the man who offered his life for his brothers. Not so the man who sacrificed his soul.

Chapter 6

Dogs

Some people don't like dogs. It's not a criticism, but I just don't get it, despite having once been bitten by a Maremma sheepdog. For those unfamiliar with the breed, the Maremma looks a little like a retriever on steroids. Hefty for a dog at up to 100 lb, it's known in Southern and Eastern Europe as a friendly and well-balanced flock guardian. Not so friendly when you run full pelt through its charges as a nine-year-old pretending, loudly, to be a one-man barbarian horde, but that was my fault. It didn't hold it against me, and after I'd calmed down from the shock of the nip, it was licking and fussing over me as if nothing had happened. I do like dogs you see, and it seems that they like me back.

Despite my affinity, I've never deliberately set out to 'own' a dog. Where I grew up, money was tight and working animals, for the lucky boys and girls whose family needed them, doubled as companions. If there was no suitable work, there was no dog, and my family were crop hands on a farm they didn't own, earning a wage which barely fed us. So, I made the most of the random canines that would trot briefly into my life, fussing over them as some people coo over babies, until they trotted off again with their 'masters', or on their own. It wasn't until I was fully grown that dogs began 'owning' me.

The first came barely a year after I'd marched into the first of many chapters of conflict. I'd chosen the life of a soldier over the farm before realising that I wasn't cut out for killing, and certainly not for dying. Cheap booze offered temporary comfort from the disdain of my more enthusiastic comrades, and I grew to crave both the taste and the oblivion. I was barely seventeen when I was adopted by a proud old Italian pointer who was both wise and sensitive enough to empathise with my hangover. He understood. His eyes told me so. He just rolled up one day, sat himself next to me as if we'd been companions for a century, and didn't leave until God whistled for him several years later. I cried for months, seasoned old squaddie that I'd become. Even then, I have never bought a puppy, or visited a shelter, or otherwise actively sought out a canine companion, but eventually one always seems to find me. Like a guardian angel, if you believe in that sort of thing. Loyally and selflessly watching my back, loving and loved, without prejudice or motive, as only a dog can. And I've needed it. Life has been long and hard. And that, perhaps, is a good point to begin to explain to you exactly where I find myself.

***

I've never trusted the medical 'fraternity'. The phrase itself screams of a casual arrogance and misogyny which seems unfortunately common across much of our established society. More specifically, I've never trusted the assured complacency in the modernity of treatments which fall out of date more quickly than low rise pants. Did you know that so called 'corpse medicine' was a disturbingly common practice across the Roman Empire? That the Romans believed in the blood of a fallen gladiator to cure epilepsy? So, as I lay prostrate on those starchy white sheets being told that 'this may hurt a little, Loman' you can forgive me for being sceptical. And as it turns out I was right. It hurt a fucking lot.

I have experienced many types of pain through my life. Of all the disparate and distinctive varieties, electric shock therapy was unique. These days there are muscle relaxants to avoid the physical dangers of seizure, and anesthesia to block the pain from the electricity. But in the eroded, asset stripped Palermo of the mid 1940's resources were thin.

Palermo has worn almost as many faces as I have. It was founded by Phoenician traders in the 8th century BC, becoming a Carthaginian settlement until being captured by the Romans half a millennium later. It fell into decay alongside the Empire, its buildings mirroring the dissolution of its society until Belisarius procured it for the Byzantines in the 6th century. For me, it is my childhood and my beginnings, and I was grateful to be returning home to the capital of Sicily following a painful excursion into the second great war - thankful and comforted by the familiarity but ashamed by my nation's choice of allegiance. And ignorant of the medical 'assistance' that I would soon endure.

Churchill once called Sicily the 'soft underbelly of Europe' and so it turned out. Lost to the Italian – German alliance two years prior to the end of the war it's people - my people - saw shame in each turn. The Sicilian loss of territory offered the allies a base in the Mediterranean - a jumping off point for the invasion of Italy proper and a turning point in the war. Society, I discovered, has little tolerance for those, like me, who have fought and failed.

I never wanted any part of the war. I had already seen too much territory won, lost and finally politicked away during mankind's first effort at the apocalypse two decades earlier. Such was my determination to avoid the violence that I went walkabout in an attempt to avoid the whole thing. I wasn't that lucky. I had worked my way up the East coast of Africa and on into Saudi, 'the birthplace of Islam'.

'Worked' is a subjective term given that I was actually searching for a quiet haven to see out the savagery - but my timing was impeccable. I hit the Somalian border with Ethiopia and the resident Italian military seemingly weeks after Mussolini had promised Herr Fuhrer reinforcements at the Eastern Front. My travels had clearly not skewed my accent sufficiently to obscure my heritage and the responsibilities that came with it, and there I was - conscripted, such that I and six divisions of my countrymen spent New Year 1943 overwhelmed by a Soviet offensive which would culminate in the loss of 50,000 lives. I could easily have been one of them, but that wasn't how it was to turn out.

Perspective is a funny thing. Most of us hope that we can 'see the other side', offering compassion and empathy to the views of our fellow travellers through life. Unfortunately, such good intent has a tendency to fall away when you're being pursued through an icy landscape by a vastly superior military force. Especially one which is brutally intent on imposing bloody vengeance on those people who had been coerced into threatening them. The Russians didn't care that I didn't want to be there – they didn't want me there either. Rumour was rife that Mussolini was losing favour with the Italian hierarchy, but our enemy didn't know or care that this would lead to Italy declaring for the Allies a few short months later. Despite my best efforts, I found myself feeling a little hatred for the enemy and their enthusiasm. It all seemed a bit too personal. Especially when it began to hurt.

I'm told that the shell landed behind me, but I wasn't conscious of hearing or even seeing the blast. The trunk of the tree in front of me just turned blinding white an instant before it and the surrounding landscape blackened and disappeared.

Heat is rarely to be expected in a tundric landscape. but I awoke choking on it. Burning hot smoke, inhaled in a whistle through a mouth icing shut as a conflicting cold congealed my spittle. The frost tore at my lips as I tried to speak through my tinnitus – a paltry effort at complaint toward the warm wet ache which flowed down my back and onto my legs.

As I've said, I have experienced many kinds of pain. This one wasn't that unusual but for being tardy in its arrival. When I look back, that first blast should have felt like I'd been hit by a baseball bat but there wasn't time for the pain to kick in. Now, though, tiny flickers of light danced across my eyes as the smoke cleared and daylight illuminated specks from the explosion. They tried their best to distract me from the agony, but it struck just as my eyes and consciousness found focus on a sky which finally pierced the residual smog. It was still dark and imposing and filled with snow.

Awareness of my injury grew alongside a deep nausea and the ringing in my ears gonging louder than the bell tower of Messina Cathedral. A childhood memory of its facade muddled into view through the ache, the gilded figures dancing across its clock tower to amaze me as a boy. I'd been astounded by the ingenuity of men and the beauty that they could create, before I returned to the present and blacked out again in deference to their baser enterprise.

When Explosive Ordnance Disposal technicians carry out risk assessments, they tend to include four major ways that an explosion causes damage to the human body. I can't bring myself to say that luck was with me that day, but I largely avoided three, these being the initial energy from the blast (direct injury), the blast wave (pressure wave causing ruptured lungs, eardrums, or being thrown around like Dorothy in a typhoon) and indirect consequences like a building falling down on you. I got number four.

Shrapnel is a nasty thing. An eight millimeter bullet creates a hole that disrupts tissue for three quarters of an inch around the bullet's path. Nasty, but by comparison shrapnel will simply tear you apart. People may laugh if you tell them that you have shrapnel in your backside. I didn't, I merely screamed as my sciatic nerve told me that my legs were probably still there, but not happy.

Somewhere amongst the throng of sensations, I felt a tug at my collar.

It's amazing how the mind can work when you're not sure which bits of you are left and which have gone missing in action. I found myself infinitely grateful that whatever was half lifting, half dragging me away from the rubble was struggling somewhat with my weight, and I was getting caught up in the surrounding debris. It was a semi-conscious indication that most of me was still attached to my body. The tugging ceased as I ended up with both legs and one arm hanging loosely and my back arched over an unpleasantly pointy shard of masonry. I tilted my head backward to see my rescuer and looked into the face of a soot covered Irish Wolfhound, all matted fur and determination. He whimpered over me for several moments before barking up an aural flag which could have brought the entire battalion running. I saw the uniforms approach before hazing back to unconsciousness.

***

I awoke to a blur of red and white, its breath warm and tinged with garlic as it sighed resignation into my face. Eventually the blur leaned away, and a crimson cross stiffened into focus on a battered, almost opaque white circle which was painted onto a battered green helmet. The helmet spoke.

'Fuck the National Republican Army, fuck Mussolini and his fucking social republic, and fuck this war' it said as it moved further away and addressed another helmeted head.

'This one's fucked' it sighed, nodding in my direction before moving out of view.

I discovered later that the expletives were the work of Doctor Filippo Russo, one of a handful of physicians who'd been sensibly allocated the role of medic in Mussolini's army. Filippo was a conscripted conscientious objector and an excellent doctor. Prior to his 'incarceration', as he referred to it, he had relocated to a backwater practice in Castelluccio, high in the Apennine mountains and far from the unsavoury militia of the black-shirts. As a twenty something undergraduate he had earned trust and respect from the begrudging provincial village whose population was ensieged by a growing xenophobia. Not surprising with Hitler barrelling his way through Europe, and Filippo's reputation for healing ultimately saw him ripped from his adopted home and posted to the Eastern front.

I heard him ask that I be made comfortable before he moved on to more hopeful candidates. I continued to flit in and out of consciousness, intermittently aware of movement around me, until the cross loomed again and I heard Filippo's voice above me.

'What the flying fuck are you still doing alive soldier?' he asked before glancing to my side and adding, without a hint of malice 'And what the fuck is this dog doing here?'

If you listened closely, Doctor Filippo had several kinds of fuck. There was a silent fuck, applicable to old ladies and members of the clergy, unsaid but still present in inflection. Then there was the everyday fuck, casually equivalent to the jeans and t-shirt we reach for on our days off. Amongst the others there was the 'flying fuck'. This was special - reserved for an occurrence which was so uncommon that the expletive was required to soar.

He frowned and screwed up his face. 'Fuck' he said again. I must have felt the need to respond since I garbled something incomprehensible about Jesus Christ. Filippo glanced at the cross around my neck and ignored my ravings, re-examining my injuries before berating himself with another filthy diatribe. 'How did I fuck this diagnosis up?' I interpreted as he looked down at me, confused at the state of my injuries and clearly upset. After a moment, the look on his face turned to determination and he called for plasma.

***

A few weeks later and here I am back in Palermo, staring at a white ceiling and listening to the incessant barking from the street outside. My canine rescuer had manipulated the ARMIR (the Italian army in Russia) with growls, barks and licks in proportions which proved appropriate to secure passage back to Sicily alongside me in a beaten-up FIAT 634N transport truck with a suspension which bottomed out over every bump or trough above six inches deep. I spent hours staring at his tongue bouncing along with each roll and jolt of the vehicle, and he stared right back at me the whole time. In truth, I would never have left without him. Maybe it was the way he looked at me with those big round eyes. Still, neither of us could persuade the medical profession to allow him into the hospital.

'This may hurt a little Loman'. I braced myself for another round with the electricity company. It may have been paranoia, but I swear I noticed a look of mild satisfaction as the doctor flicked up the switch.

To be fair, if someone had told me that they had been chosen by God, I suppose that I may have wondered who the hell they thought they were too. For several weeks I had apparently insisted upon it. A gift of confused delusion from the Russians to accompany the scarring which now decorated my right ass cheek. But the scars weren't enough for the doctors.

By this time my physical injuries had largely healed. Far from delighting in my good fortune, the doctors seemed to take offence at my unprecedented resilience. Perhaps it was because it made no medical sense, or maybe they just didn't like me. Whichever, they were intent on resolving the 'inadequacy' of my mental state in the most excruciating of ways.

As I continued to spout nonsense long after the delirium from the explosion and morphine had passed, theories had been discussed. Schizophrenia, battle fatigue, combat stress were all possibilities. It was sheer good fortune that electric shock therapy was the nineteen forties treatment for all three – good old days indeed. Psychiatrists at the time considered anaesthetic unnecessary since the electric shock produced instant unconsciousness in most patients. Once again, however, I was not 'most', and I was provided with the circulation restricting restraints usually reserved for POWs.

A fortnight into my treatment and I'd learned that I should just breathe out and try to relax while waiting for the convulsions to hit. The doctor still smiled as he hit the switch. This time, smoke swirled across the ceiling in a mocking reincarnation of the blast and Doctor Moustache – not his real name but a reflection of his most impressive trait – swooned over me. He stared down, a nibble of tobacco secured amongst the grey of that burly foliage and grinned a toothy grin while tugging enthusiastically at a Thendora cigar. He left the box, lid open, next to me and I stared surreally at the phrase 'The Bouquet of Quality' as my whole body clenched across the bed.

What to do when the world thinks you're mad? You can either believe them or believe yourself. I chose the latter and started to lie. It seemed the easiest way out of my predicament, and it turned out I was pretty good at it. Finding common ground with my carers was clearly going to be the simplest exit route and I dismissed my previous statements as nothing more than feverish nonsense with unabashed enthusiasm, even throwing in a smattering of feigned embarrassment. I played that hand from their first glimmers of belief that I actually trusted them, right through to discharge. But inside, I still had doubts. By the time I left, I barely knew which memories were real and which had been scrambled into my brain by eight hundred odd milliamps. I certainly had memories which felt real but made no sense - dreams of a past life long before the rumbling from the treaty of Versailles broke through the borders of Poland. Dreams that I kept to myself.

Dr. Moustache kept faith with his high voltage approach right to the end and swear I sensed his regret when he eventually told me that my treatment could be discontinued. It had been three months. I'd long since stopped giving him cause to question my sanity but inside my mind tumbled with self-doubt. By now, there was virtually no physical trace that I'd ever seen a battlefield. The scars on my behind had faded to a tiny dimple. Eventually that too, would disappear. It seemed that the whole event would end up being marked solely by the presence of a scruffy old mutt who was still waiting patiently outside the hospital. He'd barked and whined through each and every one of my treatments as if he was sharing the agony within his own fuzzy visage. He ran to greet me as I lurched down the hospital steps and I knew instinctively that he would continue to nuzzle my hand and sit at my side until the day that the Almighty called him to heel.

Chapter 7

Dreaming

I awoke in a swaying motion, side to side in unison with a great belching rattle which shook my ears. I reached my hand through sleep's smog, searching for a furry head, and got one, but not the one I was expecting.

Father Filippo laughed as my fingers probed at his face. I felt him flinch lightly as a finger caught a tangle of white hair and his copious beard pulled away.

'Morning Loman' he croaked through his chuckling. 'Sorry about old Ginger, he does snore a bit, doesn't he?'

Ginger continued to sway with his rhoncus from the top bunk. Filippo's description of him as 'old' seemed deliberately ironic. The priest looked ancient – a grizzled old Santa Claus handing me a mug of steaming black coffee.

'How'd you sleep?' he asked, and my eyes must have answered from their sunken sockets. 'Dreaming again?'

I wrung my hands in reply, rubbing and kneading like Lady Macbeth at that invisible spot.

Father Fillipo was genuinely intrigued. His questions invariably started way too soon, leaving my smoggy mind no time to determine its place in reality.

'Was the dog there? Which one was it? Was *I* there? I fucking love it when that happens. What did I do this time?'

I struggled to focus, and my eyes decided that the cabinet behind Filippo's head made a steadier object of attention than the Father's bobbing enthusiasm.

'Too soon?' he chuckled. 'Ok, speak later.'

If you've ever met a Roman Catholic priest, you may be surprised at just how unremarkable they seem. Outside of their special calling, they live relatively normal lives. Preparing mass, attending the sick, providing pastoral care for the congregation are all important parts of their day-to-day existence. Invaluable, but not excessively exciting.

Alongside the anticipated activities of his priesthood however, Father Filippo worked six nights a week from a windowless room at the back of his church close to Vatican City. On one side of the room, a cabinet is filled with hundreds of small statues of angels. Atop the display, he keeps a supply of sweets to hand out to his visitors. Rows of bunk beds line the floorspace. On the wall is an official looking document laying out rules of conduct for those who seek refuge from the streets at the *Chiesa di San Francesco* - the Church of St. Francis. Sometimes, it would accommodate thirty people in a night. Set next to it, offset from its neighbour in a way which bothered my OCD, was a picture of a man tending to a menagerie of creatures ranging from doves to – bizarrely – a lion. On my first stay at the church, I was convinced that the man was Father Filippo himself, such was the likeness. Filippo had smiled at my error. 'I get that a lot' - before explaining that it was St. Francis of Assisi, patron saint of animals and patron in name to the establishment where I'd slept.

I became aware of Ginger stirring above my head – an unfortunate prelude to the day and took the final moments of peace to review my dream before it drifted beyond me. I wouldn't have bothered but Filippo liked to hear about them, and I felt that I owed him something for the past two years. God knows I didn't have much else to offer.

I didn't know what drove my mind to such varied and wondrous delusions. Perhaps it was searching. Scrabbling through the darkness of sleep desperate to find a cure for itself – for me. My imagination was certainly impressive. Impressive enough to compose fresh nightly adventures sufficient to frighten the crap out of me for the whole of my waking existence. My heart pounded through the day in double beat, bass and snare pumping adrenaline through my bloodstream in a torrent that my mind told me shouldn't be sustainable. My body thought otherwise, but still allowed my brain to twist and writhe in complaint at the mildest of triggers. I laid back and tried to ignore the grip which had already begun to tighten around me. Fear of fear – an old classic, and I hadn't even finished my coffee.

I'd long since stopped trying to remember the origins of my mental state – those long-term memories just wouldn't come, and I concentrated instead on harvesting what remained of last night's trip to Palermo. This included an appraisal of which elements were 'original', and which had been driven by real life - my own personal amateur psychology. Two aspects were easy. The first probed at my back sufficiently to replicate any injury. The mattress was old, and I could feel the coils threatening to unravel through my spine. The second was obvious and distracting in equal measure, enough to undermine my musings. It also filled my heart fuller than any amount of fear would ever have the power to do.

Angus was a short haired border collie. He had the panda like facial colouring of most collies, his eyes and ears framed in black – but was mostly white, other than a spotting to his legs and a narrow saddle sitting across his back. Mainly though, he could be recognised by a gleam of understanding that shone from his whole being. That's what I thought anyway. He had been with me from the very beginnings of my memory. I *literally* couldn't remember a time without him. I sighed as he shuffled from the narrow space beneath my bunk, stretched life back into his body and began his ritualised stalking of the far side of the room. 'Here we go' I grinned.

Angus had fallen in love with Fillipo's cabinet, or so it seemed, and after a slobbery 'Good Morning' between us he trotted toward it, tail wagging frantically. He gave its legs a couple of investigatory sniffs, then raised himself onto his back legs and pushed his nose against the glass between his front paws, staring intently at the contents within.

The host of angels were predominantly gaudy trinkets from the tourist markets, brightly coloured plastics and occasional porcelain to catch the eye of the undiscerning traveller, but far from being 'displayed', each angel stared inward at an object which seemed entirely out of place with its congregants. It was a box, simple in form and no more than six inches by four. It might just accommodate a pint of milk poured within its boundaries, had its hardwood façade not been cracked and shrunken by the turning of time. I'd asked Filippo what was in it too often to revisit the question and he always gave the same answer anyway. 'God is in it, just as He's everywhere else.'

Angus for one seemed impressed by the response and gave the object almost as much attention as he gave Filippo, even while the old priest pulled a biscuit from his pocket whilst emerging from his role as barista. He mussed the dog's head as it chewed at its treat and it followed him back to me as he handed a mug to Ginger, who grumbled something before sliding from his perch with a thump and meandering off to queue for the single lavatory.

'Are your dreams telling you anything today?'

Sometimes Filippo sat with me after coffee was served. On other days it was Ginger's turn, sometimes Hettie, or any of the other souls who found a refuge from the world in Filippo's company. He plonked onto my bed and scrunched his face into its 'focused' expression, until it looked just like I was the only person in the world who mattered. I don't ever recall him asking someone he'd known for more than a week 'how they were'. His questions were far more person specific – personal – and he had the memory of an elephant. I certainly don't want to make him sound perfect and should probably mention his unfortunate tendency to snigger at inappropriate moments. Occasionally I'd get the joke, often not, but once you'd seen him snort during mass as often as I had it faded into the background like all inconsequential things. Also, for a priest, he swore like a trooper.

'Not the one from last night, no. I can barely remember it, other than that parts of it were painful.' I stared pointedly at the mattress.

Fillipo looked a little disappointed, and I racked my brain for a way to appease him.

'I could tell you about the one I had a couple of days ago. Except all I recall is standing at the entrance to a cave, pointing at something inside. I spoke to an old man. He was wearing a yashmagh – you, know, the headscarves that Arab men wear. There were some British soldiers there too. They were dressed in fatigues but just milled around smoking roll ups. That's all I remember. Wait - I did have a weird dream a few days before that.' I shuddered. 'I remember that one in enormous detail.'

I lifted my inflection in a question, and Fillipo nodded.

***

Wuhai is a regional centre city in the Mongolia Autonomous region of China. It sits on the Yellow River between the Gobi and Ordos deserts, close to where the waters dissect the Great Wall.

I sat by the East bank. It had been a cool, dry Spring, even by the area's usual standards. Still, it's people were smiling and happy as they fulfilled the wishes of Mao Zedong, founding father of the people's republic. They filled the streets, their drums banging out a repetitive enthusiasm for their sinister task. It was 1958.

Nine years after the Communist Party of China took power, Zedong initiated his 'great leap forward' - a massive social and economic campaign which, amongst other things, turned farming into a state sponsored activity.

Informed that sparrows ate too much grain, Zedong determined that China could do without such pests and decreed that they should all be killed. And the people responded.

They took to the streets, adults and children alike, to do their duty. The noise that they made filled the city and the skies above, shouting and pounding at their drums with relentless energy. The birds fled, seeking refuge from their terror, but wherever they went there were more humans to fear. Eventually, exhausted, they simply fell to the ground. Still there was no respite, and the terror continued. Time and again the survivors fought to raise themselves above the cacophony only to fall again, until each one gradually surrendered the fight and lay, panting or dead, amongst the grinding feet.

I sat within the throng. Families laughed and sang as they shuffled through the tiny bodies. One lay feet from my hands, its feathers caked and stiff as it held fast in the river's silt, staring toward the sky without hope or intent. I reached out, plucking it from the sludge, but its heart was still.

I did nothing, just leant back against the mud wall of the embankment and sighed, lamenting my place in this life. I rubbed at my hands, seeking respite from the death that I'd held, and asked a question. The same question that everyone asks, from time to time.

'Why do you allow this?'

But even in my dream there was no reply.

It took two years for the consequences to become apparent. The sparrows, it seemed, didn't only eat grain. They also ate insects. With no birds to control them, insect populations boomed, and locusts swarmed over the country, consuming all they could find.

As the food ran out, millions starved.

The Chinese government estimated fifteen million deaths. Independent calculations set that figure three times higher. Other implications of the act could not be measured in numbers.

Whether parents really did resort to eating their children - and vice versa – was never officially denied but the topic – The Great Famine - remains taboo in the country even in modern times.

I looked down at the little bird that I'd held, and was glad that when Christ returned, He would come as the lion, not as the lamb.

***

'I'm so sorry, Loman'

'Don't be. It was just a dream. It doesn't matter.'

'Pain always matters. Don't ever consider it less because it's yours'.

We sat together as the hostel emptied and the sunlight through the doorway stretched across the wall. Eventually Angus realised that his bladder was full, and he paced at my feet impatiently.

'I should go.'

'OK. But we've been doing this for a long time, and I've only just realised something. It may be nothing, but it's all I have that may be relevant to your .... condition.

'Go ahead'

'Your dreams. You must have told me about dozens since you began staying here.'

'I guess so.'

'Well .... have you noticed that you seem to be telling them in reverse order? That they seem to be going further back in time? I don't suppose it's anything really – just an observation.'

I thought for a moment before Angus whined and I got up.

'See you tonight?' asked Filippo.

'Probably'.

Chapter 8
The Library

Hettie flexed her fingers. The screen portrayed a sickly image of a perfectly formed Caucasian couple prancing down a long street somewhere along Lake Garda with the sun sinking into their heads. She squinted her determination and set herself to the task in hand.

'*Dear Suitors,*

My name is Hettie. I am thirty-four years old and still have my own teeth – some still within my mouth.

I have recently emerged from my cocoon and am unsure as to my ongoing needs and wants – but it may be time for me to investigate.

For those people who are interested, I am five feet five inches in my stockinged feet, approximately five feet five and a half in crocs. I am of slim build and my hair is the colour of the sinking sun. At least it would be if the sun was brown.

My eyes are blue-green, both the same not one of each.

I enjoy fine dining but don't have the opportunity to experience it much.

I like combat boots.

I love the sounds of the sea.

I enjoy my own company and I'm comfortable spending the day with a good book. I don't need anyone to make me complete. I don't expect perfection.

If YOU are imperfect, willing to occasionally sit behind 'Heart of Darkness' in my priorities, live within easy travelling distance of central Rome and are tolerant of people who have no idea what they want from you, please do contact me.'

Hettie sat back to review her brief epistle, sniggered huskily and pressed enter. Done.

Opening another window, she postured into a barely perceptible crouch and surveyed her territory like a frightened rabbit, guarding the little paper diary at her right hand with cut-throat glances at the disinterested academics who shared her table.

The public face of the Vatican Library is open to anyone who can document their qualifications and research needs. This was no problem to Hettie. She carried her certification within a tidy faux leather zip file, complete with carrying handle and an inlaid brass monogram of overlapping letters - H. D. E. The ring binders within had been undermined by over-use and clung precariously to a succession of clear plastic wallets, each containing a credential of learning. The first of these declared that:

'Heather Dorothy Eddy of University College, London, having completed the course of study approved by the University and passed the prescribed examinations has this day been admitted by the senate as an internal student to the degree of Doctor in the faculty of humanities, the field of study being philosophy'.

This slightly stained piece of paper had provided her access to the library building almost every day since she'd first entered the city. They must have considered her the most committed scholar of all time. At least they would have if they'd paid her any attention.

Satisfied that her journal was adequately secure, she turned a page and typed an obscenely long series of characters into the password field of her e-mail account. She had seventeen messages. Not a bad day at all. There were currently half a dozen 'Hetties' on 'Plenty of Fish.', each coloured by minor shades of the original. None of them had any intention of meeting the hopeful hearts who responded. It was just a way for her to keep warm and fill the day. And maybe it went some way toward fulfilling a need that she had no other way of discharging. She enjoyed the interaction - some of it, at least. It was safe, it was temporary, and it kept her off the street but in the world. At least a little bit. It really couldn't be anything else.

Hettie's hair *was* brown. It was matted into dreadlocks just sufficiently to tip her over the cusp of vagrancy into bohemian. It hung like coir over narrow shoulders, tips dancing lightly on the green leather padding of the library seat. She was viciously clean, every inch scrubbed red with the doubts of when the next shower may come. Beneath her layers she was military tight, her limbs sinewed through a nomadic march which meandered forward to an undefined future. For now, there was *just* now. And the library, her e-mails and an occasional bed at Filippo's church.

She clicked open her inbox and scanned the lines, filtering out the contrived, pausing only briefly at one which requested a photograph of her tits as it's opening statement. God help the poor unfortunate who ended up with that dickhead. Of the seventeen messages there were two which arched her eyebrows.

The first alleged to have been sent by 'Jose', who was six feet two with eyes of blue, the unmatched combination of presumed heritage and colouring prickling at Hettie's suspicions. A mild panic welled within her which wouldn't be batted down despite her anonymity and the ridiculousness of the whole situation. Her intellect tried to smile, scorning the unwarranted emotions which wouldn't subside. Jose continued unabated.

'*Dear Hettie*

My name is Jose. I am six feet two and my eyes are blue, both the same not one of each.

My passion is cooking, and I moved to Rome from Zaragoza to nurture my passion into a great passionate brown bear. I am employed at an exclusive hotel. I am currently on reception but get to direct people to the hotel restaurant virtually every day.

Your profile made me laugh in a way which I thought would be impossible after I singed a ganache in 2001 at the age of twelve. I barely made it through puberty.

I love pastry cooking, cake baking, bread making and constructing elaborate desserts.

I am approaching sixteen stones in weight. Unfortunately, I am approaching it from the wrong direction, 'though I still look good in my vertically striped apron.

I should very much enjoy corresponding with you in the hope that we can meet at some point. Please excuse my untidy use of 'passion' and 'passionate' within the same sentence. I only speak restaurant Italian and can only count in Spanish and English. I don't expect to keep my job as receptionist for long.

I hope to hear from you soon.

Kind regards

Jose.'

Hettie realised that her heart had calmed in the brief moments it took to read Jose's introduction. He had the potential to become one of her 'distractions', at least for a couple of months. She maintained dialogue with a dozen or so would be 'boyfriends' at any one time, limiting their interactions to an absolute maximum of eight weeks. Anything else would just be unfair. Most didn't make it that far, losing interest after a couple of messages when it became clear that Hettie would be no easy nut to crack. She put the thought to one side and looked back at her inbox.

The second message to pique her interest was accompanied by an accusatory exclamation mark, all red and bloated.

'Your medical review is now due!

Dear Ms. Eddy

You have been referred to the Madrid University Hospital for a Total Body MRI scan.

Please report to the hospital reception at 8 AM on Wednesday 14th February.

You are required to wait while the results of the scan are reviewed. Be prepared that your assessment could last up to eight hours. You will receive a text message reminder twenty-four hours before your appointment. Prior to your appointment, please complete and bring along the forms attached to this message.

All hospital grounds are non-smoking. In the interests of safety for staff and service users all visitors must be free from the influence of illicit drugs and/or alcohol.

We are a research active organisation. For further information please contact us via the hospital website.

Under the terms of your contract, you MUST attend all reviews deemed necessary by the medical review board. If you are unable to attend for any reason, please contact us immediately. All confidentiality agreements remain in place.'

Hettie's chair complained loudly as she pushed back from the desk, causing another rush of adrenaline to compliment the flush generated by the message.

'Fuck' she thought, 'At least I get to be someone's valentine'.

Chapter 9

Lies

Sara stared at the screen. A black padlock stared back; its shackle clasped firmly shut. 'This page is password protected' shouted the imagery, but there was no field in which to type the word, even if she'd known it.

There was no contact number to ring, no webform to complete, and no way to correct the error that had plagued her since the little jump in her heart had interrupted her supper.

Gambas al ajillo is easy to prepare but prawns aren't good for the digestion when you've just realised that you've transposed DNA results. It was a ridiculous error and her guts complained almost as much as Doctor Delgado would. Delgado had a nasty tendency of poking people with her skeletal fingers as she spoke, an unpleasant remnant from a bygone age which wouldn't have been tolerated if the old bat wasn't so close to retirement – or the aunt of the company's director for medical development.

Twelve months in and Sara still took hard copies of her work home before signing them off. Her university reference hadn't said the word 'genius', but it may as well have. She'd been top of her group from day one to the last day, but still questioned her ability, and her results, with an ill-concealed paranoia. It wasn't even double checking. You couldn't be the perfectionist that Sara was in just two hits. And if only Delgado would leave her alone, maybe she wouldn't be so prone to the odd mistake. But the bitch was relentless, glaring over her shoulder each morning like some kind of human drone. Almost human. She hovered like a shady parody of a Nazi commandant in a Burberry mac, one with lapels wide enough to shame every pimp on Calle de la Montera. Sara wondered whether she *ever* took the bloody thing off, even when she was sunning herself on a rock with the other lizards.

The printout was thin, despite it covering six individual specimens. Not surprising when the background information was so scant. There were no names, no history, no background on relatives or source. The identity of the client was encoded. 'Commission reference RCA1001-6J' would have been a mysterious 'name' even without the diverse and difficult nature of the samples. An antique spearhead amongst the bloodied thorn and scraps of cloth had her visualising a murder most foul, the assailant making a daring escape through a wooded thicket.

The results had been far weirder than Sara's imagined assassin and ensuring the precision of *this* report had seemed more relevant than the impossible timeframe, but 'the client has a deadline' rattled Delgado and that was that. In context, mis-typing a couple of suffixes should be understandable but her stomach still pre-empted her boss's bony assault.

In all likelihood Sara could have kept quiet and gotten away with her sloppy digitery, but that wouldn't have done at all – it wouldn't have been accurate. More to the point, it wouldn't have been *right*. She'd just need to ring the helpdesk in the morning – maybe it was just her wi-fi playing up again. 'A basement flat isn't conducive with good reception' her landlord said. 'I'm in central Madrid, for fuck's sake' she'd responded, but inside her head where they couldn't hear her. She kicked her chair back from the screen and swivelled away from the torment.

A scruffy blonde fluffball was waiting four feet away, pink eyes and nose a triumvirate of expectation. His haunches sank slightly into the piled carpet, shortening his back legs not quite enough to obscure the lithe agility.

Boris was infantile, even for a ferret. Most are playfully inquisitive, social creatures but Boris would have spent his whole life sitting atop Sara's head, watching the world with the comforting warmth of her pate warming his ass. Usually, he got as far as her shoulders as she went about the business of living, wandering the flat doing human things. Sometimes she would do things which made sense. Eating, sleeping, roughhousing with him in the deep foliage of the rug, but often she'd just do human things. Tonight, she was being especially human, and he was relieved when she picked him up and carried him to their bed. He curled himself into the gap she'd leave by her belly as she lay on her side and felt her tension drain as she found sleep. 'In the morning.' she said quietly. Then he slept too.

***

The blinds shifted slightly at the second-floor window and the low sun danced up the office wall. A couple of minutes passed and a 'phone rang down the corridor from three rooms up.

'Felipe? It's Sara.'

'Mierda Sara! I haven't even taken my fucking coat off yet.'

'Apologies. I need a favour.'

'A favour now is it? You want a favour after your no-show last night? We waited for you, you know. Twenty minutes at Ana's without so much as a sangria to kick us off. What a tight ass. I was parched you know, I ...... hang on, why are you ringing? Come down.'

'Can't. I'm at my screen'.

'Ok. I'll come up then.'

Gabriel sauntered through the door, still in his sunglasses and looking like he'd tried to remove his coat without quite managing it. And he stank. The booze sang from his pores right through his clothing.

'Good night?'

'God yes.' Gabriel grinned. 'We managed without you. What's up?'

'Take a look' Sara gestured at the monitor. The same black padlock. 'I thought it may be because I was working at home but it's the same here. Any ideas?'

The sunglasses came off. Gabriel's eyes were shrouded in black rings, and he squinted at the mild light coming off the screen.

'Its password protected.'

'Jesucristo Gabriel, that's the problem. Can you get through it? Look – it doesn't even have any options to type anything'.

Gabriel squinted harder and hovered his face next to Sara's. Jesus he really did stink!

'What exactly are you trying to access Sara? I can't just crack through it, you know? Why don't you just ring the help desk?'

'That's my next try if you can't help.' She looked at him and tried to ignore his appearance. He was a massively pretty boy but his lifestyle was already dragging at his features. That was a difficult conversation in the offing, but not for now. 'I've fucked up Gabriel. Not so much really, but you know what *she's* like.'

'Ooo, what have you done?'

'I've transposed reference numbers on my report. It's nothing really. I could fix it in seconds if I could just get *in*.'

'Oh *no*, not *that*! That's fucking terrible! ..... Hang on, that's not what you were doing last night is it?'

'Yes. I'm sorry Gabriel. I just want to get it right before she arrives.'

Gabriel began shaping his features for disapproval but lost the will halfway though. Instead, 'Mmm, ok. I still need to know what it is though. I'm not playing with police commissions, or anything from... you know, that guy from last week who made it clear that he didn't like me. Dickhead.'

'That could be anyone from last week Gabriel. And it's not the police. It's just that coded one.'

'Ah just *that* one? So, we don't actually know whether it's the police or not. It may be the fucking CNI Sara.'

'Please. Can't you just have a look at it? Before she gets in? You can do it from my workstation?'

Gabriel stared into Sara's widening eyes. He'd seen the look before. Not today, he thought, not even for Sara. 'Sorry amiga, I don't need those bony fingers up my ass either. Try the helpdesk. And fucking ring next time if you're not coming out, will you?'

And with that he replaced his glasses and ambled back to his room, shrugging his coat back onto his shoulders as he went.

'Fuck' Sara whispered and dropped the innocence from her expression.

***

'Good morning, Helpdesk. Could I take your name please?'

'Yes, it's Sara from the laboratories.'

'Thank you, Sara. How can we help you today?'

'I'm trying to access a report that I've written but there's a password screen that I can't get through.'

'Do you have the password, Sara?'

'No, I don't think there should be one. I've never been asked for one at this point before. And there's no field to type one into anyway. Sorry.'

'Ok, that sounds unusual. Hang on, yes - I've found you on the system. Are you happy for me to remotely operate your screen?'

'Yes.'

'Thank you. Please could you bring up your homepage and click on the 'yes' tab that's on your screen. That'll just confirm your agreement.'

'Ok, done.'

'Thank you. Just one moment please.'

Formalities completed, Sara waited for the moment to pass, but it didn't. It stretched into minutes, certainly over ten of them, and she eyed the door nervously, waiting for Delgado's mac to sweep in. Just as she contemplated dropping the 'phone, it beeped into her ear and a different voice spoke.

'Sara? Hi. Sorry for the wait. We've checked back through our records, and it seems that this report is security protected.'

'Yes, that's why I'm ringing. I need to get through the password screen.'

'No, I mean that *you* don't have security clearance. It's just a safety measure, you don't need to worry.'

'What? But it's *my* report. I only need to access it for a couple of minutes.'

'Sorry, I can't do that. But don't worry, I've checked with your director and there won't be a need for any amendments. Really, there's no need to worry, it's just a request from the client, I think. We'll send you a confirmation e-mail to set your mind at rest. Ok?'

'Sorry, I'm not sure that I understand what's going on. You know that it's *my* report, I already know what's in it. I only want to change a couple of digits. To make sure that the client has all of the right information. Would that be ok?'

'Don't worry there's no need. I'll get Doctor Delgado to have a word. She'll be with you soon.'

The 'phone went dead, and Sara gulped back the taste of last night's prawns once more.

***

Delgado skittered into the room looking unnaturally tiny – her coat was missing.

Sara felt her without turning from her desk. The old woman carried a presence despite the stiff narrowness of her shoulders, which extended down past her hips and stuck her pointedly to the floor. She moved as if her body jerked with Tourette's, across the room to Sara's workstation.

'Good morning, Sara. Perhaps we could have a quick word in private?' This was as new as it was troubling. Delgado never *asked* for anything. Sara rose and followed her to the end office. She caught Gabriel's eye as she followed in Delgado's wake. 'Shit' declared his eyebrows.

Delgado's office was as stark as it's occupant. Sara had seen it dozens of times but could never find the proper words to describe how it felt. She flushed a little deeper as the word came to her. 'Funereal.' Delgado's desk swamped her, framing her Lowry like form in simplistic chic. She gestured to the low seat opposite her. 'Please, do sit down,' and her face stretched into a toothless smile, skin straining at the edges in unfamiliar complaint. Sara winced inwardly as the old bat rose and wheeled her chair to face her.

'Sara, I understand that there's been a little incident.' Delgado stretched out a hand to take Sara's wrist. It could have been a clumsy attempt at comfort – a 'motherly' touch, but the claw like fingers reached further than they had any right to, clamping as much at her still twinging guts as they did at her arm.

'I hear that you've been trying to correct a minor error, and I thank you for your conscientious efforts, but there's really no need. The client has decided not to continue with the commission, and we have therefore removed your report from the system.' The smile widened marginally, but the skin held on. 'Bullshit' thought Sara. No reports were ever expunged, clients changed their minds all the time. She'd personally carried out at least ten paternity tests where the client wanted the results, then didn't, then did again.

PLONK.

A thick wad of paperwork landed in Sara's lap, stealing her thoughts. 'This is your next piece of work' chimed Delgado and began talking detail at her. The previous conversation, apparently, was already over. Sara didn't dare complain.

When she saw the old woman later that day the Burberry was back 'round her shoulders.

Chapter 10

The Truth

Gabriel lounged against Sara's sofa. The soles of his boots were muddy, and Boris sniffed curiously at the residue that had been deposited on his rug. Her friend looked like he'd been washed up on the rocks. Except there were never rocks. He didn't dilute.

'For fuck's sake Gabriel, are you going to help me or not?'

Gabriel grinned and placed his glass on the table before hoisting himself onto the chair she'd provided next to hers. 'Your bourbon is too good.'

Sara had divided the paperwork into seven neat piles. Six of the piles represented an item that had been tested. The seventh was the main body of Sara's report, encapsulating and summarising each of the results.

'What's the eighth pile?' asked Gabriel. 'That big one on the coffee table.'

'They're my photocopies. You know, just in case.'

'Nice.' Said Gabriel, 'though his face said 'Christ'. 'Ok, let's just get on with it.'

'Right. I won't go through all of the specimens in detail, but we'll need to pick out a little of the pertinent information relating to each. Then I'll explain the testing approach, and then go on to the similarities and differences relating to the whole range of samples. Finally, I'll outline my conclusions. Then you can tell me what you think.'

'I think I need another drink.' Gabriel held up his empty glass.

'Gabriel, you *promised*.'

'Ok.'

'Good, now please let me finish before saying anything else so that I can keep my line of reasoning intact.'

Sara paused, waiting for sarcasm, but Gabriel was silent. She picked up the first pile and shuffled through the pages before dropping them inelegantly in the vicinity of their starting position. Gabriel remained quiet and resisted the temptation to finger his tumbler.

'So, there were six items submitted for testing by the same client. Remember, we don't know who the client is, we've just got a reference for the commission. Testing was to be the same for all of the samples where that was possible – some didn't yield enough suitable material to warrant progressing with all of the tests.

Initial tests were to establish whatever we could about the sample itself. Radiocarbon dating, constitution of materials, whether there was anything there that may indicate that the material had been compromised, either through accidental or deliberate contamination. Explicitly '*whether it may have been deliberately made to look like something it isn't*. A few other things. And then, fundamentally, whether the sample had any DNA attached to it or within it.

Stage two was around testing any DNA – that was to include lineage – paternal and maternal – but also historic, so likely geographical heritage, eye colour, hair colour, race and the like. We were also asked to identify any peculiarities in the genetic markers, to help us to identify inherited diseases or abnormalities. We than had a blanket instruction to look more specifically at those abnormalities. I needed to consult with Delgado before proceeding to that stage.'

Gabriel held up his hand.

'Yes?'

'Sorry, *were* there any abnormalities?'

'Yes, but I'm coming to that. Delgado got even more creepy than normal when I showed her what I'd found. She looked like she was about to freak, but then just told me to get on with it. I didn't think that much about it, you know what she's like. But before I go into detail, I should outline a little about the samples. They were eclectic.... No, they were *weird*.'

Gabriel placed his glass on the floor next to him and leaned forward. Sara continued.

'Sample number one, the one I picked to look at last, didn't actually seem that interesting. It was really just a shank of metal with a pointy end. It didn't look long enough to be a spear but apparently that's exactly what it was. A Roman pilum – a sort of throwing spear used by soldiers. It would have had a wooden handle but the heel – the bit that the wood would have slotted into – was sheared off. Now, obviously you can't carbon date iron, but we did analyse the metal. The impurities within it were consistent with it being made during the latter eras of the Roman Empire.

Sample two was made up of two pieces of hardwood. Both were olive and came from the same period. There were signs of degeneration in both. One was just a blob of timber but the other had clearly been carved and had an inset rim, like it had been mounted into something. That one had traces of gold embedded within its structure.

Three was a piece of cloth. A scrap of linen with some dried blood on it.

Four was intricate, made of acacia, it was a carved box. There was a finger bone inside it.'

'Gross!' exclaimed Gabriel. 'From a dead person?'

'No, it jumped out and poked me. You dickhead Gabriel, just listen will you? I haven't told you the best bits yet.

Five and six were proper antiques. One was a reliquary, all gold with a crystal window and some painted figures moulded onto it. The sort of thing your granny would put out for Christmas. It had a long prickle inside the window.'

'*Christ's thorn?*' exclaimed Gabriel. I've seen pictures of things like that.

'I expect so. Now shut up, for fuck's sake. The gold was from the middle ages, best guess around the twelfth century. The prick was too small to test but we did pull some DNA off it – WAIT – I'll tell you in a minute.

Six was a cross, around 5 kilograms, massively ornate and encrusted with jewels. I wasn't allowed to work on that one or the reliquary, Delgado did it herself, but there wasn't much to report apart from the DNA. I don't think our insurance company would sign off any other tests. The items were deemed too valuable.

So, the results we did manage to get told us several interesting things. One, the timber samples and the spear all came from the same time period – but that isn't the interesting bit. Two, we pulled four DNA samples. The finger came from a mid-European man with black hair and brown eyes. It was dated to the Middle Ages. He hasn't been fingering anyone for around six hundred years – DON'T!' Sara cut Gabriel off before he'd even begun to form words.

'The other DNA samples all come from men born in the order of two millennia ago. They had brown hair and brown eyes, and it's likely that they were dark skinned. It should have been a minor miracle that we managed to glean even that much given the half-life of the samples, but it wasn't like that.

DNA is supposed to lose seventy five percent of its genetic information every thousand years, give or take, but the three samples we took could have been lifted from a cheek swab we took last week. Well, not quite but you get the gist. If it wasn't for the genetic markers aligning so closely with other samples from the time period, we'd have thought that they could have been dated from any time after The Beatles recorded Abbey Road. Of course, this places doubts across *all* of the findings, but that still isn't the main issue. We didn't manage to get any paternal results, but we did get the mitochondrial markers – the ones from the mother - lined up like soldiers. Gabriel, the samples all came from someone with the same parentage. It's possible that they're all from the same person. NO. Please don't speak yet, let me finish.

We tried several methods of confirming the time period of origin. Half of the tests I hadn't even done before. I went to Delgado, but she just told me to get on with it and she'd check it afterwards. I swear she wasn't even listening - God, that woman does my head in. Anyway, I still can't be one hundred percent sure that the whole thing hasn't '*been made to look like something it isn't.*' But if it is legitimate - and the reason why I need my report to be as accurate as possible - is that from the three DNA samples from two thousand years ago, one was 'different'. Oh, it still had the same markers, the same mother and the same hair colour and everything else, but it also had something extra.'

Gabriel's eyes had begun to glaze. She'd deliberately only let him have one drink, but for all she knew he may have downed a bottle of Jack Daniels before he'd arrived. For all that, he was still the best friend she had, and Sara kicked his leg and frowned, and only continued in response to his raised hands and re-affirmed attention. He protruded his lower lip and rubbed his leg as he listened.

'So, I'll re-cap. We have three samples of DNA, all from two thousand years ago and all possibly from the same person. Two of the samples were just blood. One wasn't, and here's why.

I don't know what you know about antibodies? Well, they're not supposed to exist in samples this old. I thought that it must be conclusive proof that we'd got the time frames wrong, that the samples were recent, but I really don't know what to think any more. Antibodies degenerate and recede within the body once they've done their job. That is to say they all but disappear once the disease they're fighting has run its course. These were still active. Not just active but rampant, even though there was no trace of disease for them to be fighting. I tested them. I tested them against malaria, Lyme disease and chickenpox. I tested them against HIV. I even tested them against cancer cells. They cured everything Gabriel. Fucking *everything.*'

Chapter 11

Discovery

'Hi Sara? Good, you're in. Don't go anywhere I'm coming over.'

Gabriel swaggered through the door with a billionaire's strut, wafting the report like banknotes. He tossed it down on Sara's table with a 'there you go' nod and awaited congratulations.

'How'd you get that?'

'I hacked Delgado's account. Her password is 'cunt.'

'Fuck you Gabriel, just tell me, will you?'

Boris whiffed the angst and busied himself circling the pair, eying Gabriel with a disturbingly pink glare. Neither of them noticed. He wasn't sure about Gabriel. He always petted him and played nicely but he smelt funny. A bit like Sara sometimes when she was sad.

'Fine. It wasn't that difficult, you know? It only took five minutes once I'd spoken to Beatriz in accounts.'

'Jesus, Gabriel you didn't tell her anything did you?'

'Nope, purely generic and untraceable.'

Sara squinted accusingly, then - 'Hmm. Go on then, tell me.'

'Well, it was pretty simple actually. The commission number – RCA1001-6J – well the first '1' changes depending on where the project is in terms of payment. It's an accounting tool. Zeros are pre-commission. Ones are commissioned but not complete. Twos are completed but not invoiced, threes invoiced but not paid and the number changes to a four once the finance has been received. If you're you - the one prepping the report - it's likely that you'll only ever have seen the ones. Once you've signed it off Delgado countersigns and it's issued to the client, at which point it becomes a two, and you'll likely never hear of it again. But, if the client cancelled like Delgado told you, it automatically goes straight from one to three with a time charge to cover our costs. If that was actually the case, then there'd be an invoice issued against that number in the finance section. There isn't, but there was a 'four', not in accounts but Beatriz doubles down on everything in case there's an audit. She keeps her own system alongside the corporate records. Voila.'

'Ok, I didn't understand any of that. Can I have it again, but slower please.'

Gabriel obliged and grinned in anticipation of a congratulatory hug. Or at least a nice thank you.

'Fuck Gabriel you twat. I thought you said it was purely generic. What if she blabs?'

Gabriel's grin faded.

'She won't. She's not supposed to keep her own records, but she doesn't trust the input clerks. Apparently, she got ripped at an audit last year and now she checks everything manually at the end of each quarter. Plus, she fancies me.' He grinned again.

'Have you read it? Has Delgado changed anything?'

'Have a look. But brace yourself.'

Gabriel slumped onto the sofa while Sara sat at the desk and began to read. He watched her face shift through a dozen expressions but said nothing until she was finished.

'Well?'

'Well? Well, I don't suppose I need to worry about my error anymore, do I?'

She didn't. The report was entirely different to the one she'd written. Each sample had its own fictitious biography which determined a summary in which almost nothing was found. Nothing of interest anyway. She felt sick. It still had her name at the top.

'What do you want to do Sara?'

Sara knew what she wanted to do. Gabriel saw it in her face, right up until the moment that she caught sight of Boris reclined in his rug, cleaning his face in his best impression of a cat. Then she considered her position in a world of Delgados, pushed down her indignation and replied.

'Nothing.'

Chapter 12

Requiem

Rain battered at the roof of the Church of St. Francis with a will it should not have owned.

Angus weaved himself around my legs as I waited for Father Fillipo, who was engaged in a quietly earnest conversation with Hettie. On a normal day it was possible that I could have caught the odd snippet, had I been that way inclined, but the deluge made even the thought redundant.

My eyelids felt as though they'd been weighted with gunshot. I knew I'd been dreaming again but couldn't remember a damned thing. It didn't seem important to tell Filippo that I felt weird – I always felt weird and besides, he had other things on his mind. He *did* tell me that morning that coffee was a particularly nootropic beverage. I had to look it up, but it basically means that it's a cognitive enhancer and may improve memory. It still tasted like crap cold. Not 'iced' in the way that millennials like it, just dreggy and mank. Regardless, it was free and handed to me by my friend without any expectation of payback. I glanced at his cabinet of angels and felt like shit.

I watched his face as he listened to Hettie's diatribe. The conversation had been going on for almost an hour, but he still focused like he was absorbing the death bed testament of the Pope. Right up until the point when Hettie got up, hugged him and began digging under her bunk for the giant bag of crap that she carried everywhere. Then, apparently, it was my turn.

'Thanks for staying, Loman. I appreciate it.'

'No problem Father.'

He sat next to me with a purposeful plonk and opened his mouth through that cotton wool beard. He must have noticed the jittering caress of my mug and stopped short of talking. The cup was emblazoned with a picture of a fried egg and the phrase 'Why do you have to watch what you say around egg whites? Because they can't take a yolk.' I saw Filippo stifle a boyish titter as he slid from the bed to the floor next to Angus and begin petting him. Angus reached out a paw and tilted his head in anticipation. I enjoyed the fuss made of him as much as he did. After a while Filippo nodded at the mug. 'Refill?' he asked.

Filippo didn't always wear his cassock. More often than not he'd dart around the church in t-shirt and jeans, even through the shivers of winter, but today he was in his full finery. I noticed a sheen of white dog hairs across the black as he rose from the floor. If Filippo saw them, he didn't say anything.

'Come through to the kitchen?' Filippo invited, and I followed. Angus huffed at my movement and fell back into repose.

The kettle was already whistling as we entered, and Hettie took extra mugs from the tree as she saw us. Mine was plain blue and absent humorous embellishment. I was grateful.

'Bad night?' opened Filippo.

'Yep, just the usual. It's just freaked me out a bit more than usual. Probably just the rain.'

'Want to talk about it?'

'Not just now Father, thank you. I'm happy just chilling.'

'That's good, we'll chat more when you're ready .... I actually need to be away for a couple of days anyway. Hettie's taking care of the hostel for me. I was wondering whether you'd be able to help. Do you feel up to it?'

My pause was enough to give it away. I wanted to feel up to it but didn't. I clasped my hands and squeezed, imagining my face which I knew would currently be turning into a bulging red tomato. I hoped that Filippo would read my embarrassment without me needing to verbalise - but it was Hettie who broke the silence.

'Why don't you take him with you Father? It may be good for both of you. No-one should have to say goodbye to a friend on their own.'

And that was that. A couple of hours later I was sitting in the passenger seat of Filippo's old Panda, and he was filling me in on where we were going. Angus dropped his head onto my shoulder from the back seat and looked excited.

***

'Syracuse. He wanted to be buried in his old church. He must have been happy there. I'm glad. First though we need to pick up ... whatever it is. His flat's no more than twenty minutes away.'

'What was he like?'

'I have to say that I'm not entirely sure. Father Janus was a few years younger than me. I never knew him very well and haven't spent any time with him for years. Not even when he returned to Rome. Why did he send me his note? Well, I guess we'll find out soon enough. I do remember that when I first met him, he was like a breath of fresh air. I've never met anyone more brimmed up with hope'.

'You liked him?'

'Never ask a priest to admit when they don't like someone Loman.' Filippo smiled widely 'But yes, I liked him. We were friends for a short time, right up until he'd got his parish in Syracuse. Then I suppose he just got too busy. You know how life can just get in the way? That's what I assumed. Then I heard that he'd been transferred to the Vatican archives. That was probably five or six years ago. I left a message for him, to see whether he'd like to meet up, but he never got back to me, and I didn't follow it up. I feel pretty bad about that now. Next thing I heard was a call from the bishop to tell me he'd passed away. He asked me if I'd go to the funeral, but I would have gone anyway. I *did* like him, he was fun.'

'What about his note? It sounds kind of mysterious.'

'Mmm. Not so much mysterious as out of character I suppose. But now you ask - maybe it *is* mysterious.' He threw me a look like he was about to twiddle his moustache.

Father Filippo trailed off. I was intrigued but didn't want to press. No, that's not true. I did want to press but we were stuck in a car together for nine hours and I didn't want to feel uncomfortable. I still felt embarrassed and hoped that my face wasn't still as red as it felt.

It took half an hour to get to Father Janus' apartment block. It was a quaint terracotta complex, gated with garages on the ground floor and accommodation above. His flat was on the third floor. There was no lift, but it was a cool day, and the building was well configured and clean. His flat was immaculate. Not so difficult when it's just four rooms I suppose but nevertheless, it gleamed from the terrazzo floors to the elegant coving which edged the walls and ceiling. Filippo left the key in the door and took Janus's note from the envelope it had arrived in. The stationary was watermarked, and the scribed writing looked like something a Carthusian monk would have been proud of. Filippo took care not to crease it. It sounded like luxury as the

Father unfolded it, and he absorbed its content with a melancholy determination worthy of the wishes of a dead friend.

'It's in here.'

I followed him into the bedroom. The ceiling line followed the rafters, high up into a vault which terminated at the centre of the room with a small access hatch. It was barely fourteen inches square. Henry Kissinger couldn't have negotiated a way through it and even if he did, the void above it wouldn't have accepted anything below his collar.

'Give me a hand?' asked Filippo, placing a chair directly beneath it. He removed his shoes and took my hand as he stepped up. He was still a foot short, even on tippy toes.

'Fuck.'

He mused the room from his semi-elevated position until he spotted a padded footstool. Its satin cushion sat on four ornately carved rosewood legs and its whole looked just right to bridge the difference between the bed height, a fully stretched Filippo and that tiny opening. He positioned it carefully on the bed and did his best to seat it into place, pushing down against hard springs which bobbed the thing back against his efforts.

'Really Father?'

Filippo climbed aboard, wobbling precariously.

'Thou shall not test the Lord thy God' he grinned, and I grinned back, embarrassed that the reference flew further over my head than the loft hatch.

Stretching, he grasped upward and braced – so far as possible – against the architrave which trimmed the opening. He pushed at the hatch with the other hand, rocking his Elvis legs with involuntary enthusiasm until his hand emerged from the opening clutching a small canvas rucksack which clinked as he held it out toward me. It was me who dropped it, clattering onto the bed and coming apart to strew shiny knickknacks like a giant Christmas cracker. Filippo followed them, a cascade of black and grey atop the booty, to the creaking of springs and aging limbs. He sat up, rubbing his back and grinning again before spotting the gold reliquary which perched between his legs. He stiffened visibly as his colour drained, but the expletives that I expected didn't come.

***

The road rumbled, an endless monotony of sound. Filippo had insisted that we continue on to Janus's funeral, despite looking like he may pass out at the wheel. 'I suppose it's only fair to explain a few things. At least the few that I have any fucking idea about.' he said. So much for not feeling uncomfortable.

'Father Janus's note – it asked me to pick up a few things that needed returning to the Vatican library. It didn't say what or why, and I assumed it may be a few books that needed handing back and that he'd been called away. Something like that anyway. I was going to ring him but then the bishop called and told me .... you know.

I really don't know why he chose me. I hadn't even spoken to him for God knows how long. I still don't know why. It's not the biggest question any more though. Fuck me, no. That gold container that spun me 'round? I've seen it before, or at least one like it. I'm sure that it was in National Geographic a few years ago, in an article about Sancta Colonia – Holy Cologne. Its cathedral hosted an exhibition of mediaeval relics, including the reliquary that we've got in the boot! It must be worth a bloody fortune. I haven't seen many relics close up, other than the little ossuary that I keep in my cabinet, but all of Janus's look pretty real to me. I really should have taken them straight back to the Vatican but my head was whirling and well, I promised the bishop that I'd go to the funeral. What the fuck's *he* going to say? I'll speak to him when we get there. Maybe they'll take them at the church and get them transported back. Fuck, I hope so. Janus, you asshole, what the fuck have you been up to?'

For all that was happening, it was Filippo's mention of the ossuary that piqued my curiosity, mainly because Angus seemed so enamoured with it. He perked up in the back seat, ears tilted despite the fact that I hadn't said a word. I really *wanted* to ask about it again but now clearly wasn't the time. Instead:

'Are you ok Father?'

'Bless you Loman. Yes. Yes, of course, I am. I'm so sorry. I should really be asking you. Your memory – we have plenty of time now, if you'd like to talk. Anything new to report?'

I should probably have said no but convinced myself that the distraction of listening to my woes may be useful. I didn't always act like a knob, you understand, but it was pretty regular.

'Well, yes, I guess so. I think you were right about my dreams going backwards. But they're fading more the further they go back. I don't remember half as much about them now as I did, say, six months ago. They still leave feelings behind though.' I shuddered.

'What do you mean?'

'Well, it's difficult to describe. I get snippets of what happened in them but can't string them together anymore. You know that moment when you realise you've done something wrong and your heart skips? Then your body gets flushed with heat and you feel sick? Kind of like that, but not exactly. I suppose I wake up more and more feeling like I'm the biggest shit who ever lived. It's not that different to how I've felt since .... well, always, but it's more intense. Jesus, I'm sweating now just talking about it.'

He thought for a moment, clearly weighing his words. I wish he'd weighed them differently but, in his position, well, I guess anyone would have gone the same way.

'I hope you don't mind me asking again, but have you seen a doctor recently? Could they help do you think? With your memory I mean, not just the dreams.'

I slumped back into my seat like a teenager.

'No. And I won't be bothering them again. They've never managed to do anything. The SSN chucked citalopram at me. I tried them for a bit, but they just made me feel sick. I don't want to sit in front of a psychologist anyway. How do I 'work through' something that I can't even remember? For fuck's sake I live on the streets and can't recall what happened to me beyond a decade ago. They'll just section me and then I'd top myself. I'm not mental, I'm really not - I just can't remember anything.'

I delivered the words at an alarming pace and already knew that Filippo would compensate by slowing his. I guessed what was coming and it was bumming me out even before it arrived. Filippo of all people should have known that I didn't need any more shit layered on. I wished I'd just asked him about the bloody ossuary. I bobbed in the familiarity of it all and felt sick. No doctor I'd ever seen knew when to leave it. They just kept on pushing. I braced myself - but Filippo didn't push. He just punched the buttons of his Sat-Nav and said nothing.

We drove a while then. I allowed the drone from the wheels to comfort me while I sought solace from the landscape. Father Filippo took the road down to Anzio and we followed the coastal route. It added hours to the journey, but it was beautiful. Little shards of heaven reflected off the water, piercing the winter gloom. Just after Acciaroli, in the commune of Pollica, a pod of dolphins pierced the waters and I lived in the present, just for a moment. I pointed them out to Filippo, but his eyes couldn't find them.

'You know I can offer you confession, right? If you ever wanted it? It doesn't matter what you've done, or even what you think you might have done. God doesn't bear grudges.'

'Thanks Father, I know. But I'd like to know what I'm confessing to first.'

***

The city of Syracuse is famous for its ancient ruins. Tourists come for the rich Greek and Roman history, the amphitheatres and architecture. It is the birthplace of Archimedes and was once a major power of the Mediterranean world. It boasts an impressive seventh century cathedral with a baroque façade and statuary, with origins as a Greek doric temple. It forms part of an impressive UNESCO world heritage site.

Father Janus's parish church was situated close to Villaggio Miano, a Northwest neighbourhood of Syracuse just over an hours walk from the cathedral. Its graveyard had filled a hundred years ago and not even a personal appeal from Janus's bishop could persuade the local clerics to allow his internment on church grounds. There had, in fact, been some heated resistance to the proposal. Instead, he was to be allowed a simple funereal liturgy before being transported to the local crematorium.

Filippo and I sat in a central pew behind an empty row of seats, trying to pad an attendance which was, simply, thin.

The bishop was in deep conversation with the church warden and the obvious tension within the room had quickly sidelined any attempt to discuss the riches which still sat in the boot of Filippo's Panda, and I wished that I was helping Hettie brew coffee.

Angus was being fussed over by the church warden's kids. He'd alternated between sitting and lying quietly across the rear seat of the car through yesterday's ten long hours, but now it was time to stretch his legs. He'd already punctured one football, but the children didn't care and neither did he. They chased him between the gravestones as he shook the final blows of air from its deflating carcass. Dotty, the littlest of the warden's brood had been sent back to the vestry to retrieve another toy for him to destroy, and she huffed back with a tennis ball and another bag of amaretti biscotti for him to devour. A dozen almond biscuits would sate most of us but Angus happily accepted Dotty's gift. She squeezed him as she shovelled them in, causing crumbs and slobber to shoot over Aldo and Elena with a savage belch. Elena's eyes widened as sputum dribbled down one lens of her glasses, and her pout elicited a joyous roar from Dotty's tiny form. 'Bravo ragazza, good boy!' Angus's grin widened to a toothy smile and Elena giggled as she let him lick the crumbs from her face.

Chiara had separated from the bishop, and I thanked her for her children's help as she took a seat in the row behind us. 'You're welcome' she whispered and sat back as the priest climbed the single step and placed his notes before him in the pulpit.

'Ladies and gentlemen, distinguished guests and mourners, today we gather to say goodbye to Father Janus, formerly priest of this parish and latterly curator at the library archives within Vatican City.'

The speech lasted barely ten minutes and it was obvious, even to me, that despite the pleasantries embodied within its clipped politeness there was no 'celebrating the life', 'fondly remembered' or 'dearly beloved' to illuminate Janus' existence. Chiara had even grunted, very quietly, as the priest referred to 'mourners.' I was glad when the final chord rasped from the organ's bellows. I thanked Chiara's children, and they milled as Angus jumped back into the car. Father Filippo asked her if she'd known Janus.

'Yes.' The inflection in the word sounded like a prelude but she gathered her family and ushered them back to the church. Filippo sauntered around the car for an age, hoping to catch the bishop, but he was distracted by the handful of attendees who surrounded him. Their faces held the scornful indignation of the resentful and I was glad to be in the little Fiat and out of earshot.

That evening we sat in the hotel room and laid the contents of Janus's bag across one of the twin beds.

Chapter 13

Pride

Father Filippo is not a proud man. Let's consider that statement.

Some recent studies tell us that pride makes us care about how others see us and how we see ourselves. It is presented as a positive emotion. It makes us want to feel good about ourselves and make sure that others look up to us, seeing us as competent and powerful. Some of these studies tell us that others will seek knowledge from people who show 'pride displays'. Such individuals are assumed to have expertise underlying their pride.

Filippo is not a proud man. In today's world, some people may believe that he is somehow lacking. Lacking in confidence, or charisma, or even lacking in competence, but of course none of those things is true. He shows confidence in God, and trust in His judgement. He is careful to demonstrate humility and to ensure that others recognise his position as servant, and not master. He is most certainly competent.

Sitting within a drawer of his work desk at St. Francis sits what would appear to be a random wad of papers, secured with a rusty paperclip and a yellowing, somewhat sticky, elastic band. The front sheet, innocuous and innocent, tells us something of Filippo as a boy. His 'diploma di maturita' shows a score of 98 out of 100, equivalent to A*AA, the highest grade achievable in English schools. It had never been framed or otherwise paraded and was flavoured with a spotting of powdery mould. The qualifications sitting below it tell us more.

Parcelled below the Laurea Magistrale (master's degree) sits not one but two Dottorato di Ricerca (PhDs). The first and earliest is his doctorate in medicine, followed by his certification as an MRCP – a member of the Royal College of Physicians. The second, and perhaps less surprising given his calling, is his PhD in Theology and Religious Studies. This precludes a chunky eighty thousand word thesis, printed on one side only, the premise of which is entitled 'Can the devil be saved?' If we delved into this tome in detail, we would find such questions as 'How was Satan, created by God to be wholly good and a servant to His will, able to act outside his nature and create sin?' 'Why is Satan denied the possibility of contrition and forgiveness?' 'Is sin a direct result of God's failed blueprint for creation?' Filippo's obstinate conclusions centred around there being a clear and undeniable inconsistency in the representation of God both across and within religious groups, each trying to lever Him into the confines of their own culture without ever really trying to determine the actual truth of His being. In effect, he blamed people, and those people gave him a pass. Just.

***

'What the flying fuck are we supposed to make of this lot?' He'd read the report that lined the bottom of the bag. It was crumblingly sad, and not just because it looked like it had been flushed down a toilet. Filippo looked as though he wished that it had been.

'What does it say Father?'

'It says that nothing on this bed has any doctrinal value whatsoever.'

He awaited my reply, but I had nothing to give. After a moment, Filippo interpreted. 'It says that none of these religious relics are what the church thought they were. They're all fakes. It may also be an explanation. Or an apology.'

'Really? Who from? And what for?'

'Maybe from Janus. For what he did. I don't fucking know. Not really.'

'I'm sorry Father Filippo I'm not keeping up.' Panic rose in my throat and stifled my voice. My next words hadn't reached my brain yet, but Filippo pre-empted. Or maybe he just couldn't stand the quiet.

'No Loman, you can't help.'

I must have flushed my disappointment. My face mocked the hiding of my hands behind my back where they fidgeted like a kid with a full bladder. Filippo knew the look and absorbed me into his wonderings.

'Well, maybe. It may help to talk it through, to hear it out loud. But please bear in mind that I don't actually *know* anything. It's just what's written in *that*. So far as I know it's a prop from a bad movie. They may all be props, or someone's idea of a joke. A fucking bad one.'

'Or an apology? You said it may be an apology.'

'Yes. Or an apology. Loman, I want to share this with you but it needs to stay between us. I don't really know what's going on and speculation could be damaging. I do need to speculate though, if you can handle it. I mean just *look* at it all.'

I looked at it all. Filippo was flustering and I clearly wasn't seeing what he was. It just looked like an odd collection of shiny. Something that may impress a magpie perhaps, but no one else. The gold-coloured bits looked showy and classless, and I couldn't believe that they were real. The rest just looked like crap. I sat at the desk opposite the beds and gave Filippo my face. I felt proud that he would trust me. But then my inner voice reminded me that no one ever trusted what I said anyway. Who better to share a confidence with?

'Loman, I don't know whether you've guessed this or not, but Janus's death was not accidental.' I nodded.

'He took his own life. For a Catholic, the consequences of such an act are dire. The taking of a life, even your own life, is a mortal sin that prevents the perpetrator from entering heaven. For a priest? Well, I daren't think. I still don't know why Janus picked me to collect these items. Maybe he trusted me to get them back to the church. *If* they're real. But they clearly had some relevance to him, and perhaps to his decision. You know, I've read *this,*' he held up the report, 'and I can't believe that it *wouldn't* have had an effect on him.'

He continued.

'That paperwork details a range of tests that have been carried out on the items laid out across the bed. I don't really understand all of the detail, but I do recognise a couple of the items, not just the reliquary. A few of them are more generic – the wood and the cloth – but they're all religious relics. They may be copies, but why would Janus have bothered to have me pick them up if that were the case?

The tests, according to the report, came up with a number of conclusions. The items were from different time periods or countries – that's to be expected. I mean, look at them. But what's disturbing – to me at least – is the blood signatures that were present on a number of the items.'

'Blood. That is disturbing Father.' I pretended.

'No, no that's not it at all. That reliquary is purported to contain a thorn from Christ's crown. You know the crucifixion stories, right?'

'Yes. The crown of thorns'

'Well, the dna that was taken from the samples should have indicated that it came from an individual from the middle east, where

Jesus came from, if it's to be considered authentic. But it doesn't, it's European and it's not just that. There were only a couple of samples, but the tests indicate that they're both from women. Now, we all accept that relics like these have a value in terms of faith, and who knows whether *any* of them are actually real? That doesn't disprove Christ and certainly not God, but they do provide focus and hope for people, and that's what's being undermined within the report.'

I couldn't have looked as impressed as Filippo expected and he frowned before pressing on.

'Loman, this is serious. A man has died. Janus *wanted* to believe in things like this. I *want* to but it's not the underlying reason for my faith - but people are different. Do you know how many people were affected when scientists announced that the Turin Shroud was a fake? That it was carbon dated to around the thirteenth century?'

I stared blankly, trying to keep the re-emerging panic from showing on my face. I wanted to help but Filippo was getting more and more irritated. And I really didn't know what the fuck he was going on about. Not much of it anyway. He ploughed on regardless.

'The Turin Shroud? The cloth that Jesus was buried in after the crucifixion. The only known image of the actual face of Christ. It had been revered for hundreds of years until the church allowed scientists to inspect it in 1978. They cut a corner off for carbon dating. Oh, it's still held up as an icon of faith. People still go to see it whenever it's displayed. But there's a corner of every thinking person's mind that treats it with a caution that didn't used to exist. In that sense, it can do more harm than good. *For fuck's sake.*'

The comment was directed at the papers, not at me, but it still set my hands to task, rubbing and rinsing behind my back. I'd not seen Filippo like this before. Neither had Angus, who wheeled around my legs anxiously before trancing under the bed. Filippo saw him and sank into himself, exhaling the angst and irritation in a deliberate act of will. 'I'm sorry Loman.' He huffed to his knees, ass up, and placed his hand submissively in front of the dog. 'I'm sorry boy.'

I thought that he was going to cry. Instead, he squeezed himself under the bed and lay still until I saw Angus's tail begin to pat the carpet. When they emerged, Angus was panting in a toothy grin and Filippo's fine cassock was ruined.

'I think Janus killed himself over these *things*.' He said simply, as if it answered every question in the world.

He sat on the bed for a while, stretching his feet to the floor to accommodate the mutt draped across them. When Angus shifted, he rose. 'Coffee?' he asked, and I relaxed into the normality.

We took the direct route home. Filippo said that he felt like a thief, having failed to discuss Janus's haul with the bishop, and we continued to carry the loot around in its canvas sack. It jangled clunkily as he placed it back into the boot for the journey, but Filippo didn't seem to care.

I didn't mention it to him at the time, but amongst my hand rinsing and Filippo's conjecture, one of the items had seriously freaked me out. Filippo was upset enough without me subjecting him to my paranoia, but the thing may as well have stabbed me in the guts. It looked like an old bent piece of reinforcing bar at first, but I puked myself empty after I'd touched it. I told Filippo that I'd eaten too much chocolate from the mini bar. He believed me – he'd seen me scoff down biscuits at the hostel. Filippo had said that the report referred to it as a spear head, and it still sat in my mind as the E80 toll road became the A24 into Rome.

Chapter 14

Progress

In 1996, the world stood in awe as Dolly the sheep became the world's first mammalian clone. She stood alone as a testament to humanity's creative genius – the only lamb to survive to adulthood from two hundred and seventy-seven attempts. For Enzo Delgado, the failures were irrelevant, and he pressed forward with renewed vigour.

Dolly died in February 2003, at the age of six. Her hide was scraped of fat and her skin stretched around a frame of bone and wire. After being stuffed with cotton, she was placed in the National Museum of Scotland for the public to gawp at.

In the time between her birth and her death, Enzo had been busy.

Cloning methods were improving. Stem cell technology was still a decade away, but Dolly and her sisters had raised the bar. The transfer of DNA to a viable egg cell was – given time and resource – highly achievable, and the availability of suitable donor animals straightforward.

The practicality of replicating the approach in humans - within Western Europe at least - was problematic. It was one thing to develop a viable embryo within controlled laboratory conditions, but Enzo's colleagues baulked at the idea of transplanting those seeds into real human surrogates.

As with many ethical issues, the problem was solved with money. There are always people who are willing to re-consider morality for profit and Enzo knew how to find them. Or at least he knew a man who knew a man. He didn't need to know more - only that the process itself would be carried out in accordance with his strict instructions.

The Delgado family had earnt their reputation and their riches a decade before Dolly. She was just another step toward something far bigger. Their research had begun in the late eighties but attempts to replicate the miracle they'd uncovered hit a dead end long before Dolly was even a glint in a scientist's eye. Oh, there'd been successes. More than enough to bankroll the company that he now ran. But the grail, the miracle? That remained elusive. Most people would consider the development of immunoglobins suitable to combat the menace of hepatitis, combined with vast strides forward in the treatment of influenza, to mark an extra-ordinary contribution to medical science and the world at large, but they didn't have Enzo's context. Even the unprecedented steps taken toward the eradication of HIV seemed trivial compared to the bottomless pit of riches that hovered just out of reach.

The sample they'd procured all those years ago was a one-off. A snapshot from a unique situation that was ancient long before the Delgado's had gotten their hands on it. For Enzo, forty years of his family's effort had teased at success without ever approaching the potential of the of the original. It wafted under his nose like baking cookies, resisting all attempts at replication while continuing to cast its giant shadow of hope. Enzo had grown to hate it, insofar as you can hate a 'thing', with a barely muted jealousy. Even his own 'Dolly' had proven ... problematic. He sought no justification of his methods, or their outfall. If there was ever a situation where the ends justified the means, this was it. Even though those means included Hettie.

Now though, there was a new sample, and there was new hope.

Chapter 15

The Unexpected Guest

God is a cunt. Heard that before? Good.

I suppose it needs a little context, but it wouldn't, if you knew Him like I do.

The Stones had a song called 'Sympathy for the devil'. Well, I'm not asking for sympathy, but consider the facts and you may decide that a little empathy is well earned.

Yes, Loman, I *am* talking to *you*. He thinks that his dreams aren't real you know, and who knows, maybe he's right. It's all just a matter of flavour, isn't it? I just like to throw a little spice into the mix, just to show I'm still around, and it's interesting to visit people's dreams now and again. Folk will do all sorts when they think no-one's looking.

I thought that it would be nice for the two of us to have a little one on one - away from Filippo and the influence of his tribe. I wasn't sure that I'd bother within the context of your little tale, but Janus is gone, and that word perspective is mentioned with such regularity these days that I thought I'd offer a little of my own.

So, let's cut to the chase. Jesus Christ – the editor of the biggest red top in history – the bible. And what does He say about me, leader of the opposition? Exactly what you'd expect.

'Father of Lies', 'Son of Perdition', 'Serpent of Old'. Not exactly complimentary, is it? No, but not exactly surprising either. Spin you see. Promote your own agenda whilst implying idiocy in anyone who wishes to even listen to the other side. It's ages old – but it still works.

So, let's see if you have it in you to see through the lies. There are some themes to address, but I'll try to keep things simple. Not red top simple but, well, here's hoping:

Everyone's heard of the Book of Revelation, even if they haven't read it. Within it, John the Apostle states that war is coming. The war will be between good and evil, and for the purposes of the conflict I am to be the enemy of all that is good. Not on my own, but as one of three - a 'diabolical trinity' no less. So just as God is Father in the 'holy' trinity of Father, Son and Spirit, I am to be the Father on the opposite side of the house. Except that's not quite right, is it?

Just as God is Jesus's father, he is also mine. I am, actually, his first-born son, fashioned with his will just as much as his more favoured offspring. And what does he do with me? Casts me aside for my sibling, just because I had a difficult 'puberty'. Nice. But it's not like dear old dad doesn't have form – look at poor Ishmeal, first son of Abraham, booted from the nest when a 'holier' replacement came along with God's good wishes. Don't take my word for it – Wikipedia is waiting for you. Now the Holy Spirit, third partner in the triumvirate – 'God's will in action' in simple terms. The church tells us that His will is unchanging and immovable right? So why would anyone assume that it's suddenly absent from my little team? I'd welcome it - I like the God of the Old Testament, all full of wrath and anger – humanity deserves it. I'm not looking to replace God, you see, or his Trinity, despite the bad press, I just want to be a part of it. Me, the old man and his will. That'll do for me, just so long as He lets me out of the house occasionally. That's not too much to ask surely? No? Good. Let's move on.

John stated that I am to be the opposite of God – the black to His white - total bull. One minute we're told that God is universally constant and the next that he's had a change of heart, and 'forgiven' us, between the last page of the Old Testament and the first page of the new one? It's like swapping out an actor in your favourite soap. It's never quite the same afterwards, is it? You know it's *supposed* to be the same character, but something doesn't quite ring true anymore. And are we *really* supposed to believe that the best way to mend a relationship between humankind and God is for humankind to murder His son in the most inhumane way imaginable? Fuck, yeah, that'll work. Especially in someone with a reputation for murderous vengeance.

Thinking of changing your news outlet yet? Well, if not, just listen to this. In John's apocalyptic scripture, Jesus's proposal results in the death and damnation of all except 144,000 of God's most favourite people. If we take that literally, that's 144,000 out of the eight billion souls who currently reside on this earth. Still better than the chances of me or you hooking up with Carrie Fisher – especially now that she's taken residence upstairs - but good luck, the odds are against you.

Then John describes me as 'That old serpent who deceives the world', yet here I am trying to keep things simple. Christ himself sent John the visions for the Book of Revelation. And what a mire of ambiguity that book turned out to be - so who's deceiving who?

Take verse 13.1 for example. 'And I stood upon the sand of the sea, and saw a beast rise up out of the sea, having ten horns and seven heads'. People say that the sand of the sea represents all the people of the earth seeing the beast, which is a conglomerate of ten kings - but really, why not just say that? Poor effort on John's part. Jesus' favourite disciple no less, perhaps he was a looker.

Sorry, I don't mean to get bitchy but it's not easy rising above the continual deceit. Christ states unequivocally that he's going to kill 99.9 percent of you, but still says that He's the good guy? And you lot fall for it. Are you kidding me?

So, here I am. More than happy to proclaim myself in opposition to Christ. It is my greatest wish to defeat His programme and undermine His plan for you all. Go me.

To achieve this, of course, I will need to establish my kingdom as supreme on the earth, with all the peoples of the earth (or sands of the sea, ha), brought into subjection to myself, to quote the great book. I can't guarantee that I'd be perfect, not like the 'kind and gentle' Jesus, but I can state unequivocally that I'd be a better option for those sitting outside the 144,000 that *He* chooses to take to his bosom.

So, try to think of me as an independent. Unaffiliated to any mandate but my own. Here's my pitch.

John the disciple / apostle has predicted victory for his best friend and master in the war to come. He's laid it all out in Revelations as a misty picture of dragons and beasts and a shiny Jesus on a golden cloud. If you haven't already read Revelations, give it a go – that includes you, Loman - it is, in effect, Christ's plan for world domination. After several millennia spent extolling His magnanimous gift of freedom of choice, He's finally admitting that if you don't choose Him, you're fucked.

Now, how do I hope to swing things?

Well, the first part of His plan includes turning the world to shit – *The Tribulation* – while allowing me to sit in dominance over the world. Then he'll sweep in, blaming me for everything that's gone wrong, and lock me away for a thousand years before doing away with me entirely.

For the uninformed, He'd certainly appear the conquering hero, but clearly, *I* don't see the ending the way He's dictated it. So – what to do?

I see little point in fighting the initial episode. If God chooses to elevate me to a position of power – great – I won't even bitch about it. What I don't like is Christ's assumption that I'll roll over and give it all up so that He can live forever with His handful of favourites, all telling Him what a good guy He is for murdering the other eight billion souls and me on top.

Here's the alternative, still based on the words from the book of God. There's always a *little* truth thrown in with the spin after all. Remember the seven heads and ten horns, rising from the sea?

The symbolism of the sea is revealed by John in Revelation 17:15: "*The waters which you saw, where the harlot sits, are peoples, multitudes, nations, and tongues.*" So, my reign arises through the peoples of the earth from the mass of the world's humanity. That really narrows it down, doesn't it? But we're getting there slowly.

For God's explanation of the seven heads and ten horns, turn to Revelation 17:9-13. The heads are seven mountains. Mountains in the Scripture often represent kingdoms or imperial powers (have a look at Psalm 30:7; Jeremiah 51:25; or Daniel 2:35 if you're so inclined). Revelation 17:10 specifically says that of these seven kingdoms, five are fallen, and one is, and one is yet to come.

The world as we stand today has seen only six great imperial powers: Egypt, Assyria, Babylonia, Persia, Greece, and Rome. The one which existed in John's day was Rome. Five imperial powers have fallen, and one is - that was Rome. God said there was one more yet to come - a great power to rise up, and from it will come the empire of the beast (Revelation 13:11). Little old me.

Now, this is all very well but I sense your eyes glazing over. Well, while the world waits for another superpower, and has looked suspiciously at Russia, China, and in fact almost anyone with the clout to stir the pot, it doesn't seem able to grasp the obvious. Let's see how you do, Loman, with the wisdom of two thousand years to draw upon.

Which group has grown in wealth and authority, unchallenged and unabashed for centuries? Quietly or otherwise dictating policy and process across nations? Which group has set itself on high, looking down upon the people it purports to serve? Which group has shamelessly interpreted and undermined the intent of Christ's life for its own benefit? If you haven't already guessed, then shame on you.

The *Church of Rome*. This great new world will be born of the Church of Rome - God's own fucking people! Filippo and all his little pals, inadvertently elevating me on high. It really is sheer poetry. And what's my role in all of this? Absolutely fucking nothing. I don't need to do a damned thing except wait – the bible tells it so.

Have a think about that as you wake up inside the church of St. Francis.

Chapter 16

What's in the bag?

'D*ear Hettie, thank you for your most recent epistle. Your messages lift me as a souffle rises.*

I long for the day when your hair will radiate its brown luminance upon my face and your crocs squeak knowledge of your presence to my soul. I have been practicing my boulette d'avesnes for that wonderous day. Please tell me when it shall be.

I have happiness to share. Having left my role as concierge I am now a junior chef at the Moderna Hotel Roma. I aspire to greatness, 'though they currently have me on the spuds. They shall be mashed in your honour.

I am working the supper menu but can meet you any lunchtime or Tuesday / Wednesday evening that you name.

Your aspiring friend

Jose'

Hettie smiled wanly. Jose's messages were getting shorter, but she could hardly blame him. He'd hung in there for longer than most – in fact, longer than all – she'd cut off contact with the rest as she realised that she could genuinely like him, and now only he remained. A forlorn hope of joyous normality which faded with the winter nights.

The e-mail she was anticipating hadn't arrived. No admonishment, no demands. No threat of legal action or in fact any consequence at all. 'I should probably be pleased' she forced but realised that her situation would never be that simple. She'd often wondered what they'd do if she declined to attend her medical, but never, ever thought that it would be nothing. Nevertheless, there was little she could do now but await their response.

She clicked open the search bar and scrolled down. There seemed zero point in looking again, but that hadn't stopped her the last time. Or the hundred before that.

'Spanish Birth Certificate search'

'Family history search'

'Spain Civil registration records'

'Italy Civil registration records'

All meant the same to Hettie. He was missing, and she didn't know where he was or what had happened to him. Nor even if he'd kept the name she had given him. 'Gamma.' The brightest light in the universe. Physicists may have told her that her interpretation of the word was not technically correct but that wasn't really the point, not to her anyway. She liked the representation, and she enjoyed the thought of him relaxing into his name as a long-haired teen with a spliff hanging easily from one corner of his mouth. That, of course, would be years away yet. Years of typing the same words into a search engine.

'Fuck it.' Her hands abandoned their hovering. What was the point? The chances of finding him were next to nothing even if she'd had a job and a home and a 'normal' life. *Her* chances were a million miles even from that. Fucking Enzo. The architect of her life. She was glad that she'd finally refused to accommodate him. Fuck their 'research' – she'd done her time as a fucking lab rat.

Swooping up her belongings she turned from the desk to stride purposefully for the door. A half dozen steps before tumbling across a ransom desk. Its suited, bespectacled bald head creased at the neck in anticipation of impact before returning to its reading. 'Sorry' she mumbled, reverting to her usual unassuming gait, which looked very much like an animated apology. 'Fucking Enzo' she thought again.

***

The walk between the Vatican Library and the church of Saint Francis is barely a mile. It usually took Hettie twenty minutes to lug her belongings between establishments, but tonight was cold, and she widened her stride, fighting her irritation as the buckle of her rucksack bounced incessantly off her thigh. The chill hadn't quite emptied the streets but the normal bustle along the Via Giulia had been replaced by an eerie stillness which clung ominously to its flanking structures. The long street had a feeling of dark oppression despite its reputation for high fashion, and its towering facades fish eyed Hettie's focus to a distant end which seemed just a little too far to be comfortable.

Trailing footsteps are an unwelcome addition to such an environment and the slap at her thigh grew faster.

'Christ, girl, chill.' A personal admonishment for unwanted fears. Rome's nightlife produced all sorts of people. Hettie was used to most of them. Some tried to steal her stuff, some pissed on her in her sleeping bag. Some hit. Regardless, she determined that her mind at least should stay free from their influence.

She slowed her pace and paused outside the Church of Santa Maria dell'Orazione e Morte, standing obstinately rigid opposite the image of a winged skeleton that had been embossed onto the masonry, inches from her face. She had seen it a hundred times, but her disdain had been immediate. Why *would* someone build a church with the sole intent of terrifying its congregation? Inside, through a door to the left of the main alter was a chamber decorated with human bones and skulls. Hettie had never seen it, but Father Filippo had told her that it had given him the 'heebie-jeebies'. He didn't use one 'fuck' to describe it. Somehow, it painted the picture even darker.

'*What's in the bag, Missy?*'

'Fuck.'

There were two of them. A 'fatty' and a 'skinny'. Unfortunately, there was no-one else. No passers-by or even a hint of movement from further down the street. Just them. And her.

'Nothing. It's just my clothes and some papers. You can look if you want.'

'We can? Well, that's very accommodating of you. I guess we should. Just to be sure that you don't have anything dangerous in there. Something that you could use to attack us with.'

'Why would I do that?'

'Well, *look* at you, girl. Now look at us.'

Hettie looked. Both men were smartly dressed. The 'gent' on the left, the one who spoke, was immaculate. He was puffed with a casual arrogance, as if his ego stood on tiptoe, and looked like he'd dressed for the theatre. He wore no overcoat despite the cold, and his blazer was fastened at the waist with a single button. His hair was slicked. If it rained, the moisture would never have bothered his skin, but he barely looked 'greasy' at all. He could have stepped straight out of a silent movie.

The other man was shorter. Still taller than Hettie, but a good four to five inches less than his imposing companion. He wore a smart but simple suit below a military styled overcoat which swung open over his belly. He grunted as he tore Hettie's bag from her grasp and ruffled through the contents before handing her file of certificates to his partner.

'What's this? A doctorate in philosophy? Not yours surely?' Hettie didn't reply. Whatever they'd decided to do, it was already fixed. To fight or to flight? There were only two of them and she was pretty sure that she could outpace one of them at least, but the file that hung so nonchalantly from the stranger's fingers was her identity, and she wasn't quite ready to lose that along with everything else.

'So, Hettie. Are you ready to come to your appointment now?' The words accompanied a clumsy grasp for her wrist and chubby fingers closed limply in an underwhelming attempt at restraint. Enzo.

'Christ Enzo, *really*?' Her heart rate slowed – just a little. What an entitled fucking narcissist. It would be easier to just go, but *this*. Fuck the little shit.

She twisted easily and grabbed at her file, which hit the ground with a ringing thud as the spring clips finally gave way and her education strewed around her feet. She looked up as the tall man looked down. It could have been *his* face embossed on the church wall and she realised that Enzo wasn't her immediate problem. This was something that he enjoyed. She ran, hearing no more than a half dozen stumbling footsteps before bounding beyond the trailing sound.

A half mile later and her run became a jog, then a walk. There were no footsteps behind her. The ineptitude of her would be assailants had switched down her adrenaline and by the time she spotted Ginger waiting at the hostel steps she felt unexpectedly calm.

'Alright?' he asked, and she realised that her life had been stolen and fear clamped around her like cramp.

Chapter 17

Hettie

We arrived back at the hostel in the early hours. True to her word, Hettie had opened up and the place rocked with the varying rhythms of two dozen sleeping destitutes. Most bunks were taken but it didn't matter, neither Filippo or I could sleep anyway. The hour I managed draped over the tiny kitchen table had done more harm than good, and I felt sick in a way which made my reaction to the spear feel like thanksgiving.

Hettie was up. Filippo had noticed the marks on her wrist within minutes of our arrival. He may not have looked so closely if she hadn't been pacing like a parade. She was just settling at the little table as I was abandoning my final attempt to nod off and rubbing goop from my eyes. It appeared as though I'd entered the conversation just as it got interesting.

'They took my certificates. And my diary. All my passwords were in it for fuck's sake. My boots were in there too. I've had them since university.'

'Do you know who they were, Hettie?'

'Yes. I mean no. Not personally, but I know who sent them. Enzo fucking Delgado.'

I didn't recognise the name, but it was clear that Filippo did.

'Have you contacted the police?' Filippo looked like he knew the answer already, but I suppose it was a question that needed to be asked.

He hunkered visibly into his chair awaiting the response. When it came, it was surprisingly mild. In tone, if not in language.

'What the fuck for? What fucking good would it do? Oh, Filippo, you of all people should know what the police do when people like me go to them. A great, big, aporophobic fuck all.'

Filippo wasn't swearing. I guess you can have too much of a good thing and Hettie was spreading it pretty thick. I didn't dare ask what aporophobic meant but looked it up later. *An adverse reaction to or rejection of the poor or underprivileged*. I guess you needed a philosophy degree to use it in real life. I considered retiring to the dormitory but didn't want to risk straying into her line of sight.

'You can't just leave it Hettie. You can't let anyone just assault you without repercussions. No-one should be allowed to get away with that.'

'It isn't no-one though, is it? It's Enzo Delgado.'

She breathed steeply before offering a solution. It wasn't received well.

'I should just go to the fucking appointment.'

'You're not actually serious? Not after this, surely? I wouldn't be going within a million miles of the man. If you're sure – if he's *actually* tried to steal you off the street, Hettie. What would someone like that be capable of behind closed doors?'

I was waiting for Filippo to bring the police back into the discussion, but Hettie glanced in my direction. She'd noticed my emergence from sleep and clearly hadn't reckoned on an audience. I guess that my half-conscious self must have been more tolerable than the open-mouthed interloper who was now gawping in her direction. A line of drool spilled down one corner of my bottom lip, completing my discomfort. Now really *was* the time to get up and hide amongst the snoring majority but her stare had pinned me. I jittered. Hettie decided to plough on through my indecision.

'He won't do anything. He just wants to prod and poke like he always does. I don't believe he'd try to hurt me, not in a violent way, anyway. He's just stupidly obsessed with his 'research'. And he needs me. Or at least he thinks he does. You know, there was a time when it made me feel important.'

Hettie ejected angst in a drawn-out exhalation before pulling back the air with the voracity of a free diver. She was building up to something and now focussed on me despite my efforts at a frozen defence.

'Can I trust you Loman? I mean really trust you?' Father Filippo wasn't asked. I nodded passively and she responded.

'I'm not proud of this, you understand. But I need to tell someone. And I need help getting my stuff back. I can't get into the library without it.' I blinked through my lethargy and glanced at Filippo, who seemed impervious. Maybe God's people don't need sleep. The room next door heaved with the rumpus of at least a dozen constricted nasal passages – enough to have been distracting even if I'd been wide awake – but Hettie was off and there was no turning back.

'Father, you've heard some of this before, but there are things I've left out. You'll see why when I tell you. Loman, I'm only sharing this with you since it's clear that you think you're the shit on God's shoe. So maybe we have something in common.'

'Do I?'

'Oh, don't bother trying to deny it. We all hear you yakking on in your sleep. You have problems. Hopefully that'll make you sympathetic toward mine. At least you believe that some-one gives a shit.'

Filippo looked hurt.

'Sorry, Father.'

'It's ok, Hettie. Carry on.'

But Hettie wasn't quite ready and sidled across to the kettle. Its whistle filled the minutes before she handed mugs to me and Filippo. Mine came complete with a whimsical illustration of a fly and a line of text which read 'What do you call a fly with no wings? A walk.' Filippo eyed the picture but didn't laugh, and Hettie began. Once she'd started, she flowed. I admired her fortitude.

'Filippo, you already know that I'm tied into a contract with a medical research company run by the Delgados, but you don't know how it all began:

Enzo Delgado. Company bigwig and minor genius. After all this time he can still surprise me. I really *don't* mean that as a compliment, but it wasn't always that way.

I lived with mum and my stepdad in the London suburbs until I was twenty-two. Some people think of 'London' as posh, but we lived yards from the M25. The noise from the lorries rang your ears constantly, even at night, but I liked it. It dampened the tumult of the world, and I slept better there than I ever did anywhere else. My stepdad - Greg - was funny. He was more obsessed with understanding the physical world than I was about NSYNC. He worked as a lecturer in statistical mechanics and read every article and research paper he could find with physics or mathematics in the summary note. He cried when he heard that Stephen Hawking had died – he disappeared upstairs but I heard him through the bedroom door. Anyway, he'd bang on about string theory and multi-universes at every meal. I can't remember a Sunday roast that wasn't served with gravity or dark matter or electromagnetism. I still associate sage stuffing with quantum mechanics. I really loved the philosophical aspects - you know, that there might be another me out there somewhere, but the technicalities – the physics – never really bothered me. Somehow, I still chose the three traditional sciences to study at A-level and ended up flunking the lot. I thought that dad would be livid, but he just shrugged it off and told me I was still young.

I mulled my future for a couple of months, then got a job as a hotel maid. It was more boredom than an actual decision and it wasn't meant to be a long-term thing. The job description said 'housekeeper' but the manager – he was called *Mister* Armstrong - made sure that we knew exactly what we were, right down to those stupid frilly mobcaps that Victorian cleaning ladies used to wear. He was my first proper experience of a misogynistic dick. At least one that I couldn't just walk away from. We called him Sherlock because of the stupid tweed cape he'd wear, but we should have just left it at 'dick'. I stayed on regardless. I told myself that I'd study in the evenings – you know – to get my education back on course - and that a job with no stress would be ideal. But I ended up just knocking around with my friends at the hotel. Three years later I was still doing it.

Enzo appeared one evening. It just happened to be in one of those interludes where I thought that if I didn't do something soon I'd end up scrubbing toilets forever. He was sat at the bar as I was heading home. I'd seen him staring at me earlier that day, but I didn't pay him much attention. Lots of men stared at me in those days – occupational hazard – I just learned to ignore them. I was more worried about Sherlock. I knew there'd been a complaint – something about items missing from a mini bar. It wasn't me but that had never stopped him - he loved an excuse to wear his 'stern' face. He'd jackboot toward us whenever he saw the chance to make us miserable and as soon as I hit his eyeline he came at me like he was the Schutzstaffel, all bloated with petty spittle. Enzo never did say whether he'd intervened on purpose, but I was grateful either way.

'Excuse me sir, but I was just about to ask this young lady to join me at the bar.'

Now, one of my study books for O-level literature was Oliver Twist, and there's a certain look that I always imagined appearing on the master's face when he's told. 'Please Sir, I want some more.' A look of such astounded indignation that it could only exist on the face of an individual who'd become grotesquely bloated with their own self-importance. That's how Sherlock looked, just before he deflated into sycophancy so sickly that I nearly laughed in his face. He must have considered Enzo a 'very special' guest indeed.

'Would that be alright with you?' Enzo continued, turning his back on Sherlock as he addressed me personally.

So, I wouldn't normally have accepted a drink from *any* stranger, let alone a client where I worked, but I saw Armstrong's face and a ten-minute conversation and a polite goodbye seemed like an easy escape route.

'Thank you, that would be lovely.' I replied with a smile at both gentlemen.

And that was it, I was his. Not in a sexual way, never that, 'though to be honest I could easily have been persuaded otherwise. He never seemed interested though, and I really didn't mind. He was fascinating, sort of like my stepdad without the boring bits – sorry Greg. Ten minutes turned into two hours and a promise to accompany him to dinner the next evening. To me, he was sophistication personified. I explained why I'd agreed to have a drink with him within the first two minutes, and he just asked if I was ok, then wafted it away, like he already knew he had me. The rest of the time we talked through the arguments for and against assisted suicide – prompted by my suggestion that he should have bought Sherlock the drink and slipped something into it. It was entirely unexpected and lifted me despite the morbidity of the topic. It was the first decent intellectual conversation

I'd had outside the family home since I'd folded my first bedsheet dressed like Mrs Doubtfire.

The next night we went to the Ormar in Mayfair. I'd walked past it a handful of times on my way to the park. It was neat and lightly colonnaded like many of the buildings around it, but gave no impression of vulgar opulence. I'd still never have actually considered going in – I never went anywhere that didn't have prices in the window – but it never really seemed as posh as its reputation. At least not until we actually sat down. In an instant we were surrounded by waiting staff, and the woman on the table opposite us wore earrings that pulled at her lobes like fishing weights. 'Do you think they're real?' I asked Enzo before realising how stupid I sounded. He glanced behind him and eyed them with the dedication of a pawnbroker before turning back to me. 'More real than her nose.'

That evening was as breathtaking as the first. Enzo told me about his work, and I told him about my failures. We talked until his offer came out like it was the most natural thing in the world. 'You want to return to your studies? Well, I need some volunteers to help me on a new testing programme. It wouldn't take much of your time, and in return I could finance your attendance at the Universidad Complutense de Madrid. They're partnered with one of the research establishments that we sponsor here in London, so you could continue your studies there once you've had enough of Spain'. It was the offer of a lifetime from a guy I'd known less than forty-eight hours. Of course I said yes.'

Hettie paused and tilted her head slightly in my direction. She looked a little like Angus when he expected a treat. She may have been waiting for me to say something, or maybe was just pausing for breath. Either way, I only managed to glance down nervously and swill the grounds in my mug while Hettie set herself for round two.

'Madrid was a mystery. I struggled with Spanish almost like I struggled with physics, and it was only a peculiar predisposition toward my chosen subject - philosophy - that kept me on top of my course. My conversations with Enzo tempered down over the first couple of months until I only really spoke to him when I visited his labs at CTBA – the Cuatro Torres Business Area. It's essentially a sprawling industrial estate with his building at its centre. It was enormous, but so were the other buildings. Apart from a sign on the door, it was almost entirely anonymous. The first time I visited, Enzo sent a car to pick me up to help me find it. By the fourth time he didn't even collect me from reception. I don't think he liked me any less, he just liked his work a whole lot more. And that was where my problems started.

I didn't know the city at all. I'd visited a handful of places with Enzo. They were all really expensive and eating bocadillos out of your college dorm isn't quite the same as Arroz Caldoso con Bogavante served with a Canaletto Pinot Grigio. I started running up debts. I didn't want to go to him for help, but I couldn't even afford the flight back to London. My cards were maxed out. I knew I was being an idiot, but I was lonely. And bored. Mum was so proud that I'd finally got a place at university – she'd told all her friends about me studying in 'a European capital' - like London wasn't one - and I didn't want to let her down. So, I found another option. Or it found me. I grabbed him with my free arm as one of his clan was pulling blood from the other one. It hurt, but he was already on his way out and I needed his attention. I got it, but Enzo didn't offer the money for a flight. He offered something else.

His programme had hit a dead end, or so he said. I think that his idea of a dead end must be different from most peoples since his company was running up the IBEX – the Spanish stock index, but that didn't seem to interest him at all. He talked at me like Ahab talked about his whale - like he'd lost something and couldn't rest until he'd found it again. He spoke with such passion; like he was searching for his soul, and I felt for him, despite his ambivalence toward me. For the next forty minutes we talked like we had at the Ormar, and I almost forgot that I owed close to fifteen thousand euros. I was worried for him - right up until he suggested that there was a way around my problems.

With hindsight I suppose that I shouldn't have been shocked. Surrogacy. He made it sound as though he was doing me an almighty favour. Nine months with my feet up, getting paid to relax and feel good about the joy I was bringing into some sad couple's lives. What a fucking politician he was. I don't even remember why I said yes, I just remember that it felt like the most natural decision in the world when I did.

Enzo arranged it. He carried me along on a great wave that felt like a holiday every time he spoke to me. He was present during the embryo transfer and made me feel like no-one else meant a damn to him. It was only afterwards that I felt like a cow with a plastic syringe stuffed inside of her. I followed the same cycle through forty-one weeks. I knew that I was just expensive livestock, but I still drifted on cloud nine for an hour after each visit. Christ. It wasn't until I'd handed my boy over that I realised I really was just a prize cow. He handed me a banker's draft for twenty thousand euros and a cattle class plane ticket back to London - the one I'd asked him for ten months earlier. Oh, and a list of instructions extrapolated from the contract that he'd had me sign. The reason why I now get e-mails telling me '**Your medical review is now due**.'

Hettie stopped. I looked up from my mug and tried to think of something to say that didn't sound like a platitude. Filippo rescued me.

'How did you end up in Rome, Hettie?'

'That's another story.' she said.

***

'I still need to get my stuff back.'

Hettie harangued Father Filippo as the last of the night's guests passed through the door and back onto the street. By now, even he was flagging. A couple more hours draped over the table had done nothing to lighten the rings of black which shaded his eyes. The weight of the funeral would have dragged at him even without the lack of sleep but the heft of that bag, left unattended in his antiquated Fiat, couldn't be tolerated for much longer.

'Just hang on Hettie. I need to make a 'phone call.' He left her at the table and sat for ten minutes in his office. No one could have called it a vestry – it was far too small – but it did offer space for a telephone and a moments peace. When he was done he hauled his lethargy back into the kitchen and shook everything but his friend from his being.

'Hettie.' he invited.

'I'm sorry Father. I know I'm being needy. I *am* needy. I don't know what to do.'

'It's alright Hettie. Why don't you just pick up where we finished. I still don't know how you got from Madrid to Rome. You said that you had a ticket back to London. Why didn't you just go home?'

Filippo had his listening face turned up to full and smiled gently though his beard. It was barely visible through that copious mass but always seemed to be encouragement enough. Hettie still hesitated, wincing over her words.

'There's more I need to tell first. About Enzo. And about what an idiot I've been.'

'Go on. No judgement here.' Filippo lifted his beard to expose his dog collar, tugging slightly at the tuft of grey filling his hand. Hettie went on.

'I knew that the programme was centred around a new drug – one with the potential to treat multiple diseases, not just one. Sort of like penicillin when it came out first, but penicillin on crack. Sorry Father. That was the actual phrase that Enzo used. No-one explained much more than that, not in terms I could understand anyway. It was in the paperwork I signed, but I was so excited to be out of London I barely read it after I hit the word 'immunoglobins'. I just know that they tested my blood before they began injecting me with stuff. They wanted to know whether I had any genetic defects to understand how they may affect their results. I didn't think too much about it, I just let them prod and poke me for a few hours a week. That was pretty much it. I never had any adverse reactions other than a sore arm when the doctor stabbed at me looking for a vein. And they kept paying me. Not enough as it turned out.

It wasn't until I was pregnant that Enzo came clean. He told me that I'd had an 'unusual' reaction to one of the tests. He said it was a liver infection. He didn't tell me that it was Hep B. That would have been bad enough, but it wasn't the Hep B that you pick up on street corners. This was a new and particularly virile strain. One that meant that I 'shouldn't engage in sexual activity with anyone, in any way, ever, not even with a condom.' Bad enough for anyone who'd actually tried having sex.'

She trailed off, waiting for Filippo to catch up. It didn't take him long.

'You were a ...?'

'Yes. I was a …… The only one in Madrid with a sexually transmitted disease.'

'But I thought you said that you would have. With Enzo, I mean.'

'I did say that, yes.'

'Oh, Hettie. I'm so sorry.'

'Don't be. Not yet anyway. There's more to come. Now, how I'd managed to pick up this little blessing is still something of a mystery. The laboratories were always meticulous, and I can't believe that they'd somehow mixed needles or samples or whatever, but that's only a part of it. I didn't find out until after I'd given birth that women aren't supposed to be 'first time mum' surrogates, and I don't know why Enzo would have suggested it for me. There was still a bit of me that hoped he'd arranged it especially to help me, but then I remembered how hard he'd touted the benefits of surrogacy and finally realised that helping people other than himself isn't really in his canon. What he did say is that the baby would have Hep B too, and that he'd make sure it was healthy and received the care it needed before he arranged for the transfer to adoptive parents. And after everything that had already happened, I *still* fucking believed him. Except that time, looking back, I *chose* to believe him, or at least some of me did. Even though I knew what he was. The thought of being *alive* seemed terrifying enough at that point, never mind being a mum.

And that's where I am. He insists that my little boy is safe. In a loving home, being looked after by 'good people'. And he *still* says it like he actually expects me to believe him. And idiot that I am, I still do. When I'm there in the room with him I *do* believe him. It's only afterwards that I remember that he's a manipulative cunt. But you know what worries me most of all? His research is more important to him than money, or fame, or people. *Any* people. And if he can make *me* do the things I've done with a few well-chosen words, what the fuck would he do with a *baby*?'

Filippo waited, but there was really nothing else to say. Hettie just took herself to the dormitory and lay down to sleep. It was a little miracle that Filippo hadn't had to lay down first. He took the bunk next to hers and succumbed, still in his cassock and still covered in Angus's hair. The room was quiet and the two slept until the sun had slipped well past its apex.

***

Father Filippo was back in his jeans and t-shirt and had showered before Hettie had woken. Uber Eats had turned up with a rattle of the church door that could have made St. Francis jump out of his picture frame. Hettie selected Arancini stuffed with peppers, tomato and mozzarella. It was Father Filippo's favourite.

'You know Hettie, you could still go to the police? I'd come with you. They ought to do something about the mugging at least.'

'It doesn't matter Father. I don't care about my stuff really. There's nothing I can't get 'round, not even my passwords, and all my certificates are scanned. And they wouldn't believe me about Enzo. I'd just be making trouble for myself.'

'Then what about Enzo? Maybe I could speak to him?'

'Thank you, Father. I appreciate it but with all due respect I don't think your collar would impress him. I'm not sure that he believes in that sort of thing.'

Hettie was talked out. There was still more to tell but the rest probably wouldn't have added much anyway, except to make her feel even more ridiculous. And what could Filippo do anyway, even if he'd known the way she'd search and search every day for a child which, for all she knew, had no official records to find. Maybe he *was* with loving parents. Enzo didn't always lie. But who really knew what Enzo would stoop to?

Of course, stabbing him with the needle hadn't helped her cause. It broke right off in his arm, and she'd been glad, until the police turned up. Then he told them the truth. She'd been a voluntary test subject – paid – and a voluntary surrogate – paid – and had gone psycho when she found out that she'd picked up Hep B and wanted the world to think that it happened due to a dodgy 'test'. She tried to argue her side, but when it came out, well, it didn't actually sound much different than Enzo's version. And what about Enzo? It seemed that he was the only realistic hope of finding her boy, so she kept going to her appointments, all except this last one. Even then, he'd sent what everyone would construe as a conciliatory message. 'No hard feelings, I'll *expect* you at your next consultation.'

'I still want to help, Hettie, if I can?'

Good Fillipo. She'd heard him have the same conversation with at least a dozen fellow destitutes. She already knew his answer, and the reasoning behind it. She knew that he'd say no and feel horrible for saying it.

'You could let me stay here Father, in the church? Call it my home? If I could only get registered as an official citizen, I could access social services. They may open an investigation for me. They'd at least insist on visiting the labs and Enzo's home. What do you think?'

Filippo twitched and stared at Saint Francis. He stared back accusingly.

'I think you already know the answer to that, Hettie. I'm sorry.' The response was always the same – it had to be - but it never got easier.

'Please, Father. I don't need to live here. I just need to show that I have an address in the city.'

'I'm really sorry Hettie. The building is registered as a night shelter. You can stay here as often as you like but you can't 'live' here. It wouldn't be fair to let one person stay without offering the same to everyone. And there's the insurance company and the revenue agency, and probably half a dozen others. They'd make us close the shelter. The bishop wouldn't let me, even if I wanted to. You know that. Maybe I could speak to social services with you?'

Filippo droned on and Hettie tuned out. It really was quite hopeless, that was becoming all too evident. It wasn't Filippo's fault, and in all honesty, she'd known what the outcome of their conversation would be before they'd started. But she'd still needed to hear the words. Now they were just two people feeling uncomfortable about a conversation which might as well be over, and Filippo was dragging it out. She watched him talk and noticed a remnant of mozzarella bobbing in his beard like a little yacht in a windy sea. At least their breakfast had been good. She gave him the courtesy of waiting for him to finish before getting up to leave.

Chapter 18

The Miracle

'For God's sake boy, just get the damn thing in there.' It was a phrase that Beatrice Delgado had used on multiple occasions, though this time it referred to the needle that had been left hanging half out of her arm. She batted Enzo's hand to one side and slipped the drip expertly into a strand of the wispy blue web which covered her forearm.

Enzo clenched his jaw for the fiftieth time that day. It ached liked he'd worked his way through a kilo of chewing nuts – those hard old toffee ones that lasted an age for a fifty pence piece. His aunt had always been a crotchety old bag, but she'd gotten increasingly worse as her muscles thinned and her skin yellowed and sagged. He could possibly have felt sorry for her, if she'd ever shown him an ounce of proper affection, but their interactions had been limited to uncomfortable hugs and an isolated pinch of his bottom as he'd entered puberty. She was his father's sister, and that came with an air of entitlement that stretched all kinds of boundaries. His mother said that she'd been 'an adventurer' as a young woman, but he hadn't understood exactly what that meant until he read the reams of complaints that had been filed against her, once he'd overtaken her in the company's hierarchy. One had used the word 'misandry.' The dictionary offered the following advice:

MISANDRY (meaning 'hatred of men') was originally considered the converse of its counterpart MISOGYNY (hatred of women). This is no longer the case. While MISANDRY has retained its original meaning, MISOGYNY has broadened in meaning to cover an additional sense involving sexism.

Beatrice didn't hate men, that was clear from the nature of the complaints. She did however have a tendency to comment on the 'freshness' of the newest male interns in a way which would have been considered unacceptable had the sexes been reversed.

For her part, Beatrice loved Enzo. Not in a 'family Christmas opening the presents' sort of way of course - that type of unfettered affection was more befitting the uneducated, or at least the 'ordinary', and she was neither of those. No, she enjoyed him as a composition. A diluted approximation of her brother's zealotry for success watered with his wife's mincing need to appease. The combination had given him an edged silver tongue with the capacity to advance the firms objectives. A useful trait to be sure, and fortunate, since she doubted that the boy used the organ for anything else.

'I'll be back in a couple of hours to check on you Aunt Beatrice.'

Enzo checked the flow of drugs through the catheter. Beatrice insisted on an IV drip as the method of delivery, complaining that the alternatives 'made her piss sting.' It may have been true. Her liver had withered years ago, giving her a jaundiced hue the shade of English mustard. He'd never liked the taste of that either.

Beatrice had been receiving her treatment since the nineties. She had little doubt that she'd be long gone without it, but the real miracle – to her at least – was that the company was still around to offer it.

***

In 1988, an international team of scientific experts performed radiocarbon dating on snippets of a famous shroud purported to bear a faint but venerated image of Jesus Christ. One of those scientists was Rocco Delgado, medicinal chemist, managing director of the Delgado Research Establishment, sister to Beatrice and father to Enzo.

Once the tests had been completed, three of the wise men sat triumphantly before a chalk board upon which had been scratched the figures '1260 AD – 1390 AD'. They may as well have written 'FAKE' in foot-high capitals. Delgado was not amongst them, since he had already engaged in work of a more faithful nature.

The sample tested by the mainstream had been extracted from the bottom left-hand corner of the shroud. Rocco's had not. Some years later, one of the three men who announced the results stated that he believed that the specimen he'd studied had in fact been part of a medieval repair carried out after a fire had damaged the relic, but this was taken in most quarters to be an attempt by the church to re-investiture the item to its former holy rank. Or, perhaps, that the scientist in question was merely attempting to find some comfort in faith as his years advanced. Whichever it was, it held little interest to Rocco, who had given credence to the authenticity of his own piece of the relic during the intervening years, through his obsession alone.

While his counterparts had gloried in identifying the age of their sample, Rocco had insisted that each woven strand in his possession should be individually subjected to the widest spectrum of x-ray, gamma ray, ultraviolet, infra-red, radio wave, microwave, alpha radiation, beta radiation, ionising radiation - in fact every type of ray, wave, radiation or scrutiny - available to science. What he found was miniscule in scale, but a miracle nonetheless. A tiny sample of human blood containing DNA from a male of middle eastern descent, and bound to it, a population of immunoglobulins - antibodies. The sample was ancient, but its community of cells and proteins thrived as if they had been deposited mere hours earlier. The DNA told a story. A man with dark hair, dark skin and no defects. No heart condition or cleft palate, no club foot or bald spot. No defects, and no illnesses, at all. But it was the proteins – the antibodies within the blood - that moulded Rocco's infatuation. Since it was they that held the potential to cure the world.

A dozen primates had benefitted from the precious substance. Each had been injected with a different disease. Diphtheria, polio, meningitis, mumps, the common cold amongst a handful of others, and each had been cured, but not just of their primary ailment. All had been tested following treatment and had been found clear. Not just of disease, but of all illness, disorder and genetic deformity, right down to the eradication of scar tissue. Put simply, they had been made perfect. A true miracle. Unfortunately, despite all his efforts, Rocco was just a man, and men cannot replicate miracles. Antibodies drawn from the test subjects showed promise, but did not repeat the full effects of the original. Once the source material was all but gone, the Delgado corporation placed the experiments on hold. It owned a raft of information. It understood *what* the sample had done, but not quite *how*, and all attempts to reproduce the results with derivative material had failed.

A few years into his work Rocco brought Enzo under his wing. The boy was young, but bright. A true prodigy, and his eventual successes escalated the reputation and stock of the Delgado corporation by a factor of ten. The company thrived on the new lines of research which emerged, but even Enzo couldn't get near the perfection of the original sample.

***

Beatrice relaxed her arm at her side and settled to the monotony of her treatment. It seemed just a few years ago that Rocco would administer the drugs. It was hard to accept that he'd been gone a quarter of a century. Dead of ischaemic heart disease at fifty, despite the wealth of knowledge he'd accumulated. She grinned at the irony. Now she – and the corporation - was left with Enzo, and the boy hadn't made one millimetre of progress toward finding a cure for her, despite the incentive she'd given him. That incentive was a woman - Heather Dorothy Eddy. Hettie to Enzo, but apparently very little else. He hadn't fucked her. He hadn't fathered her. She was nothing – a little tic that he'd picked up on his travels, and not worthy of her keep given the unchallenging test regime that Enzo had selected for her. Still, Enzo had enjoyed *something* about her, at least for a while, and on that basis alone she *could*, perhaps, be useful to Beatrice.

Beatrice had caught Hepatitis in her twenties. Hardly surprising given her lifestyle, but people rarely feel that they deserve the consequences of their indiscretions. In some ways, Beatrice could be considered justified in feeling that she was a victim. Many people own an immune system voracious enough to eradicate the disease, but Beatrice did not. It could almost be said that the situation was representative of her place in the world.

She was well off, if not affluent. She was clever, if not gifted. But she was Napoleonic in her entitlement. She'd grasped position and possession from her family name since well before the age of consent, and when she discovered that she'd fallen foul of the filthy virus, well, her family owned a fucking medical research establishment! They *would* find her a cure. Except they didn't, not even after Rocco had stated prematurely – thankfully privately - that his research would make the rest of the medical profession superfluous.

It hadn't, of course, but his work had, in a small way, changed the world. It had changed Beatrice's world – she was still here, even though her organs rotted inside her and her body now resembled a palliative stick insect. By the time Enzo brought Hettie's glowing visage through the office door she'd decided that the boy needed one final kick up the backside to concentrate his unfulfilled potential, and switched out a clean needle with one drawn from her own wizened vein.

She'd hoped that the opportunity to save a beautiful young girl would be a greater incentive than an aged and unwelcome family obligation. It certainly seemed to concentrate his efforts, 'though not sufficiently to generate any actual success, and she'd watched as his frustration grew well beyond her own. Now, he was more obsessive than he'd ever been, and even she baulked at the empirical games of medicinal poker that he'd embarked upon.

Chapter 19

The end, the means

Enzo sought refuge from his irritation in the obvious place. He'd spent three years manoeuvring to remove his aunt from the organisation, but memories were long, and she was the last remaining child of the founding member. He knew that time would assist in the task, but his head still throbbed with latent frustration. Only as he entered his laboratory, a storey underground, did the veins at his temples begin to subside. He slumped himself into his chair and accessed file RCA1001-6J, now simply retitled 'GAMMA'. He typed his password almost before the black padlock hit the screen. 'dr0frankenstein', all lower case. His aunt would not have approved.

He had waited decades to complement his research with fresh samples. Not *his* samples - cheap knockoffs of the original - but the authentically miraculous material that his father had squandered on fucking chimpanzees. Even Enzo hadn't had the nerve to use the very last remnants remaining from the shroud. At least not immediately. The Vatican had denied all requests to re-access the relic and he'd been left with one hundred and twenty odd pages of text and an ever-decreasing circle of research. Gamma was a last throw of the dice, the thirteenth primate, and a living gift from the virtually deplete samples of blood from the Shroud of Turin.

He still couldn't quite believe that his aunt – or at least her team of elevated paternity testers – had found more. The same blood. The same DNA. And the same anti-bodies. Not from the shroud, but from some random relic presented for testing by a librarian cleric. And now here it was, locked down here with him under the ground in his own personal vault. He could have cured another dozen specimens with this new material, maybe more, given modern techniques in refinement and application. People, not primates. He could have cured his aunt, along with a further gaggle of nobodies, but what did the world need with another dozen healthy chimps? The likelihood of their antibodies – their blood – yielding the perfect healing storm of the original was no greater than it had been all those years ago.

Enzo had calculated that a maximum of thirty dried blood spots could be sourced from the sample extracted from the spear head. Around 600 milligrams of material – maybe 300 droplets once solutes had been added. It was infinitely fortunate that his aunt hadn't grasped the full extent of what she'd had before the work was passed 'upstairs'. So far, he'd used ten of those spots. The material taken from the shroud was gone, but based on the text prepared by his father, there was no difference in the chemistry of the spear sample from the one drawn from the shroud. Not one iota of distinction between the two. Same material, same tests, same results. A holy grail of healing in a handful of irreplaceable drops.

But there was hope of more. Gamma – Enzo's very own Dolly – one which proffered a brimming receptacle of material alongside an inherent ability to replenish itself. But even he presented an enigma. No, not an enigma, another fucking failure. The same sample of blood which had provided the original antibodies also offered up the DNA which had forged Gamma. The boy's own antibodies *should* work in the same way. The potential was surely there, even though Enzo hadn't quite managed to replicate the miracle itself. He still retained hope in the boy despite the skip full of sharps that had been expended. But the process was slow - the child needed time for his blood count to normalise between donations, and six weeks was simply too long to wait.

And so, there was Hettie. The child's mother and the obvious answer to his problem. Same recovery time, four times the volume of blood. A transfusion of red blood cells from mother to son would minimise the recovery time of the child and allow Enzo to widen his research. At least it would have if Beatrice hadn't fucked it up. What a stupid, withered, pointless old cunt she was. If there was ever the slightest possibility that he would have wasted one of those precious sample spots on his unsavoury aunt, she'd sabotaged it in that one egocentric act. Now Hettie, the cleaning girl from London with her second-class philosophy degree, would receive number eleven of his thirty samples. The cure for her Hep B. And with it, the gift of perfect health, forever. He just needed to locate her.

***

Ollie rubbed at the soft scab. It was nothing, but still stung like a bite from a carpenter ant – those big black ones that feed on smaller ants. They'd invaded his uncle's farm one year when he was just a boy, building a nest inside the seat of the burnt-out Alfa GTV which still sat forlornly at the side of the old man's house.

The rusty binder rings had nipped his pinkie as he'd finally managed to snap them shut, and the morning's rain had penetrated his gloves, staining his hands a mottled grey and dampening the little nick which sat at the apex of his wrinkled finger. But what really hurt was the drumming earful he'd received from Delgado when he'd handed over the file without its owner.

‘Snap out of it you fat Ciambella. He’ll get over it, he always does.’

Santo reclined into the deep leather of the coffee house sofa and surveyed his comrade. There was little wonder that his friend had selected the higher levels of the wingback - he'd never have raised his heft from the plush comfort that Santo has chosen for himself.

The window seat of the Greg café offered views of the Trevi fountain, but Santo ignored the river gushing from the ancient aqueduct and eyed the girls in their long skirts and trousered suits. ‘Mio Dio,’ he thought, ‘I’m not sure I can last out ‘til summer.’

‘Stop calling me fat, you puffed up magnaccia.'

'Ha. At least the cap fits!' replied Santo, running his hand along the slick of his greased back mane. ‘Why not just drink your coffee and enjoy the scenery? Look, there’s one for you.’ He gestured toward a dumpy pink woman in stretch shorts and over-sized sunglasses. She was half obscured by the see-through umbrella which sat over her head. ‘American. She may even be grateful.’

‘Ever the gigolo aren’t you Santo? All meat and no veg.’

‘Ha. What the fuck is that supposed to mean? Jealousy put you off your game, fat man?’

‘Don’t get smug. You know you were just lucky right?’

‘I don’t need luck. Look at me. A new Sinatra for a new age.’

‘Gesu Cristo keep your voice down, will you? You’ll get us murdered.’ Ollie sought out disapproving eyes, but if the Mafia was present that day, they had bigger fish to fry than Ollie and Santo.

‘Fuck them. And fuck you, Ollie. *I* do what *I* want.’

Santo pulled the slip of paper from his jacket pocket and leaned forward to waft it under the big man’s nose. He could have read the words if it had been an inch further from his face, but they blurred out of focus with a slap against his nose. It didn’t matter – he knew what they said.

'Half of that should be mine.'

'Why the fuck would I give you half? I asked you to come with me, but you wouldn't get your fat ass out of bed.'

'Morning mass isn't the place for men like us, Santo. You should have more respect.'

'I have respect fat man, that's why I went. And that's why God repaid my faith with this.' Santo wafted the cheque again before returning it to his pocket.

If God had really intervened that day, then Ollie didn't understand why. The poor girl they'd accosted so unceremoniously on the streets would be better off staying there. She'd certainly be better off sitting in the Vatican library where Santo had followed her that morning after church. It really had been a chance in a thousand that he'd spotted her along the Cortile Belvedere, and another one in a half dozen that she hadn't spotted him back. He'd given up counting when she'd returned to the building next morning after a night on a bench in the Parco della Mole Adriana.

'Tell you what,' said Santos, 'I'll buy you dinner tonight. That should come to at least half anyway. Ha.'

Ollie considered his retort, but his partner had already found another oblivious young girl to ogle. He returned to his scab, berating his choices and his company.

***

Gamma was small for his age. Enzo occasionally forgot that he came from a time when men were considered tall at five and a half feet. He watched the boy sleep, tucked away inside the bespoke 'creche' that had been constructed a floor beneath his laboratory, and wondered what he dreamed. Did he have some inherent memory of a past life, lodged inside his brain as a cellular gift from his progenitor? Enzo hoped so, and imagined the conversations they would have. Perhaps those discussions would come sooner than he'd imagined. He'd need to bring the boy out of sedation once his mother arrived. Her wrath was already coming and there was little chance of her playing well if she found out that her child had been kept asleep for the first year of his life.

The boy had been declared free from hepatitis at his first round of testing. It was a singular piece of good news from a raft of disappointment. His blood contained similarly voracious antibodies to those that had been present on the spear, but where-as the blood from Gamma could be forged to battle, delay, and sometimes even cure certain select viruses, it was far from the same all-encompassing well of remedies that Enzo had hoped. Perhaps Hettie had been a poor incubator for the child, somehow diluting the full potential of the material during gestation, but Enzo had found no evidence to indicate that Gamma's blood was in any way different from the original sample. Except, of course, for its limitations in delivering the miracle which Enzo craved.

Enzo re-appraised his approach. He re-appraised from basics, and he re-appraised from each point from basics until now, until the thoughts churned at his head in a never-ending cycle of exasperation. He was missing something – maybe something simple - and one eureka could plug the gap.

'Antibodies are proteins that protect you when an unwanted substance – a disease – enters your body. Produced by your immune system, antibodies bind to the unwanted substances in order to neutralise them and eliminate them from your system. They remain active until the disease is irradicated from the body, at which time they become dormant but remain present and able to re-activate should the disease return.

It is possible to transfer antibodies from one person to another, avoiding the need to wait for the body to produce its own antibodies since the donor material can fight an invading disease with immediate effect. This treatment using samples from Gamma has irradicated every disease that it has been tested against but left the treated individual vulnerable to future attacks. The original sample offered infinitely more – it engaged with the recipient's own system on a genetic level, allowing their body to recognise and replicate the voracity of the donor material, ensuring that it was henceforth primed to eliminate all invading disease without the need for further medical assistance.'

Enzo had extrapolated several strands of investigation from his studies of Gamma but had thus-far concentrated his efforts on two.

The first recognised Gamma's ability to identify foreign substances immediately - and therefore begin the action of fighting the disease before the symptoms of illness had an opportunity to manifest. This went some way to explaining the constant active state of the original samples.

The second related to how Gamma's antibodies worked with the body's other immune responses, allowing his system's defences to remove 'invaders' more efficiently.

Both offered the possibility of replication if Enzo could understand how Gamma's system worked to maximise the benefits of each element. But Enzo knew that this wasn't really the point. *Every* element of Gamma's physiology meshed perfectly together, in a way that shouldn't exist in the natural world. It wasn't just that each part of him was perfect. Each perfectly contributed to and complemented the whole. The actions of his body *were* perfect. *He* was perfect. And as much as Enzo knew what was happening, he couldn't *make* it happen.

There were four pictures above Gamma's crib. Four chimpanzees. A weird choice, unless you understood the context. Enzo's father had selected four chimpanzees from his original test sample to exclude from vivisection. None had suffered a single day of illness in over thirty years. Perfect health, free from pain, free from discomfort, free even from the greying of time as their bodies grew old. They were the miracle that Enzo sought for the world.

'You've a lot of work to do little man.' thought Enzo, as he cracked open the lid of the incubator and removed the catheters from his veins.

Chapter 20

Restitution

Anyone can visit the Mater Ecclesiae Monastery to attend mass in the chapel. A ticket on the metro costs only a couple of euros and an easy ten-minute walk from Ottaviano station will see you along the Viale Gregorio XVI in the Vatican Gardens and deposited into the chapel building.

The 'Mater Ecclesiae Monastery' was founded by Bishop of Rome, Vicar of Jesus Christ, Successor of the Prince of the Apostles, Head Honcho and multiple other titles for the Pope. If you check out the facility online you will be informed that it had been founded within Vatican City for 'Poor Clares et al', an order of cloistered nuns. Officially it was commissioned to house the convent - to pray for the Pope in his service to the church. Why it was necessary for the incumbent nuns to be replaced every five years was never clearly understood. Neither was the expansive footprint of the building, being far too large for triple the number of sisters actually accommodated.

Twenty years of invocation later, it was announced that the convent was to be permanently disbanded. The Pope no longer required the prayers of the order - a conundrum that the clergy deemed appropriate to ignore. The building was adapted – the result of a series of refurbishments – and a new set of occupants moved in. Some of these moves were widely reported, others less so.

Officially, amongst other uses, the facility has been home to Pope Benedict, the first pontiff to retire from his position in six hundred years.

Unofficially, there have been rumours of floors filled with racks, and shelves, and cabinets, and closets, as if some hoary collection required room to grow under the hushed protections of the Vatican.

***

The Corps of Gendarmerie of Vatican City – the Vatican police force - could be expected at the Mater Ecclessiae Monastery no more than three times per year. At these times, they would attend security training for public appearances by the Pope, alongside their colleagues in the Swiss Guard. But this was not one of those times.

His Excellency Leonardo, Bishop of the Diocese of Ostia, Holy See and Dean of the College of Cardinals, greeted Filippo at the door. He was a man of advanced years and retarded politics and tutted disapprovingly at the bag slung around the shoulder of his subordinate. If a priest can look shifty in full robes and vestments, Bishop Leonardo was managing it, flitting his gaze behind and around his colleague from behind the doorframe.

'Is that it, Father?'

'It is, your Grace.'

Leonardo led Filippo deep inside the building to a stark room containing a graphite grey meeting table enveloped by eight chairs, jammed tightly beneath it. The older man rattled the seat at the table's head until it shook loose and seated himself before gesturing to Filippo to do the same.

'Well, let's lay them out, shall we?'

Filippo followed the instruction, carefully removing each of the six relics and spreading them so that they sat equidistant from one another. Leonardo examined them, one at a time, taking an age to view each angle, crevice and detail, before setting them back to their original position on the table's surface.

'Thank you, Father. You may leave them here. Please come with me.'

Leonardo pushed the chair back from the table, shuffling to free its leg, which had become entangled once more with its fellows. Filippo fought down the overwhelming urge to help him, and allowed the old man to muddle out of his entrapment. Once extricated, he stepped forward and placed a hand on Filippo's arm, the same way he had for the last dozen years. A deep furrow had creased into his forehead.

'Leonardo. Am I in trouble?'

'I hope not, Filippo.' He replied, before cupping his hand to his colleague's ear and whispering. 'Ask me afterwards, in confidence of course.' Filippo checked behind them, just to be sure, but there was no-one else within earshot.

Leonardo's eye flickered and Filippo thought that he saw a glint of mischief in the awkward subterfuge. He took position behind the bishop as they passed through the door and out into the corridor. Leonardo's feet dragged at the carpet, and the two shuffled along like a stunted schoolboy crocodile, until they reached a small office with an antique desk and a 'Barista Express' coffee machine on the sideboard. Filippo eyed it hopefully as he sat at the visitor side of the furniture, but Leonardo made no offer and no moves toward it.

'Thank you for returning the articles, Father Filippo. Are you able to offer any information regarding their absence?'

The question sounded loaded, and Filippo choked down an expletive. He didn't always remember that his friend was not what he had been, and that his phraseology could now be clumsily ill considered. Filippo had seen him berated mercilessly by a shinily beautiful young visitor to Vatican Square for welcoming 'her' to the city. He'd cried afterwards, distraught at his failures and his years. It's always sad when people accelerate beyond the old.

Filippo relayed all that he knew, as concisely and accurately as he was able, and showed the bishop the note that he'd received from Father Janus. Leonardo swallowed heavily.

'Were you aware that Father Janus had been experiencing some problems before his death, Father Filippo? Problems that the church had been forced to work hard to ameliorate?'

'Not really Your Grace. I hadn't spoken to him for several years.'

'Then you know nothing of the tests that he commissioned?'

'Only what I read in the report. The one that was in the bag.'

'So, you read the report?'

'Yes.'

'And what did you make of it?'

Filippo wasn't sure what he was being asked. The questions were formulaic – premeditated and delivered with an awkward inclemency. Was Leonardo trying to be *stern*? He wasn't entirely sure, but it didn't change the answer anyway.

'I found it upsetting.'

'Of course. It is always upsetting when our faith is brought into question. That is why I must ask you to keep our discussions and the details surrounding our holy relics entirely confidential.

Father Janus had been unwell for some time, and we cannot allow his actions to undermine belief in the authenticity of artifacts which have been valued through hundreds of years. We have no idea of the credentials of the company procured by Father Janus, particularly in the areas of historical and theological interpretation. So far as I'm aware they are a medical research company with a specialism in paternity testing. We cannot allow mere opinions to 'upset God's applecart'. Do you *agree* Father?'

Filippo did not agree, and may have said so but for Leonardo's emphasis on the word itself. He didn't like the implication that he should deny the truth for some undiscussed 'greater good' but also didn't believe that Leonardo was the instigator. And what would be the point in upsetting the old man?

'I am God's servant.'

'Thank you, Father. As we all are.'

Both men sat. Was that it? Had Leonardo finished whatever he was supposed to be doing? Filippo couldn't tell.

'Leonardo, what's going on?'

'Thank you for your time, Father Filippo. Now, can I offer you a coffee?' He exhaled deeply, and relaxed the frown that still left a visible crease.

'What the fuck Leonardo? Are we done? *What* have we just done?'

Leonardo ignored the question and reached into his drawer for a sachet of grounds. He dropped them onto the filter, spilling a few onto the floor and cabinet.

'Milk?'

'No. Thank you.'

'Good, I don't think I have any.'

Filippo finished half his cup, and Leonardo abstained.

'Now, if you're ready, you can walk me back to my priory. I'm not as steady on my feet as I used to be.'

The two men sauntered slowly through the Vatican gardens and Leonardo commented on how green everything looked so early in the season. Once they'd walked beyond its walls, the subject changed.

'Now, shall we discuss things informally? I was never good at officialdom, anyway.'

'Was that supposed to be official Leonardo?'

'Yes, and you'd better take it seriously. The cardinals are not happy.'

'Ok.'

'Ok, listen up. Janus was in trouble, and not just with the hierarchy, but spiritually. You know what he did – that he ended his life - but he didn't just do that. He'd been in trouble for some time. We had him moved to the Vatican from his parish so that we could administer to him, help him, but also to protect the church from his actions. He'd started telling people that they should stop looking to God, that He'd abandoned them. But the things I can't tell even you, *those* are the things that make me shudder.

But it's not just Janus, and *that's* the real problem. The church is losing, Filippo. There are over twenty sects within the Catholic church alone, not counting all the other Christian groups, and none of us seem able to agree on anything. And while we argue amongst ourselves the world dissolves into war and greed and poverty and pestilence and, well .... *shit.*

The Holy See have become paranoid. A few of them were always half convinced that the world really is two minutes from Armageddon, but now the rest are following suit. They're worried that if God can allow a priest – *a Roman Catholic priest* – to fall so far then the rest of the world really is doomed. I'm scared Filippo. And I'm not alone.'

Leonardo grasped Filippo's arm and pulled him close, cupping his hand to his ear once more.

'Do what you can, Filippo. While you can. Be God's servant. I will too, I'm just not sure what *I* have left.'

Chapter 21
Guardian

'Guardian' never really had a name. It's just difficult to reference an animal without calling them something, and I was never really sure exactly *what* he was. He stood around forty-five centimetres tall at the centre of his back, but his pointy ears added half that again. To call him brown would have understated his beauty. He was shadowed gold, with a patch of white emblazoning his chest. He walked with an agile bounce which betrayed the brawn beneath his coat, and his howl sent chills through the rocky valley which stretched almost to the town of Nag Hammadi, some two hundred miles South of Cairo. He was, I suppose, what the locals would have called a prairie dog, but could have been a mongrel, a jackal, or even a small Egyptian wolf. He never came close enough for me to be entirely sure.

I suppose I could have called him 'watcher', or 'overseer' and either may have better described his interaction with me than my chosen moniker, but neither had the ring – or the gravitas – of the animal, and I wanted to share those attributes through his title.

He was there within a day of my arrival in the desert, and never left except for odd occasions when he would lope off into the heat and return with food that he'd scavenged or caught. I hoped that after a while I may gain his trust, but no matter how gently I sidled toward him, or how often I threw scraps to encourage him, he would always meander away, maintaining the distance between us.

Christ had been gone for five hundred years, and the battle for ownership of his words had been fought for most of them. Adoptionism, Gnosticism, Marcionism sat alongside the more recognisable modern theology of Eastern Orthodoxy and Roman Catholicism, each claiming their place as the pinnacle of God's holy agenda.

Once, as a young man, I'd been told that 'God is all the answers to all the questions you ever wanted to ask.' I took this phrase more literally than I now suppose it was intended, and marvelled at the thought of someday sitting in His presence, understanding the mysteries of the stars. Why the winters were cold and the summers so, so hot. Why thunder always followed the lightning, and why my best friend's dog sometimes rubbed his butt on the grass. Years later, I assumed that a better interpretation would be that 'God is all things to all people,' with the comforting implication that God, whatever He, She or It is, could love you regardless of the nuances of your beliefs.

I never could settle myself to the exclusionary approach of most religious factions, each proclaiming God as their own personal property with an arrogant self-righteousness which condemned all outsiders to eternal suffering and damnation. Even irrelevant tweaks in perspective were disparaged as mortal sin, regardless of their potential to bring more souls to believe. So, when the Catholic Church determined through their Nicene Creed to eradicate all alternative thoughts on God, and His son, from history, I determined that I'd be fucked if I just stood by and did nothing.

I had never spoken personally with Christ the man, or even heard him speak, but people who had said that he would free the world, and you didn't do that by enslaving its thoughts.

***

Nag Hammadi sits on the Nile less than one hundred miles from the shores of the Red Sea, but the land between them stretches with rocks and caves and sand, and not much else. People immediately associate the desert with heat, and that's true, but live in it for a season and you'll realise that it is actually a land of extremes. Extreme heat in the day, extreme cold through the night. An endless dearth of water until a flash flood wipes away everything it touches, then sinks to oblivion, down into the thirsty earth.

A multitude of creeds and backgrounds travelled its barren countenance along padded trade routes, but no-one ever stopped to search the crooks and fissures which lined its craggy face. At least not for the four months that I validated its solitude. Only Guardian looked on as I searched for a suitable refuge – a home with security from errant eyes and protection from the intemperate perpetuity of creation. Not a home for me, but for the cargo I carried. Thirteen leather bound codices, each offering a view that the church of Rome had determined surfeit. I didn't agree with everything that they contained, but they were still someone's opinion – someone's faith – and that was between them and God, not them and Loman.

The sun belched heat through my yashmagh on the day I deposited the books. Even the haze of mist which hung across the valley roof could not obscure it. I had been one hundred and eleven days in the wilderness.

Guardian stared from the shadow of a twisted juniper tree. Its trunk had cracked and whitened but leaves still spiked obstinately at its crown, offering muted shade as the morning sun cleared the sky. He sat upright, flicking his shaggy tail where it crossed over into the searing heat. We'd eyed each other across thirty yards for sixteen weeks. He no longer retreated with each footstep of my advance, but still milled in irritable discomfort if I strayed close enough to invade his peace.

I would be leaving him soon. Once the books were safe. And I wanted him to know how I'd valued his company. I buried my treasure in a sealed jar at the base of a cliff, obscured from the extremes of the elements, before whistling my intent and launching my hopes across twenty of those thirty yards. A shard of cured beef rolled to a stop on the baking ground.

He looked up, sniffed the air, but did not advance. Instead, he circled the tree before settling back on his haunches. 'Get it, boy' I shouted, but he sat, unrelenting, as if awaiting some great revelation. I called again. 'It's right there. Get it,' and he woofed his reply, before his great pink tongue lolled loosely from an expansive doggy smile. It took an instant to realise that I was not the root of his attention, before the sun was dwarfed and the desert blazed, but not with fire.

The hairs of His head were white as white wool, white as snow. His eyes were like a flame of fire, his feet were like burnished bronze, refined as in a furnace (Revelations 1:14-15).

I heard a story once. The tale was told by an ageing farmer who grew olives on a tiny scratch less than thirty miles from Jerash. He'd never seen the city and I suspect that the story was the only one he had, and that I was the thousandth person to hear it.

One day, when he was a young man, his father had sent him to check the trees for aphids. The bugs posed little threat to the crop but fed on sap from the bark, and the resultant scars left the tree open to infection and damage from frost. The farmer strained his eyes to find the tiny pests, seeking to please his father and help his family, and his pupils grew large despite the sun which raged above him. He sat for a while to find his focus, blinking tears as his eyes adjusted. He closed them for a moment and placed his hands to block the sun, and as he did the sun was overwhelmed. The sky blazed as if all the air within it was set alight, exploding upon him like the wrath of God, until he realised that the light came from a single point, not far from the sun itself. He saw this light through his hands, and through his eyelids. It lasted no more than the time it took to turn his head, but left spots in his eyes which would not blink away as he hurried home. His family had all seen the light, and although the farmer's spots faded with time, his brother had been looking toward the sun and his eyesight never returned.

The desert glowed with the brightness of a supernova, but did not hurt my eyes. It left no scars or spots, despite a luminance which permeated the rocks and the earth that they stood upon. And within the light, I saw the image of a man. His eyes were as a flame of fire, and upon his vesture a name. King of Kings.

I stared until the vision left me and did not turn away until I knew that it would not return. When I looked for Guardian, he was gone, and despite staying close for several days, in the hope that I would spot him watching me from behind some rock or tree, I never did. I think of him sometimes, and when I do, I remember him with his lolling tongue and beaming grin - but know that they were never meant for me at all.

Chapter 22

A familiar respite

Ginger had woken and left before coffee. It was almost unheard of, and the quiet tranquillity meant that I slept way beyond the dimming of clanks and chat from the little kitchenette. Filippo laid a hand on my shoulder to wake me.

'I took Angus outside to pee. I hope you don't mind.'

I looked at the clock. Quarter past ten. Then I looked at Angus, who looked pissed.

'I'm sorry Father, I'll be gone in five.'

'It's ok Loman, why not stay for a while? I have croissants.'

'Ok. Thank you.' I smiled, despite my embarrassment. Maybe if the room had a window I'd have woken, but the only daylight glowed dully through an internal door to the nave, and I guessed that it was raining in the world outside.

'Dreaming?' asked Filippo, his voice inflected with hope, and this time I didn't disappoint.

'Yes.'

'Fucking excellent. Just let me get the bread from the combo and I'll be back.'

Filippo returned with a tray filled with hot croissants, strawberry jam and black coffee. It could have been a commercial for Hotel Artemide but for the greasy flakes around the waiter's whiskers. I guess he hadn't checked the mirror.

I relayed my exploits with Guardian and the desert and was disappointed when Filippo didn't seem enamoured by my tale. In fact, he looked a little sad.

'I'm sorry, Father. I thought you'd like this one.'

'The codices of Nag Hammadi. I don't think I'm the right person to advocate for Gnosticism, Loman.'

Then we both looked a little sad, and I stared through the doorway at the gloom.

'I know what you mean about individual belief.' Filippo offered. 'There are several aspects of biblical interpretation that I believe are widely misunderstood. Just look at St. Francis over there.' He gestured at the picture.

'The exorcism of the Gerasene demoniac - the miracle of Jesus casting a legion of demonic spirits from a man into a herd of swine, who promptly drown themselves. The story appears in each of the gospels of Matthew, Mark and Luke but John told it slightly differently, in a way which didn't result in the demise of the innocent animals. It's my hope that John was the one who got it right.'

Angus perked unexpectedly, the way he did when I picked up a stick, and padded on the spot. Maybe he thought something interesting was coming. I perked up too, and Filippo ran his hand down the length of his beard just as he did when he was prepping a sermon. He looked surprised when it came away greasy.

'Humanity has been gifted with dominion over the earth. We are told this not only in Genesis 1:26 but also in Psalm 8:6 - but it is a gift that we have abused. To be fair, there may be some legitimate mitigating factors - words do not always translate exactly between languages, and biblical sources all tell their stories slightly differently. Still, John has intimated that we have fundamentally strayed from the role that God intended.

The word interpreted as 'dominion' in Genesis can also mean 'subdue'. Now 'subdue' can mean all manner of things, depending on how you apply it. It can mean overcome, or quieten, or to bring under control. In this context I and many others believe that bringing under control means 'to manage' on behalf of God. Unfortunately, mankind has read 'dominion' and taken it as permission to rule the earth and everything upon it - and has ruled with oppression. And it gets worse.

With the authority to manage comes the responsibility to manage well. There is an inherent accountability in the command to subdue the earth. The word 'subdue' doesn't have to imply violence or mistreatment; it can mean 'to bring under cultivation' - yet man chooses to misinterpret the heart of the words. He has ignored his opportunity to cultivate love, trust and mutual benefit, in favour of abuse, which he inflicts upon the land and the creatures who live upon it.According to many theologians God trusted man with stewardship of the earth in the hope that he would learn to love all things - to understand and cherish the unique qualities that each possessed. When God gave humanity dominion over the animals, it was to care for and tend to them, helping them to realise their fullest potential. Instead, we have assumed that God's act in setting us apart from His Kingdom is permission to treat it however we wish, placing our needs so high above that of His creatures that our treatment of them has become obscene. I can't even say the words 'foie gras' without feeling physically sick.

Humankind treats God's creation as its own, literally consuming its beauty and ignoring its value, just to satisfy its own gluttony. This, of course, is wrong, and there are warnings of the consequences.

We forget that God maintains dominion over the *whole* of His creation, including us. Do we really want to reap what we sow, when what we sow is cruelty, destruction and death?'

Filippo paused to relax the tenseness which had developed in his shoulders. He looked slightly embarrassed, and a sheepish grin spread across his features.

'Forgive me, I'm preaching. I know that I'm merely presenting my personal beliefs – but in my defence, that is the exact nature of faith. Suffice to say that I think that in giving us a taste of *His* responsibility – of what it is to be *Him* - God hoped that we would be brought closer to Him. Instead, we've moved further away than we've ever been. Doctrine has muddled God's intent – and in this instance the church has failed in its duty to provide humanity with the guidance it needs.'

Filippo always spoke to me like he thought I was infinitely cleverer than I was. I took it as a compliment, but sometimes I got what he told me, sometimes not. This time I sort of did but wasn't sure how to respond.

'I ate some sausage last week. I'm sorry.'

Filippo laughed.

'I don't know about that. I'm not a vegetarian. Sometimes I think I should be, but religion doesn't often give clear answers. It's about your own conscience, and your relationship with God.

Just imagine leaving your child in the care of a trusted aunt. The aunt may smack the child if it's naughty. It may have seemed perfectly acceptable to the aunt - she'd been smacked when she was small, after all. You'd still love the aunt, but it wouldn't stop you being disappointed and upset at what she'd done. Maybe that's what it's like for us. God still loves us even though we hurt His creatures, which He also loves. It's not the best analogy but it's the closest I can think of for now.

I don't suppose that any genuine Christian would agree with destroying rainforests or bringing species to the brink of extinction –

that's obvious. As for taking the life – the single life - of another of His creatures to satisfy our tastes, well, perhaps that would be a case of *hurting* God, rather than bringing his unadulterated wrath. You must understand though that these are only my thoughts.'

You know when you wrack your brain for a clever phrase? Something pertinent which leaves your friends clear that you've been following them, when in fact you've been struggling to keep up the whole time? And then you blurt out something totally inappropriate, just because it's the first thing that comes into your head?

'What exactly *is* in that box in your cabinet Filippo? It's not *just* God, is it?

I'm not sure that the words ever actually passed through my brain on the way to my mouth, and I gasped audibly at my own audacity. Filippo frowned. His brows furrowed and my heart sank deeper than the red on my face. He *never* frowned, not even when he was thinking.

'You know, it's been two years since anybody's actually had the nerve to ask me that.'

'I'm sorry. I didn't mean to. .....'

'Well, now you have, do you want to take a look?'

It wasn't the response I'd expected. Filippo's frown still lingered but I didn't reckon my chances on ever having the nerve to ask again. I nodded.

Filippo sauntered across to the display case and opened the door. I expected its hinges to creak like a coffin in a Hammer Horror, but it opened smoothly. He carefully moved the angels to one side, deliberately and slowly as if each had given conditional permission, then picked up the box with a reverence close to adulation.

'Be careful' he whispered, handing me the precious object. Its edges felt worn in my hands - cherished - and I cradled it like a fledgling chick, frightened that my clumsy grasp would damage its fragile form. I glanced sideways and Filippo nodded, and I lifted the lid.

'WHAT? What the fuck is this?' I asked, and Filippo laughed like the proverbial cavalier.

'Thanks Loman. I was wondering how we were going to get past my preaching.'

Inside the box was a small roll of euros, around sixty, and a sachet of dog treats.

'It's my swear box,' said Filippo. 'It pays for the coffee. The dog treats are for Angus. I had to hide them in there to stop Ginger from taking them. Fuck knows what he does with them.'

I hardly ever swore in Filippo's presence. He was a priest, after all, despite his own obscenely potty mouth. 'You fucker' I said.

'*Flying* fucker.' He corrected, and handed Angus one of the treats.

Chapter 23

Heat

Only Angus seemed relaxed, curled up in the doorway and snoring as if God Himself was personally watching over him. The dormitory baked. Rome had hit thirty-five degrees and there were no windows to open.

'Jesus. It's supposed to be fucking March.' Filippo used Christ's name as an address, not an expletive.

He'd just dropped the 'phone and seemed relieved. Hettie had forgiven him, and he'd agreed to meet her at Villa Doria Pamphili. It was a landscaped park a mile or so due South of Vatican City.

Filippo sat with his back to the sun, watching picnickers spread across the grass of the old Roman estate, oblivious of him and his worries. Sweat stuck his clothing all over him, and he shifted his sunglasses down his nose to wipe the perspiration from his eyes. He'd taken Angus. The dog had milled 'round his legs at the mention of 'park' and was panting on the seat next to him following a round or two with a tennis ball.

Hettie approached and Filippo smiled, beckoning her to join them on the bench which was clearly designed for two. They huddled together for a few short moments, until the heat of the day became unbearable, and Angus levered himself away to sit on the ground in front of them.

They sat amongst the throng of birds and traffic and children playing and adults laughing. It seemed quiet.

'Peace doesn't come from silence - it comes from this' said Filippo, waving his arms at the host of activity. 'I come here sometimes, to remind me what it's all for.'

He laughed as a handful of kids stared at Angus. When he nodded permission they descended on him, all giggles and happy smiles as they jostled to pet him. Angus rolled over, exposing his belly, enjoying the love bestowed upon him.

'I'm leaving Father.'

'I suspected. People from the hostel don't ask to meet outside the church if they're intending to come back.'

They sat together peacefully, drinking in the warmth and the sounds of joy around them. A swift touched the ground in front of them, its stumpy legs padding at the grass in a clumsy waddle before it soared effortlessly back to the cloudless sky. A little while later, once the children had been called back to their parents and the sun had lowered a little, it was time for words once again.

'Where are you going Hettie?'

'To him. Enzo.'

Filippo sighed. 'Why, Hettie? Why the fuck would you do that?'

'It's not just him. He has Gamma.'

They sat a while again, but the sounds of laughter had gone with the people.

'He gave me a laptop.'

Filippo looked at her. She was glowing red.

'One of his henchmen gave it to me. In the street. With a flash drive. It had pictures of Gamma on it, and a message. They returned all my certificates too.' She stared at the old boots on her feet.

Filippo raised a furry eyebrow.

‘I know Father. I’m an idiot. But he’s not all bad, you know.’

Filippo raised both brows.

‘Look, I have the chance to see my son. And not just see him but *be* with him. Be part of his life. Plus, my Hep B has started to affect my liver. Enzo told me. He’s willing to help me. That’s why he wants me to stay with him and Gamma.’

‘You’re going, aren’t you?’ The eyebrows had lowered.

‘Yes.’

'Will you come back? I mean at all?'

'I don't know Father. Probably not. I mean, I didn't exactly get what I came here for did I?’

‘I’m not sure that you ever finished that story, Hettie.’

‘No. Maybe not. But at least there I'll be with *him*. I want that more than anything.'

‘Will you contact me? As soon as you're able? Just to set my mind at rest?'

'Yes. As soon as I'm able.'

After Hettie had left, and the spring sun had faded, Filippo sat left alone on his bench. He hadn’t noticed before, but his heart pounded. Angus had sat at his feet through the extremes of the day, quietly waiting through his friend’s distress. Filippo met his gaze and patted the empty seat at his side, and an instant later he was no longer alone.

Chapter 24
Motherhood

Gamma would not stop crying. He'd bawled his heart out for six weeks straight and there was no sign of his clamour slowing down. He'd cried when Hettie first saw him, more when she held him. He cried when he was hungry, and cried when he'd been fed. Hettie rocked him, cuddled him, sang to him and sometimes cried with him, but he never stopped until he'd worn himself to sleep.

'He hates me.'

'He's a baby. I don't think hate is on his agenda.'

If Enzo was offering consolation, his tone didn't suggest it. His work had been easier when the child just slept. He didn't blame the boy for bawling when he took his blood, he still moaned less than his aunt, but that was once a week. The rest of the time was just irritating and would have been unbearably distracting if he hadn't had the foresight to secrete him away on the floor below his lab.

Hettie was different. She spent every waking hour milling and shuffling between him and the child. In fact, everywhere except the accommodation he'd provided. She must have covered every square inch of floor at least a hundred times and he severely regretted making himself and his lab available to her.

'Enzo ....'

She stood in the doorway, a vision in snot and puke. Shards of yellow coloured her hair and her eyes pimpled through sunken black.

The boy was with her, bundled inside a purple sling sheath which hung a good eight inches lower than it had appeared on its wrapping. It dragged at Hetties neck and the boy's arms bustled from the edges like two limp bananas. He was still bawling.

'Hettie, I need to work. Why not just give him to the nanny? We're paying her enough.'

'No, Enzo. He's mine. I just need some help.'

'That's what the nanny's for. I'm not the child's father Hettie.'

'Is that right? Well, if you didn't want to be 'the child's father' then why the fuck *did* you adopt him?'

Enzo dragged himself from his desk and joined Hettie at the door. He positioned himself to prevent her entering, but she noticed his subterfuge and bustled past him in an expansive flourish. She plonked herself into the seat he'd vacated.

'Look, you invited me here. The least you can do is give me ten minutes of your time. Then you can get back to *this*.' She wafted a hand at the desk, and one limp banana bobbed with her movement.

'Ten minutes.'

'Yes. Ten minutes.'

'Well then, we'd better get on with it.'

Around ninety seconds later, Hettie spoke.

''What's wrong with him?'

'He has Hep B. You gave it to him.'

'No. Why does he cry all the time?'

'He's a baby.'

'Fuck you, Enzo. Don't you care at all?'

'Of course I do. Why do you think I spend half my life sitting in this lab? I can't do anything unless you let me find a cure. A cure for both of you.'

'Why isn't the treatment working? The one you stab into us every other day?'

'It is. You'd be worse without it.'

But Enzo still didn't know why his work wasn't, well, working. Oh, it had worked on Hettie, but that was the newly acquired sample, and not actually his *research* at all. The antibodies had done their job and she'd soon start to feel fitter than she ever had.

In the meantime, he kept on stabbing. Gamma and Hettie, as often as medically possible, but despite having four times the sample material to work with, and four times the breadth of investigatory activity, there was still, as yet, no worthwhile progress toward achieving his 'miracle'. Maybe if Hettie knew that she'd leave him alone, but of course he wouldn't be telling her, so he muddled along and tried his best to appease her, however difficult that had become. The child was fine, at least physically. He'd been tested to within an inch of his life and while the tears gave some small concern, they hadn't undermined his health, or his yield.

'Look Hettie, I'm getting close to a breakthrough. I know you're worried but he's just doing what babies do. Really, why not just take an hour or two for yourself. I brought the Nanny in to help you as much as for Gamma.' He smiled. 'Now, your ten minutes are up, and I need to work. Please just give yourself a break.'.

Hettie *needed* a break. From *Enzo*. And from this place. She couldn't and wouldn't take Gamma from the labs, he was far too ill, but maybe a few hours away would help her mood, and maybe that would help her interactions with her son.

The streets aren't a good place to live, but they have their blessings. Freedom. The ability to be yourself, say and do what you want within a context of no money and no food, and right now that seemed better than sleeping in a laboratory where the lights never dimmed. One day, when Enzo had found a cure, she'd take Gamma and they'd travel the coast in a beaten-up camper. The gulls would mew and steal their croissants as the waves rolled and the wind whipped sand around their ankles. He'd surf and swim and wear a blue and white coral necklace and never cry again. And maybe she'd even meet a Jose, who'd do it all with them.

Chapter 25
Connection

Hettie bowled through the corridor with a sixteen-inch MacBook Pro tucked under her arm. It had Gamma as its screensaver, eyes shut and sleeping like he'd never made a peep. She'd opened it one evening a week or so after her arrival, once Gamma was down, and worked through the apps out of sheer boredom. She'd been granted an account with an attached card in her name, but other than Disney plus and Sky Movies, pretty much nothing else worked. She'd tried to download her old dating account, but it wouldn't load, even with the passwords she'd remembered. But she wasn't done trying.

There were no external connection points on her floor, just the company network, and she kicked her way through imaginary surf as she strode toward the lift.

'Good evening.'

Hettie recoiled slightly as the lift door opened and a slightly downtrodden imagining of Henry Cavill greeted her.

'Jesus, I'm not that bad, am I?'

Gabriel grinned. Then stopped once Hettie began to bawl like her son. Weeks of frustration leaked out of her.

'Christ. I guess I am. Are you ok?'

'Yes, I'm fucking brilliant. That's why I'm embarrassing myself in front of a preening dick.'

'Jesus!'

Geckos have a strange mating ritual. David Attenborough alone must have made twenty documentaries about it. First, he postures, a slow and intricate dance, switching between pairs of opposing legs, one pair for standing, the other for show. This culminates in a series of nudges, increasing in urgency as his furore begins to flow. Then he bites, clamping his jaws onto anything that may offer the necessary leverage. His passion rises, and if she's lucky, he lets out a screechy exclamation of appreciation, before reaching an explosive climax of reptilian ecstasy. We should all feel dirty for watching.

What we don't often see is what happens when the male is rejected. How he slopes away with jerky lamentation in his little gecko footsteps, and frustration in his weird swivelling eyes. That was Gabriel. And Hettie laughed. Right in his face. It took a long thirty seconds for her to stop. Gabriel looked bemused, and a little bit hurt, but caught his reflection in the mirrored button surround and shrugged. Maybe he should have showered. He looked at Hettie, bewildered, as she held up the MacBook to his face.

'Know anything about computers?'

***

Gabriel plugged the laptop into the socket below his desk and gestured to his new acquaintance. Hettie sat at Gabriel's workstation and accepted the invitation, pounding at the keyboard. Eighty messages! One glance at Gabriel, who shrugged his agreement, and she turned away to begin her trawl. She was looking for Jose but was waylaid by a singularly ornate entreatment. Monotype Corsiva script font. It shouted from her scroll like a mediaeval fop.

'Dear Hettie,

You fill up my senses, like a night in the forest.

The words are not mine, but could have been, had I written them.

I have not contacted you for several weeks and must apologise for my tardy approach. My 'Plenty O' Fish' account has been hacked and my profile and picture cruelly adjusted to resemble Dame Edna Everage. There's no way she could pull off my buzz cut. I attempted to intervene but had been excluded from all editing features. Admin took weeks to address the problem, but I am now addressing you through my new account reference, 'Jose 2'.

Since we last spoke, my dauphinoise has been referenced on page fourteen of 'Kitchen Help International – Rome Edition' and I have been promoted from potatoes - oh glorious day. I am now free to work with vegetables of my own choosing. Last week I turned a simple carrot into a chocolate souffle through sheer determination.

My Italian is also improving, I think, and I am now more pizza than paella. I consider myself a delectable Hawaiian, 'though that may be doing Nicole Sherzinger a mild disservice.

I must confess my disappointment at your absence from my inbox.

I sometimes feel that I am a Welshman, and you a wheel of cheese, cascading away down the slopes of Pen Y Fan, bouncing and tumbling across its ragged form. Tell me truly Hettie, shall we one day become a Grana Padano or will we forever be no more than congealing curd?

Your aspiring friend

Jose'

As Hettie enthralled through her messages, Gabriel quietly retired and whispered into his mobile. 'Get down here Sara. I've got a mad woman sitting at my desk.'

***

Sara arrived as Hettie was finishing, and she swivelled to observe Gabriel and his friend exchange the same glance that she'd seen from people who'd passed her by along banks of the Tiber. The eyebrows up questioning of sympathetic distrust.

'Look, I'll go. Just give me back my laptop.'

Sara scanned Hettie's ensemble, before eyeing the £4k computer. 'Where did you get that?'

'Please, just give it back and I'm out of here' She looked at Gabriel. 'I thought you were trying to help me.'

Gabriel looked at Sara again.

'Maybe we should call security?' she suggested.

'No. NO. Please don't do that. Enzo gave it to me.'

'Enzo? You don't mean Enzo Delgado, do you? Why would he do that?'

'It has pictures of my baby on it.'

'That's bull. Why would he give you a laptop just for that?'

'Look, I can show you.' She beckoned to Gabriel. He looked to Sara again before handing the machine back to Hettie. She opened it up and turned it toward them. Gamma shone from its screen.

'So what? That doesn't prove anything.'

Sara rooted in her pocket for her mobile. Her jeans clung around her hips and her hand stuck at the wrist as she tried to lever it out. The struggle lasted less than ten seconds. It was long enough.

'Please, wait. I can prove it.'

***

Gamma was asleep. Hettie discharged the nanny before beckoning Gabriel and Sara into the room. The three exchanged awkward glances as they passed in the doorway.

Gabriel looked bemused. He'd only ventured below ground level once before and that was with Anaisha at the Christmas party two years ago. He flushed with the remembrance as they strode down the corridor and passed the cupboard door. Neither woman noticed.

Hettie picked Gamma out of his sleep and the boy began to wail. Gabriel's bemusement rose as Hettie did her best to comfort the little man, but he still belted out a tuneless aria of yellow spit.

'He's been like this for months.' said Hettie, battling to avoid adding to the cacophony. The boy took on a violet hue and spluttered bogies down his mother's back.

'Purple crying.' said Sara.

'What? What did you say?'

'Purple crying. My brother's baby had it for weeks.'

'But ...... Is this *normal*, then?'

Gamma continued to wail.

'It's *loud*.' smiled Sara. 'My sister-in-law 'phoned the paediatrician half a dozen times before the woman got pissed off and told her to chill out. It's not that common, but some perfectly healthy babies go through a period of bawling their lungs out. They're not sure why, but it goes away by itself in four or five months, tops. Bianca actually went to church to thank God when it died down. First time since she was twelve, she said.'

If there'd been a knife involved, Sara would never have survived. Fortunately, the only damage was to her lipstick. Hettie bounded at her, and kissed her full on the lips, dragging pink lacquer an inch and a half across her cheek. The baby squeezed between them, peeling his head from between their chests to deposit crusty blobs of burnt ochre onto Sara's navy shirt.

'Nice' she thought, remembering why she barely saw her nephew for two full seasons

Chapter 26

A change of heart

Sara descended into the pile of her lounge carpet while Boris clambered gracelessly across her face.

'Jesus, Boris, be careful, will you?'

She settled back and stared at the crack in the ceiling. It had grown through the winter, tracing an unswerving path from cove to cove. 'How much will that cost?' she pondered, wondering how hard the landlord would crash her deposit if she were forced to leave.

Hettie had relayed a woe-some tale that would have shocked her six months earlier, but Sara had been introduced to the shady side of the Delgado corporation and her stroll to the office had become an increasingly reluctant trudge.

Report 'RCA1001-6J' still lived in her head. Just last night she'd dreamed of a knock at her door as the police arrived, batoning past poor Boris to reach her bedroom with a warrant in one hand and a broken metal spear in the other. A little voice had cried 'Help me!' from her toilet before manifesting in the lounge with the spear hanging limply from their back.

In the morning, Sara wondered whether the voice belonged to the person who'd commissioned the report, or her own conscience prodding at her to challenge the lies. Whichever it was, neither had persuaded her to act against the deceitful activities of her employers.

Hettie. The girl was an enigma. Sara believed that she may be border-line bipolar. She lurched between emotions like a sidewinding snake, and sometimes had the venom to match. But she was in trouble, and it wasn't her fault. It was Enzo's. His aunt's nephew, so it seemed. Sara had seen him up and down the corridors and he once held the door for her as she entered a meeting room that he was vacating. He didn't look like a cunt, but they rarely do.

Now Hettie had joined her nightmares, squeezing her baby between them until waves of chunky vomit spewed through her home, carrying poor Boris on its crest and out into a starless night. The time was coming for a decision, and she wasn't quite sure what she should do. Maybe the answer would come to her in the night, but dreams are just dreams, and dreams don't mean anything, do they?

Chapter 27

Forgiveness

John shuffled his backside in the sand, forming a shallow crater to cradle his buttocks. Reclining, he accepted the gift of the morning sun and gave thanks for its warmth. The river drifted lightly over stones turned smooth, and he opened his eyes to watch its flow. It eased forward with the comfortable gait of a soul which had found its peace.

He glanced upstream and remembered the time before Him. The time before He had honoured John with his gift. It was less than a year, but seemed so distant that he could barely see it. Later, they would call it the gift of tongues, but it was far beyond that.

From the instant of receipt, his thoughts had been more than his own. The turning of the world drove them. His insights shared more than mere words. A bounty of understanding, comfort and hope dwelled within him. He knew truth - beyond the context of belief or law – as if he gazed directly at the heart of righteousness. Yet even this describes the practicality and not the gift.

The gift was freedom. Freedom from the insecurities which undermine us. Relief from the never-ending search for our place in the world. An unquestionable understanding of who we are and our purpose on this earth, and the means to share in that purpose. John thrived in his role. More than that, he was moulded to form the best and most complete version of himself. He was happy. He didn't need more, but had received it, nonetheless.

As Peter had been His rock, John had been His friend - and friends are sometimes given more.

John had been a baby when he'd met Him. Even now he was young, his whole life before him, and he barely considered the time that he'd been given. Time, and youth, and the energy that it gives. Not forever - what sane person would want that? But enough. Enough to see Him again, on this earth, at the time of His return. Enough to share His wisdom across all the lands and all the peoples of creation.

That end was beyond his sight, and he followed the flow of the river with his eyes. The water stretched toward the Gulf of Aquaba, and beyond to the Red Sea and the open waters of the Indian Ocean. Finally, the world. The analogy escaped his guard before his consciousness blocked the thought.

'*Stop it*!' John chuckled inwardly and returned to the present. God wasn't that pretentious, and anyway, for now his reach was restricted to Loman. Given what he'd learned of the man in the few days since they'd met, that was going to be challenging enough.

***

I first met him on a balmy May morning, maybe a year after the rising. We were both in our mid-twenties, but he could have been in his teens. It didn't even look like he'd started shaving.

He smiled at me as I approached, 'though he had no idea who I was or what I would ask of him. He'd arrived at the Nabataean trade centre at Petra a month or so prior to my appearance, spreading his message across the diverse human mosaic which coloured the city. He welcomed me as an old friend, in a Catalonian dialect that reminded me of my mother.

Everyone who knew John loved him. I loved him. Jesus had good taste. A few weeks after we met I asked him how he'd learnt such fluent Italian, and he explained his gift – the gift of tongues. The language to spread God's word absent barriers of nationality or education. His description was comically close to an enthusiastic critic's description of watching 'It's a Wonderful Life' at a provincial cinema in Pruszkow, near Warsaw, centuries later.

There was comfort in his presence, and I followed him. We moved South from Sela – Petra, they call it now - in the Southwest corner of modern Jordan. I'd heard of his preaching, this man who had outlived Christ, and I hoped that he may have words to ease my pain.

'I killed the light of the world, and the guilt is crushing me.'

I was lucky it was John. Anyone else may have shoved a blade through *my* ribs. I wittered in the hope that he would forgive my act. Instead, he stayed silent, tolerating me as I clung to his presence.

After a month I was boring myself, relaying the same old lament to ease my soul. I talked through the crackle of the evening's fire and replayed His death again, until the glow in the embers faded and the night grew cold.

'What have I done?'

I spoke the words aloud, though their echo chased through me. Remorse. Plain and black, and unencumbered by selfish guilt. The purity of regret. And then John answered.

'Is it restitution that you seek Loman? Do you want to go back? Back to before? Would you erase your actions, and return Him to the world? Or do you want to move forward?'

A spark of hope peered nervously from behind the shadows.

***

I approached the river. Its banks were steep, and the morning cast shadows on its face. They moved as its features ebbed, and the darkness on the water frowned. '*All* who repent will receive forgiveness through His sacrifice'. That's what John had said. Even I, who had ended His life.

John saw me and rose. He could have hated me. He could have shunned me. Instead, he led me to the water's edge.

Some two hundred years from now, John would inspire a Greek bishop to set down a summary of the resurrection and its relevance.

The Lord therefore ransomed us by his own blood, and gave his life for our life, his flesh for our flesh; and he poured out the Spirit of the Father to bring about the union and fellowship of God and humanity, bringing God down to humanity through the Spirit while raising humanity to God through his incarnation, and in his coming surely and truly giving us incorruption through the fellowship which we have with him.

John would tell that same truth for two thousand years. But as they came from John, all complexity, all ambiguity, was taken from the words.

The incarnation. God sent his son Jesus to live with mankind to bridge the gulf and heal all ill will between us. *Ransomed us by His own blood.* He accepted Jesus' death as the price to free mankind from the grip of sin. *Poured out the Spirit of the Father.* He declared an abundance of forgiveness and renewed love for each of us. *Incorruption through fellowship.* And He re-made our relationship through our trust in His son.

A new beginning for everyone. Even for me.

'Have you received Jesus Christ as your Lord and Saviour, and will you obey and serve him as your King for the remainder of your life?'

The enormity of my sin enveloped me, crushing in its constraint. The forgiveness, the freedom which was offered by this man and his God was beyond my deserving. I was a child again, reaching for his father's hand.

'Please.' I replied.

Please. John had not expected it, even after a multitude of Christenings. Hope without expectation. Trust without demand. He shook, moved as if the Spirit flowed from the waters and into him, filling his being as the sun had filled him with its warmth. He looked at me and I felt the heart of the words as he spoke them.

'Because you have professed your faith in the Lord Jesus, I now baptise you in His name, and in the name of the Father and the Spirit.'

And then, finally, some semblance of peace. Christ's hope for the world, living through John. At my remorse, contrition, and the seed of faith that he observed growing in me. He lowered me into the waters, and when he raised me, we were as one. Brothers in His spirit.

What neither of us could have known was that God Himself, observing this tiny moment in time, had been moved to bless me. He blessed me as Christ blessed John. A life everlasting? Not quite, but youth, health, and of course time - in a way of His choosing, at least. Time to repent, but also to recover, and to achieve retribution in my own eyes as well as His. All of this flowed from John into me as we embraced, before each of us recognised the sun upon us and we re-entered the world.

Chapter 28

A day in the life

I don't suppose it's a bad thing to occasionally reminisce over your time heading up the mountain pass with Hannibal - or Kate Bush in her leotard - but my dreams seldom hung around that long, sinking back into fuzzy obscurity within minutes of awakening. You know when you wake up having fallen in love in your dream? Your heart full for them and the image of their face stinging with reality? Give it a couple of minutes and nine times out of ten their face has disappeared; you shrug off the feeling and get out of bed to empty your bladder. Last night's dream wasn't like that, and I was keen to share my little revelation with Filippo. Perhaps it would redress my little foray into Gnosticism. The one that he'd taken so badly.

Filippo, on this day at least, had other ideas. Bishop Leonardo's words rang in his ears, and he hadn't heard from Hettie. 'Do what you can, when you can' is pretty onerous in the context of anybody's life, but say those words to a priest and you could end up driving them insane. Filippo, for the moment at least, was just venting in his usual manner.

'Fucking percolating fuck.'

I looked at his swear box and questioned its volume.

There was nothing wrong with the percolator other than the time it was taking, and that hadn't changed since yesterday, or the hundred days before that.

'Can I help, Father?'

'Yes. Do you recognise this?' Filippo pulled a sheet of folded A4 from his pocket, straightened the creases and plonked it into my hand. It showed a logo - a series of letters DBRE, all in capitals, tied through with a rope which then cast a half circle above them. An eagle sitting atop it would have made it vaguely nazi. I didn't recognise it.

'Well, I do. The letters stand for Delgado Biomedical Research Establishment. It's the same organisation that prepared the report that Father Janus commissioned. It's also the place that Hettie's gone to find her baby. A man named Enzo Delgado is the CEO. He's the one that she said she was going to see. I looked his name up on the internet and saw *that*.'

Filippo flicked a finger at the piece of paper in my hand.

Ginger was banging around the kitchen looking for something that wasn't there. Filippo strode through, handed him a blue note and said 'Just buy some Ginger. I'm all out.' I heard them wonder to the outer door and the muffled intonations of a conversation that I couldn't make out. Angus' ears pricked up and he stopped licking his belly, staring through the door at the activity.

'Ok boy?' I asked and he smiled broadly.

Canine behaviourists refer to a dog's smile as a 'submissive grin' and align the expression with an attempt to illicit a positive reaction from their owners. Essentially, we like it when we see an expression that we recognise, and the dog learns that it can result in petting or treats. I think that's bull. There was nothing submissive about Angus when he smiled or at any other time. I reckon he just liked stuff.

Filippo returned with an authentic peaked quiff, streaked with brown. It looked like a home dye job, but he'd actually run coffee grounds through his hair. It was standing up and to the side off a head which was clearly spinning. He'd taken a pre-marital meeting with two young things in his tiny vestry the previous evening as a hostel regular played chess with a new face. The new face must have been a sore loser since they ejected the board from the table just as Filippo was escorting the couple around the lectern in front of the pews. A lone pawn jolted through the back-room door and rolled pitifully up the aisle between them, coming to rest against Filippo's boot. The face was still offered a bed but vacated in the early hours, waking the establishment as he crashed through the vestibule doors with a tin of stolen baiocchi under his arm.

'I should try to help her. But I have a sermon to prepare for Sunday and Signora Scamacca's got influenza again. I need to visit. And who do I trust with the hostel?' Filippo floundered through a long list of potential failures. He hunched as if shielding from the bludgeoning guilt of each one and looked lost. He needed help. He needed my help.

By now, you may have guessed that I was pretty useless in a crisis. The constriction of fear squeezed thoughts of anything positive so tightly that they often fled my mind before they'd even feathered my consciousness. Today, though, I felt buoyed by my dream. 'Why don't we go together Father? To try to find her? Ginger could open the hostel, he's always here first anyway. And you could 'phone the Signora and write your sermon on the way. I can drive.'

Filippo was sceptical. Ginger didn't talk much and of all the people who used the hostel, there weren't many that Filippo knew less about - other than the fact that he could do with having his nasal passages looked at. He drifted between rooms for an hour – I presume while he cogitated – and ended up in front of the picture of St. Francis. It had been knocked off centre and tilted like a curious dog. He tried to straighten it, but it sloped back to its jaunty angle. 'What do you reckon?' he asked of the crooked image. 'Shall we wing it?' Angus barked, and Filippo laughed.

'Ok. Looks like we're going.'

Filippo insisted on completing a round of house calls and Angus and I waited for him at the church.

That evening Ginger arrived at five. It was still hot, and sweat dripped from him as he shuffled in his pocket. His hand emerged with a brown note and some odd coins which he handed to Filippo before they exchanged more muffled words.

Filippo must have peed a half dozen times before we finally hit the car. 'It's a long trip.' He explained, handing me the keys. An evening haze sat over the city and the dome of the Basilica contorted in the heavens. The heat from the car hit like a sledgehammer and Angus danced around the door on tippy toes. He jumped inside when prompted despite accusing eyes which questioned my sanity. I opened every window and we relaxed into the oppression as best we could, three of us longing for the relieving vent of movement. Filippo shuffled in his seat. His bladder had other ideas.

'Hang on, I need to pee again.'

Angus huffed as Filippo disappeared inside. When he returned, he was clutching two cones of stracciatella and a bowl of ice cubes which were already melting. He reached behind me, dripping cold water down my back and across the rear seat. A moment later I heard Angus crunch and I drove onto the road with my mouth still full of ice cream, hitting sixty before Filippo's bladder could refill. Within minutes we'd hit the E80, and we were on our way to Madrid.

Chapter 29
Shepherd

Shepherd remembered his name, but couldn't remember the last time he'd heard it. He remembered his ball, and his bed, and the voice that would soothe him, but did not know how long it had been since he'd lost them. Sometimes, when the sky was dark and the noise went quiet, he would listen, in case they were calling from far, far away, but if they were, he could not hear them.

He looked for them through the streets and the turning of the earth, day after day sniffing at people and places as his paws turned raw. When, like today, the burning heavens beat hard enough to hurt his eyes, the ground hurt too. It burnt his pads and made them sore. Sometimes they would bleed, but it was too hot to sit and lick, or to groom at all, and he'd lope between shadows, seeking refuge from the big voices and the bigger sun. All glared with equal disdain.

When they shouted, he would run, but they didn't always shout. Sometimes, they would kick, and when they kicked, it hurt. Once, a voice had kicked his tummy and stamped his tail. His tummy stopped hurting now, when he ate, but his tail was kinked and ached where it bent.

Yesterday, a voice had followed him. It was tall and big and did not shout, and Shepherd ran. He ran through parks and dodged through roads where cars run too fast to escape, until he'd found a valley – a concrete leat – and hid as damp rose through his body, turning his fear to sleep.

When he woke, the air around him smelled of rot, but he could not smell the voice. He lapped at the murk around his feet to soothe his throat and scrambled from the depths. He remembered his bed, and his ball, and sniffed. The pangs of morning squeezed his belly. The emptiness gurgled and his eyes were dark despite the sun. He shook the pain from his body and the road steadied.

He skirted the high streets. The bigger dogs would scavenge there but he was not big, and the voices never fed him. They chased him from their stalls and doorways and shook objects in his face. He tried the alleys, but the bins were empty, and he could not chase the rats. His collar, frayed and faded, hung loose and rubbed his neck, a clinging remembrance of a different life. He slept again.

***

Ginger worried. The little boy had lain still, a darkened stain beside Fontana del Moro on the Piazza Navona, rigid and withered. He was matted with filth and mange crusted across his snout and dimpled his neck. It was red and sore and caught the sun where burrowing mites oozed moisture from his skin. Excrement hung from his tail and backside, dried with smutty dust. He'd breathed relief as the tangled mass had risen and run.

A year earlier Ginger had slept there too. The same sun had scorched his eyes and cracked his skin. The same people had walked by, gratefully oblivious to the pain in his bones and his heart. But Ginger was not one of them.

He'd seen him twice more. Yesterday was close. Close enough to see his eyes. One was bloated red and tiny white strands slithered from beneath his lids, obscuring his sight. The other was deep and sad and wet with loss.

Last night he'd taken the picture from the wall while the others slept. He'd sat behind the pews and revelled in its truth. He hadn't read the name – he couldn't – but he saw that the animals loved him and that he loved them.

He'd risen early, and prayed to the picture that when he saw the dog, it would look inside him and would not run. He shuffled the treats in his pocket. They were biscuit bones and hearts and little dogs with smiling faces which smelt of fish. He pushed them tight inside his jeans and blinked through the vestibule at the street, and began his search again.

***

The sun still shone, and Shepherd did not know why the ground felt cold. The bins smelled full, and he thought that he may fill his belly, but he was tired, and could not rise.

A rat tickled his feet and sniffed his nose. He bared his teeth and tried to growl, but his voice rasped and frothed and the rat bit. He howled inside and saw his shoulders broad and strong, lifting him to run, but his body did not move. His senses ebbed and his pain lessened, and he heard the squeaks as more rats came.

'No! Fuck off. Fuck *off*.'

Shepherd smelled the voice, but could not raise his head and the darkness in his eyes would not go away. He pricked his ears and tensed against the blow, but all that came were hands smoothing his fur, and the smell of fish.

Ginger lifted the boy and cradled him. Mange touched his face and shit streaked his jeans, but he did not care. He wrapped him in his shirt and felt the sun sting at his naked back, and carried him out of the alley.

Chapter 30

Ginger and Shepherd

'I'm sorry. We can't take him.'

Ginger stared at the man. He looked kind, and his eyes *were* sorry. There were cages behind him. They lined the floor and the wall, and each one housed a dog. In the adjacent room, there was a similar provision, filled with cats.

'Will you wash him?'

'Yes, we can wash him, even treat his mange and those worms in his eyes, but you know, at this stage it may be kinder just to let him go.'

'No. Wash him.'

The man washed him, then rinsed him in a green gloop which looked like spirulina. It stank like boiled eggs and Shepherd wretched as it was rubbed across his snout. Then winced as the man reached his tail.

'We can reset this, but he'll need an anaesthetic.'

'I don't have money.'

'We don't charge. We just need to make sure that he'll have a life. Someone to look after him after we're done. Can you do that for him?'

'Yes.'

Ginger held him while the anaesthetic took hold.

'How long?'

'He'll be asleep for the operation, but he'll be drowsy afterwards too. He won't really know what's happening for twenty-four hours.'

Ginger smoothed the little dog, lumbered into his shirt and left to open the hostel.

***

Shepherd lifted his head. The room smelled strange. It tinged his memories, and he saw a bath and sink and a floor with cold white tiles. Then he realised that the smell was him.

He was on a bed, but it was not *his* bed. That had been soft and deep and held his toys. This bed was soft, but it was lined with something stiff, and shed the wetness when his bladder leaked.

He was awake, but his head felt like sleep, and he closed his eyes again.

Some hours passed, and Shepherd woke again. His eyes felt clear. The crawling in them had gone and he could see things to his right, and to his left. His tail was sore, but no longer ached as it had, and his coat had been groomed, and felt like it had when he'd had his ball.

His smell remained, but more smells had come. There was food next to him. It crunched and flaked and tasted of fish. And he smelled the voice. It sat with him, and Shepherd tensed, but it did not move. The voice was quiet. It did not shout, and did not kick. It just sat, and watched. And sat, and watched. Until Shepherd slept again.

When Shepherd roused, the voice was close. It spoke, but gently. It soothed him, as he had been soothed long ago, and when it reached, its touch was light and slow. It offered food, and Shepherd sniffed and ate, and drank, and believed that the voice was kind.

When Ginger wrapped his arms under him, they felt soft and deep like his bed. The man was warm where his chest throbbed against his side, and when he placed his chin upon his head, Shepherd slept again.

***

Ginger unlocked the church. Filippo's vestry was small, but quiet. His desk was sheathed with blankets, a kaleidoscopic cube of drapes and folds which offered shelter from the world beyond. Beneath, a further pile lay five tiers deep, and two bowls were placed inside, one with water, one with boiled rice, steamed vegetables and white fish. A rubber bear was placed upon the makeshift bed. It had a black nose and eyes that smiled, and a belly which squeaked when it was pressed. And next to the table, for when his boy felt better, a little red ball.

Chapter 31

Reunion

A whirling smoke penetrated vents and seals, a sinister wraith to blacken our arrival.

'Fuck me, that stinks.' Filippo threw his shoulder forward and cartwheeled his wrist, desperate to find relief through the open window.

It had taken twenty minutes to find the entrance, a creeping slog of signs and turns and mini roundabouts to conclude our day and night of travel, and the car didn't like it. Angus didn't like it either and sneezed as the swirling spectre escaped through the passenger side of the vehicle.

If the others were complaining, I wasn't. Madrid sat at a pleasantly balmy nineteen degrees and felt like ice cream compared to the unseasonal oppression of Rome. Angus and I both needed to stretch our legs and began an easy wander toward the city centre, leaving Filippo to conduct the business at hand.

Modern Madrid is a city of history and culture. It is considered a mecca for artisans and historians and boasts over seventy galleries and museums. Dali studied at the San Fernando Royal Academy of Fine Arts through the nineteen twenties, before fleeing the continent to escape the onset of the Nazi Invasion. Our route included the Dolmen de Dali, the only city monument in the world designed by the famous surrealist. It features a weird looking man with a ball hanging in place of his stomach. Angus looked impressed.

El Retiro Park has been described as 'the lungs of the city' and sits centrally within the municipal boundary, fitting neatly inside the M-30 ring road which feeds traffic around its urban veins. It was founded by and for the Spanish monarchs of the seventeenth century as a place for recreation, leisure and entertainment. To provide the facility, the Count Duke of Olivares purchased the land on behalf of King Gabriel IV. At that time, it covered around half the area of the city of Madrid.

Angus was not interested in the history of his surroundings and splashed through Retiro pond in front of its crystal palace, an imposing glass pavilion and conservatory containing centuries of art and a monument honouring King Alfonso XII. He smiled at the frowns of human denizens from a half-submerged squat. Wet fur spiked his snout, and he offered me the same nonchalant grin when I tried to call him from the water. He was in 'that' mood, and we had three hours to kill before we rejoined Filippo at the car. I pushed my ass into the bench and tried to relax, and contemplated a slow dawning that I was a very minor act in Filippos play. That was fine, but I quietly hoped that at some point my contribution may be more than that of a badly qualified chauffeur. It was the first time that a thought for my future outweighed the dreams of my past for as long as I could remember.

The Fuente del Angel Caido – the Fountain of the Fallen Angel - was just a short walk away past Monumento a Ricardo Codorniu, but I didn't see it. My boy preferred to stay close to the water.

***

Filippo pushed through an anonymous single door bearing the same vaguely Aryan decal he'd shared with me a few hours earlier. It was unrecognisable as a primary entrance until he'd passed from the lobby into an expansive space with a high ceiling and a circular reception desk at its centre. Toilets, a cafeteria and a small museum outlining the history of the company were situated around the edges of the room. A row of sixth form seats offered comfortable waiting against the curvature of the wall. The space was overseen by two sectorial galleries which led down via individual staircases. Each gallery had five or six doors, behind which sat the administrative functions of the DBRE.

The top of the reception desk was made of a mottled black stone that Filippo guessed was marble. There were several screens inset at the inner perimeter, but only one facing out to the foyer. The word 'Visitors' glared from its surface. '*Do you have an appointment?*' The first hurdle. Filippo pressed 'No'.

'Can I help you, Sir?' The receptionist appeared with clasped hands and the buoyant air of a shopkeeper.

'Yes, thank you. My name is Father Filippo Fabbri. You completed a report for us earlier this year and I wondered if it may be possible to have a few minutes with the author please? Her name is Sara Amato.'

The fingers separated and flitted breezily across the screen.

'Yes, I have her. She's free of meetings. I'll just give her a quick ring for you.'

A brief conversation later and Filippo was offered one of the posh school chairs and an invitation to browse the company's achievements while he waited. It would be a few minutes, then someone would come to speak with him. Fifteen minutes later and he felt eyes from the balcony bead him with a sniper's intent. A slight woman in a large jacket began her descent.

'Sara?'

'No sir. My name is Beatrice Delgado. I am Sara's supervisor. Please come with me.'

Filippo followed Beatrice upstairs to the first floor and on through an internal corridor to a second stairwell and a lift which, if its signage were to be believed, had no 'G'. A further floor up and their walk continued, through a single door to a seat next to a pretty young woman with reddish hair and nervous eyes. Filippo smiled before scanning the top of Beatrice's expansive desk. It was lightly strewn with pens and a paper notepad, and her laptop was closed. A hard copy of Janus's report sat directly before her with an empty mug at its side. He wasn't sure, but a pastel shade of ouzo may have wisped his nostrils. There had been no conversation between reception and Beatrice's office, and Filippo eased at the sign of humanity, which was in no way evident in the woman herself.

'Now. This is Sara. How can we help you, Father?'

'Thank you. Would you mind if I asked about a friend of mine before we begin? I believe that she's been a guest of Enzo Delgado and I'd hoped to catch up with her during my visit. Her name is Heather Eddy – Hettie.'

Sara shivered and Beatrice stiffened, her frigid stare clagging the space between them. Filippo was surprised that the breath from his words didn't tail upward through the freezing scene. If Beatrice had seemed intractable, any ambiguity dissipated with Filippo's enquiry, and her glare pitched straight at his forehead.

'Sara, would you mind returning to your work, please? I'll call down if we need anything from you.'

Sara rose, her focus anchored on the exit. She barely held her pace in check as she exited, exhaling in her retirement, as if she'd slipped the shackles of clandestine intent. Filippo thought he heard her sigh through the door.

'Before we move forward, could you explain why Father Janus is not visiting us today? The original commission was in his name. Perhaps you could clarify the reasons for your involvement, Father Filippo?'

What *is* the difference between a smirk and a sneer? Most thesaurus will imply that the two are interchangeable, but that's not strictly the case. A smirk, according to literary experts, is the genuine smile of a narcissist, a sign that they have, or are about to hurt or undermine you - and are pleased about it. It is an expression of their own feelings of superiority but put simply, relates to how an individual feels about themselves, not about their 'quarry'. Conversely, a sneer emerges from feelings of contempt. It is directed at the recipient and can accompany the emotions of rage and anger. It is driven by how a person feels about their 'victim.' It is rare that both can be expressed simultaneously, but Beatrice was an unusual woman.

'Father Janus is dead.'

All expression slipped from Beatrice's face.

'I am currently representing the church in terms of this commission.'

Filippo had already concluded that he'd get no help from Beatrice in finding Hettie and had no wish to complicate the episode by delving into the detail of the report. He doubted that any 'ordinary' priest would have felt comfortable discussing the theological implications of its findings. *He* certainly didn't after twenty hours in his old rust bucket. His backside still ached. He cursed the ten hours of daylight he'd spent staring out of the car window, assuming that he'd 'wing it' when he arrived. He assumed that he may at least get a few moments to think, that Beatrice's next comment would be a polite expression of regret at Janus' passing. He was wrong.

'I see. Then perhaps you could explain exactly what you'd like to know.'

'Thank you. I understand that you've prepared the report in a scientific way, exactly as we would expect, but in the eyes of the church the conclusions you've reached may have some spiritual as well as secular significance. It's important that we fully understand the context for the series of tests that you've undertaken before considering how we may deal with their implications. Essentially, I'd like to understand the possibility of errors in the results. Not in terms of errors in the process, but the parameters that exist for interpretation of results and the possibilities for alternative conclusions. Are you able to help with that?'

Given the circumstances, Filippo felt pretty pleased with his efforts. Nevertheless, the sneer returned. Beatrice didn't even try to hide it. It was followed by a distastefully patronising outline of the reputation and proficiency of the Delgado organisation, so expansive that Filippo wondered whether the company should be considered for consecration. Beatrice was, however, especially careful to indicate that while all the findings of the Delgado 'empire' could be trusted implicitly, there were always doubts and inherent assumptions that must be made when dealing with items of such age and Lilliputian quantity. Essentially, she didn't commit to anything at all.

'I understand that all this must be frustrating Father. But if I may, I would like to offer you a further service, should you need it. I am willing to provide a comprehensive testing regime, free of charge, for any further items that the church may hold, so long as they fall within the same broad categories of origin as the original samples. We have a long-standing relationship with the Vatican and would be happy to help establish dates and origins which may prove more useful in your quest for validation, should they actually exist. I hope that this may be of some interest and may go some way to making your visit worthwhile.'

And that was it. Filippo was dismissed, along with his beliefs, in a single phrase. Beatrice smiled, and called Sara back into the office to escort him from the building.

***

It's easy to forget what good company dogs can be. On the odd occasion that Angus would trot with Filippo to the park I genuinely felt that part of my soul went with him.

Dogs fall in love far more easily than humans do, and their capacity for loyalty and forgiveness is a beauty which rivals the best sunrise that God ever created. My boy's presence turned a walk through concrete streets to a vision of Angel Falls, with every stranger's face smiling their joy in my direction. At least that's how I felt once he'd stopped being the little shit he'd been for our two hours in the park. When he got the fidgets again, around a quarter mile from the car, I got a little edgy.

The closer we got to Delgado's car park, the worse he got. He whined and bounced and pulled and almost slipped his lead until I wrapped the leash around my wrist and picked him up, carrying him as he jiggled in my arms. He didn't seem distressed, but something had his wind up.

It was only as we rounded the corner that I found out what.

***

'I'm sorry if I made you feel uncomfortable. I hadn't meant for things to happen that way.' Filippo's apology did little to calm Sara's discomfort. If anything, she seemed even more nervous than she had in Beatrice's office.

'Don't worry,' she said as they approached the foyer, 'just follow me.'

She guided Filippo through the outer door and along the sober walkway which led to the car park.

'Really?' he thought, 'Right to the car? What the fuck do they think I'm going to do out here?'

But Sara didn't stop at the car. She coaxed him along with a 'Please.' and he followed along a narrow gap between two buildings which opened into a covered courtyard with a few tables, a vending machine and some chairs. A grizzled man with shiny eyes appeared through a pair of garage doors. His briar pipe stood erect through gritted teeth, and he spoke with a voice which surely came from a spaghetti western.

'Thanks Luis'

'No problem, Bello, *you're* welcome here anytime.'

Luis dropped a spanner and wiped grease from his hands. He winked with intent and Sara tutted loudly and smiled as the old man returned to his engines. 'I'll get the kettle on' he shouted as he disappeared behind inside. 'And I'll let them know you've arrived.'

Sara pointed and Filippo eyed the table. 'Client waiting area' scowled from a greasy sign and he scanned the building questioningly, wondering why the fuck he was here. The answer was immediate.

'WOOF!' Angus barrelled into the priest as he finally escaped my hold. He lapped at his face before settling for a hand which Filippo extended as he took a seat.

'Hello boy, what are you doing here?'

'He's with us. Hello Father, it's good to see you.'

It was Hettie.

Chapter 32

Bad Medicine

Beatrice stomped through her own personal minefield, with each footstep a bitter explosion of distrust. Why the fuck *was* she still shrivelling in her skin while Hettie pranced through the office like Mary Fucking Poppins?

Enzo. Of course it was Enzo. Her nephew paraded his cure around the building like his elders were either too stupid to realise or too impotent to act. Well, fuck him.

His lab was unlocked. It often was since Hettie had clawed her way under his skin. The situation made no sense, but Enzo didn't act without reason and maybe the sense was secreted within his workstation. She slid down the staircase once the evening's stragglers had left, and she'd seen her nephew's car disappear with the day.

Enzo was no fool. He changed his password almost daily, but Beatrice had talents of her own. If he'd spent an ounce of effort on company etiquette, he would have realised that password override was a privilege he should have kept for himself. She tapped. Doctor Frankenstein. She almost laughed. Maybe the boy had something to him after all.

Beatrice typed, her bony digits stabbing at the keyboard with unnatural grace. Passwords and padlocks fell away, and she forged through the company database with cold precision. The system took longer to load the files than she took to invade them, their simplistic firewalls doused with an intuitive fluidity. Once she'd accessed the first, the rest toppled. Each file was labelled and cross referenced so that the monkeys they contained could almost have followed them. The boy was meticulous, but not very imaginative.

'Hettie.' The girl was cross referenced two dozen times. 'Gamma', 'Dolly', 'Hepatitis', 'Antibodies', all scrolled from the page in a wave of tumbling opportunity, but a little further down the screen, one word grabbed like a Sunday headline. 'Miracle'. She caressed her hands like Fleming's Blofeld, and the smirk crept back across her face.

Everyone exhibits narcissistic tendencies from time to time, whether it's bragging about yesterday's triumphant dessert or enjoying attention at a family get together. Narcissistic personality disorder is something else. Symptoms are severe, occurring across multiple situations and environments, they make relationships with others difficult, if not impossible. The mental health sector uses an acronym to remember the nine traits of NPD. The traits are 1. Sense of self-importance, 2. Pre-occupation with power or success, 3. Entitlement, 4. Can only tolerate people 'of note', 5. Interpersonally exploitative, 6. Arrogant, 7. Lacking in Empathy, 8. Craving admiration, 9. Envious of others or believing that others are envious of them. The anacronym spells SPECIALME, and Beatrice was certainly that. So much so that she was struggling to understand just how she could access Enzo's files with such extraordinary ease, but couldn't wrap her head around their content.

'Fucking boy needs a lesson in plain language.'

Beatrice was far from inept. She was a competent chemist, and the nuances of analytical and biochemistry were embedded through years of repetitive application. But original thought? Well, perhaps not so much.

Her issues were copious. The samples relating to the recorded 'miracles' were physically locked down. The intricacies of the experiments were difficult to decipher. Many of the test results were disappointing, even though the chemical composition of the samples seemed identical to those which had been a success. What she didn't consider was that she lacked the technical proficiency of her nephew. She just wasn't bright enough.

Life's realities can leave an unpleasant taste, especially for the Beatrices of the world, who've grown to assume the privileges of wealth and family. A fancy school and a limo are armour against all manner of inadequacy, but papered cracks and false assumptions hold no sway with proteins or platelets. But life's realities held no sway with Beatrice.

There were three cultures labelled for direct use in Enzo's refrigeration unit. None had come from the 'miracle' source, but each type had demonstrated healing qualities, and, more relevantly, each was cross referenced to Hettie and ready for immediate application.

Beatrice prepped all three and relaxed into Enzo's seat. It was too big and angled forward in a way which tipped her ever onward toward her endeavours. The infusion of drugs would take several hours to assimilate – Beatrice estimated eight – and Enzo's appearance could not be discounted. Her bodyweight was low for the volumes she'd prepared but her body had adjusted to the process through years of cantankerous obstinacy. The headaches and nausea she'd felt from the outset had dissipated to a mere inconvenience, and four hours would manage the risk of interruption. She placed a large glass of water on the desk beside her and stabbed the needle into her arm.

Under proper supervision, the majority of people cope well with intravenous treatments. Infusion reactions can include fevers, chills, flushing, rash and muscle aches, as well as headaches and nausea, but these are generally not severe and can improve with analgesics and antihistamines. In formulations with a high sugar content blood sugar levels may be temporarily raised, but this can be avoided by slowing the infusion rate and ensuring that the body is well hydrated. Finally, because a high volume of medication is absorbed, blood pressure can be elevated, and existing heart conditions worsened.

Beatrice experienced none of the above, but trouble still erupted from her gut like it was Trevi Fountain.

Gastrointestinal infusion reaction is unpleasant to witness, never mind experience. Usual protocol dictates that where acute reactions occur, the infusion must be stopped immediately, but that's difficult to achieve when you're doubled up with cramp and sloshing around in your own crap. Even if she'd been able, it seemed doubtful that Beatrice would have denied her 'cantankerous obstinacy' the opportunity to win. She'd never succumbed to the opinions, or the wishes, of others, even where the actual facts weighed against her, so why the fuck would she start now?

She reached for the glass, but slumped to the desk. The table-top swam through her vision as she struggled to find focus, and the glass toppled from the surface as her hands found it. It bounced to the floor without breaking, and Beatrice wondered at its survival. She tried to lift her head, but merely shuffled the papers that Enzo had strewn across his workstation. Perhaps the boy would yet arrive to interrupt her efforts. It *would* be just like the little ass. She remembered him as a youth, just months before he'd given himself to intellect. God, she would have fucked him then. Her hands on his throat as he erupted with boyish naivety.

Her bladder released. An expansive fluidity to spread her mess across legs and buttocks. A swift jerk at the needle may have ended the episode, but Beatrice was beyond that. Still, she was surely too hardy, too resilient, too 'right' to succumb to failure, and she twisted and turned and writhed through the stink, all the while assuming that the world's complaisance would rescue her.

By the time she was dead, it was hard to tell where Beatrice ended, and all of her shit began.

Chapter 33
Machinations

Madrid's cuisine is famous for amalgamating the specialty dishes enjoyed across the many eclectic communities of Spain. The city contains some of Europe's most unique restaurants, but neither I or my companions could afford any of them.

We squeezed around an undersized table for four and stared at the soggy tapas. A skinny waiter with dark rings shrouding his eyeballs had set the meal before us. He'd smelled of cigarettes. The pinch was tightened by the presence of Gabriel, who had dragged a chair between Hettie and I and squeezed his shoulders against both of us. Hettie was enjoying the company, if not the food, and asked how my memory was before launching into a tenuous theory whilst awaiting my reply.

'I have never subscribed to the theory that we only use ten percent of our brain capacity. We use different parts of our brain for different functions and at this stage in our medical understanding only God knows what capacity the normal person has to expand their knowledge, fulfil their 'potential' or however you wish to describe it. Nonetheless, the brain is a finite organ with the same physical limitations as our liver, heart, or the rest of our body. It can't operate beyond the potential of its design. Now in most people I'd expect the brain to protect itself, or at least 'make room' to a certain extent by diminishing old and unused thoughts to make way for new ones – the reason why we can recall faces without names or vice versa - but what if *your* mind doesn't work that way. From what you've told me, your dreams exist in as much detail as if they'd actually happened. I guess that you already know that the brain stores information by rearranging the connections – the synapses – between neurons. Maybe *your* brain is resisting this change in order to retain your subconscious memories. Under those circumstances, eventually you're just going to run out of space. In simple terms, your brain is full, and it's been necessary to lose part of your memory just so that it can go on living.'

Sara looked bemused. Filippo bypassed the diatribe. 'How are you, Hettie?'

'Better than I was. Sara's been keeping me sane. It's just a shame that Gabriel is such a dick.'

'Hey!' Gabriel spat croquette across the table. I thought that it would be the end to his contribution, but he'd latched onto Hettie's theory.

'So, Loman, have you ever dreamed of Cleopatra? Or Helen of Troy? Were they really the beauties that history portrays?'

I sort of got it - he was enthralled by my subliminal existence. Filippo was too, but at least he never assumed that my dreams were more than my mind playing its fanciful tricks. Gabriel's assumption that I must know everyone from Genghis Khan to William Shakespeare simply because I'd dreamt through the timeframe would wear thin pretty quickly. I took Filippo's lead.

'Really Hettie. How *are* you doing?'

'I really mean it. Sara's been keeping me sane. If you'd asked me how I was a fortnight ago I'd have puked over your lunch, but things have been better. The detail would put you off your food, and I wouldn't want to spoil all *this* - but I basically thought that Gamma hated me for leaving him, and Enzo's been, well, he's just been Enzo – but the whole thing's been easing down. I'd almost say that I was happy. Well, that's not *exactly* true. I'm as happy as I can be under Enzo's 'regime.'

'Yes. Enzo's *regime*.' Sara cut in. 'That sums the man up. I thought his aunt was a cunt, but he really is a rancid, herpes riddled, half eaten peanut sized prick – sorry Father.'

'Ha. Peanut prick.' Gabriel contributed.

'That's fine. He certainly sounds like a prick.'

The table paused. I don't think Sara or Gabriel had heard a priest use the 'p' word before. Just wait 'til they'd seen him burn his mouth on a quesito.

'You know, Father, I do need to tell you something.'

'For fuck's sake Sara, can't we finish our food first?' Gabriel lost another morsel. Sara was clearly in the habit of ignoring him.

'Actually, it may be better if I showed you.'

***

The home Sara had made was a reflection of her. It was as easily handsome in jeans and a ponytail as a little black dress. Either may have been worn with warm stripy slippers that reached all the way to the knees. Her lounge should have looked chaotic. Her pastel blue sofa breached the perimeter of her deep green rug. The rug sat atop generic wooden laminate which was edged with authentic Carrara marble skirtings. It shouldn't have worked, but fell together like old schoolmates.

Angus liked Boris, but it wasn't mutual. Ten minutes and a scratched nose later I took him for a stroll and left the others to it. 'I'll come with you!' exclaimed Gabriel, and I braced for another interrogation of my subconscious. Hettie came too, and walked with us for fifteen minutes before hugging Angus and turning back toward the Delgado building, and Gamma. Gabriel threw his arms wide and beckoned her in. 'You can fuck off.' She threw him a finger and strode back to her life.

'Recognise this?' Sara handed Filippo her copy of the report.

'I think so.'

'I bet you don't. Have a look while I put the kettle on.'

What can you tell from a piece of paper? Weight, brightness, finish, opacity. All of these impact on print performance and the assurance of quality. But it's just finery, isn't it - the emperor's new clothes. The paper in Janus's version of the report had the lustrous feel of grandeur. The cover had been embossed with the Delgado crest, and the whole thing presented in state-of-the-art UV print, but it still crumpled to nihility in Janus' bag. Sara's print was thin. You could see the text through the pages and the ink was sketchy and clogged. But Filippo had learned from a legion of parishioners not to judge rectitude on appearance.

'Do you understand it, Father?'

'I hope so, but tell me anyway.' And Sara did, just as she'd told Gabriel.

Filippo had been pretty comfortable with his comprehension of Janus's report. Sara's insights were something else. He followed the themes, and her summary was succinct and coherent. But when she began layering – tier upon tier of reasoning and methodology and background – it became clear that he'd never be a pharmacologist.

He read it again, asking questions as he went. Eventually he bit into his lip and asked what he was thinking.

'Is it Christ's blood?'

'That's your decision Father. I just follow the facts.'

Filippo's face fell. A temporary ebb in his wave of expectation.

'It says here that the blood – or the antibodies within the blood – will cure anything. Isn't *that* a fact?'

'Well, no. Not really. It doesn't actually say that. It says that the culture of antibodies prepared from certain of the samples – more specifically one sample – has previously unknown healing properties. Actually, all of them do, but this one in particular had wider applications and much more significant outcomes.'

'Significant outcomes Sara? That's like saying that Christ's existence on earth resulted in the healing of a paralyzed man. Let's give it the context it deserves. It's a miracle. A full on bona-fide miracle. It *is* isn't it?'

Sara relented.

'Some people may say that.'

'The blood of Christ. '*In him we have redemption through His blood.*' *That's* what it says Sara. And this is the proof. Living fucking proof.'

'Look, Father. I understand what you want this to be, I really do, but my beliefs are different from yours, and I haven't written anything to deliberately suggest that. My parents did the Hare Krishna thing, at least until Thatcher came along and screwed with their karma, but I don't know what God is. I don't know *if* God is. Half the time I'm not sure what *I* am. I'm excited by these results. And yes, in your shoes I'd probably be drawing the same conclusions as you are, but I'm trained to record my observations and comment on the secular possibilities. I'm *trying* to be professional.'

'Of course. Yes. Thank you. I'm sorry, Sara. This must all be difficult, given the actions of your employers. I'm truly grateful for your help.'

'And I don't need platitudes. My employers are shit, and I already hate myself for not trying to find Janus, never mind not telling someone how Enzo's treated Hettie. But the fact is that I don't even clean under the sofa, even though I know that Boris craps under there. I'm just trying to do my best. And *that* thing hasn't helped.'

Sara flicked fingers at the report while Filippo finally remembered Father Janus. The colour drained from him like a flushed cistern. He'd totally forgotten him. The man had killed himself over a fucking lie. And here he was giving praise for the act of it. And poor Sara, a young girl just trying to live her life, caught in the middle. She *had* done her best. And she looked knackered.

'I'm sorry, Sara.'

'It doesn't matter. I just want it to be over.'

'Of course. I'll leave as soon as Loman gets back.'

'No, Father, that's not what I meant. I wish I could just fuck off to Thailand and set up a beach bar.'

'Mmm. I guess that Gabriel may want a discount?'

Sara smirked.

'Boris wouldn't like the sand. Go on, Father, let's just get it over with. I feel a second wind coming.'

'Sure?'

Sara shrugged. Filippo thought twice, but his excitement was back.

'The miracle cure. It came from the spear head?'

'Yes.'

'Then why didn't the others work in the same way?'

Sara's second wind puffed out.

'Look, I'm sorry Father, I don't know. Everything I know is already in the report. It was enough for Delgado to expunge the whole line of research from the company records. I'm more than happy to tell you what I do know - but I don't know everything.'

Sara glanced at the door. Where the fuck were the others?

'Shall we stop, Sara? It wouldn't be a problem. Maybe I should just read the report again?'

'No, we can't. Not yet. You should know about Hettie.'

'What about her?'

'She may not tell you herself, but she may need your help.'

'Go on.'

'She's been subjected to something. She told me that Enzo had given her some sort of treatment that's supposed to be helping her. She had an illness when she came here. It was getting worse, but now it's under control. At least that's what Enzo's told her. *I'm* worried that it may be something to do with the samples he's cultured.'

'You mean her hepatitis? But that's good, isn't it? That it's under control?'

'I don't know. It depends how he's done it. *If* he's done it at all. We can't trust what he says, or what he does. It may be nothing, but I wouldn't put it past him to try something new, some new drug, just to see how it works out. He's definitely been injecting her with something, and hepatitis like Hettie had doesn't just 'go away.' Her situation is just too closely related to the 'miracle' concept for us to ignore. It may just be my own paranoia, but if he *is* using Hettie as a lab rat, I'd bet big that the drug he's using hasn't gone through the fucking Agencia Espanola de Medicamentos Productos Sanitarios.'

***

I knocked at the door while Angus sniffed at Gabriel. He'd insisted on buying a cold six pack from the licoreria, just as refreshment for our efforts. I'd had one. Regardless, Hettie heaved him through the door with the jerk of a tugboat. 'You're staying here tonight' she told him, and even his leering grin didn't dissuade her.

Coffee and quiet later, Sara offered us the living room. It was tiny, but under the circumstances, it was personal and generous, and we gratefully accepted. We heard a noisy rummage from her bedroom, and she emerged to throw two blankets and a pillow over the sofa.

'You can use the cushions too. I'm sorry, I don't have more.'

Filippo still had the report. He ran fingers over Sara's words. '*it is my opinion that the specimens presented originate from the same progenitor.*' It was a simple line, tiny in form and with a bubble of dried ink half obscuring the words, but for Filippo, it *was* the blood of Christ, filling a void that had eaten away at his faith, despite his protestations.

'*Thank you,* Sara.'

She believed it was the most heartfelt gratitude that she'd ever received.

Chapter 34
The Hill

There is a green hill far away,
without a city wall
where the dear Lord was crucified,
who died to save us all
We may not know, we cannot tell
what pains he had to bear
but we believe it was for us
he hung and suffered there
He died that we might be forgiven
he died to make us good
that we may go at last to Heaven
saved by his precious blood
There was no other good enough
to pay the price of sin
He only could unlock the gate
of Heav'n and let us in
O dearly, dearly has he loved
and we must love him too
and trust in his redeeming blood
and try his works to do.

I stood at the foot of the cross, looking up. He seemed far away, and the height dizzied me. A single gasping sob unsteadied me, and

I turned away, seeking balance. I hadn't noticed that the sound had come from my own throat. Silence fringed my existence. I had turned the world to mute. No people spoke, or horses whinnied, or even birds sang. Unnerved, I tightened my grip on the spear as the sticky warmth reached my hands.

I felt no anger or bitterness toward me. I was nothing. The extra to His lead. No backstory to my life was required, 'though my act had emptied the world. He was gone. His body ragged heavily, knees bowing as they swayed. A final decaying movement bequeathed by my thrust.

Something squeezed my shoulder.

'Loman, we should go.'

It was Gaius. He was my friend - a fellow foot soldier and member of my tent group. He eyed the crowd nervously as I fixated on my deed.

Weeks earlier we'd grinned like little kids. Our posting was a hundred miles from war, and no more than a handful of backwater insurgents to manage. Our role was to offer comfort to the local Prefect. 'Wear your uniforms and be seen.' Simple.

I never expected to kill that day. I just saw no reason or benefit in the suffering of a man who was already dead.

'Loman, *come on*'.

We turned from the scene and followed the track down the hill. It was lifeless and dry, battered by footprints. I heard my spear thump heavily at my feet before it tumbled away, muffled in the soft sand. Gaius glanced nervously behind, but there was no baying mob, nor even a murmur. No punishment at all.

I listened through the silence, searching for the end to its emptiness. It came with a gust - a universal sigh which breathed dust at my eyes. I rubbed at them, and my perception turned red, stinging with the touch of His blood.

'Wait!' I cried, grasping for Gaius through a blitz of fluttering tears, and I felt his hand lower me to sit. It took just moments for my sight to clear, and for a crown of sunlight to reacquaint me with the world.

'What have I done?' I asked.

It would be a year before I met John, who would tell me.

Chapter 35

Ginger

The car sounded asthmatic. Several visitors to Filippo's hostel had suffered from the affliction, especially through the summer, even though pollen struggled to negotiate a route so far into the city. They'd sneezed and coughed and whistled though the night, unintentionally sharing their insomnia with the room. The fiat sounded worse. To be fair, the poor vehicle had looked sickly as soon as we'd entered Madrid. The little hatchback seemed forlornly inadequate amongst the SUV's and buses which muscled their way through the congested streets.

Some chance encounters are part of God's plan, at least that's what Filippo said - and Sara's friend Luis was an excellent mechanic.

'We cannot leave our vehicles unserviced for four years, senor. Their souls may not survive the neglect.' He appeared genuinely hurt. He changed oil filters and adjusted points – a nostalgia which made his heart sing – and soothed the vehicle with a bedside manner that suited a paediatrician. God only knows how we managed to persuade him to limit his repairs, but he finally accepted that we didn't have time for a full resuscitation.

'That should get you home. But please get the car to your garage once you get there. I've left a diagnostic on the back seat.'

The car flew. It roared with Lamborghini conviction, and we revelled in its happy gait as we zipped along the A6. I didn't share my dream with Filippo. I was enjoying the bounding inertia and didn't want to risk the moment by revealing that his travelling companion had ended his Lord and saviour, at least in my mind's vision.

When did my dreams become visions? I never did give much thought to their title, they just were. For a decade I didn't conceive that my excursions may be different from Filippo's sleeping hours, or Ginger's, or Hettie's - like a person with colour-blindness traverses their whole life without ever knowing that the world sees red to their green. I couldn't say that all my dreams were especially vivid, or memorable, or even noteworthy, 'though sometimes they were to me. I didn't know whether their manifestation was related to my lost memory, or even whether they were some kind of memory in themselves. Hettie would have her theories, no doubt. But they did give me a sense of who I was. They didn't *feel* like mere stories that my subconscious told to help me work through the joys, or terrors, or even indolence of the day. I didn't live my life through their messages, there often weren't any. But they also weren't just a run of unconnected televisual repeats, played out in my head as an anthology of recollections in glorious technicolour. They felt personal. I connected with them, and within them. I never experienced the sense of third person 'observance' or 'looking in' that many people describe of their dreams. It was always me, right there in the centre of it all. Whatever else they were? Well, maybe God knew. I doubted that anyone else would.

'Jesus Christ!'

I heard the shout pierce my eardrums as Angus's head jolted into the gap between the seats. He offered a brief but toothy smile to my face in the time it took me to thank God for ensuring that I'd anchored him to the seatbelts with a proper harness. He sat back down and grinned. The jolt had lifted my backside, but turned out to be no more than an overly firm application of the brakes - Luis had changed the pads and Filippo hadn't adjusted.

'Christ!' Filippo moved to the abridged version as I sidled back to my starting position. I was just relieved that we hadn't ended up in the back seat of the Seat Arona which finished up the queue of traffic that had formed in front of us. Filippo was still sidling when he repeated his expletive.

'Christ!'

'I know! I nearly peed myself.'

'No, no, not *that*.' Filippo squirmed like he'd already peed himself, but it was a eureka that had begun to flow. 'The miracle - the miracle cure. It has to be!' And it looked as though the pleasantries of the trip were about to get serious again.

Filippo described what he'd read in Hettie's report, and added her verbal embellishments where he thought it may be useful. I understood *some* of it.

'It's the spear. The spearhead is the only example of Christ's blood which results in the holistic treatment of disease. Yes?'

'Yes, that's what you said.'

'Well, what makes the spearhead different from the thorn, or the fragments of wood, or any of the other relics?'

'I don't know, Father. Tell me.'

'Well, it wasn't the crucifixion – the cross – that actually killed Jesus, and the crown of thorns was placed on His head prior to the cross being raised.'

'Yes.'

'So, the only sample – the only sample of His blood – which was deposited as a result of his death –came from the spear. The spear which killed him.'

'Ok.' I replied, hoping to catch on.

'So *that* blood. That blood which flowed after his death, is *the* blood. The blood of the sacrifice. The whole reason for his time here on earth. What else could it be?'

He found first gear and the car growled back into motion. His face shone with a euphoric glow that you never want to see on the face of a person who's driving you down the middle lane of a foreign motorway.

'Should we pull over Filippo? You look a bit flushed.'

'Yes, yes, sorry. I suppose I am. There's a junction ahead. I need to pee anyway. You probably shouldn't have mentioned it.'

Filippo signalled to change lanes and laughed. I wasn't sure whether it was wee related or whether he actually believed he'd landed on the winning number to doctrinal roulette. I was far from an expert, but thought at the very best that he may have picked black or red. It just didn't feel as though his ball had quite nestled into the exact number.

'What about the resurrection?'

Filippo pulled into the service station car park and turned off the engine. He seemed genuinely gleeful at my attempt to engage.

'Yes? What about it?'

'Well, you said that that the blood was miraculous because it belonged to the sacrifice. But I thought that the bible said that Jesus was reborn in perfection at the resurrection. So, for the blood to be perfect, wouldn't it have needed to come from Jesus after the resurrection?'

I watched as the blood drained from him. It seemed to be happening a lot lately. He looked a little crushed, like I'd just refused his offer of a date and he was trying to face it out. He didn't say anything, and I swivelled in my seat to check on Angus. He was eying us both in the same way that Filippo watched Ginger that time he'd turned up rolling drunk and peed in the sink, long before he'd poured his final vermouth down the very same plug hole.

'One to ten Father. How pissed off would you be if I said that I wasn't quite feeling the religious significance in the same way as you are?' His face fell further. Not so easy considering its starting point.

'Mmm. Honestly? Maybe about a nine. Ten if today had been a Sunday.'

I cracked open a coke and swilled it 'round my teeth - caffeine works in all sorts of forms. What I hadn't told Filippo was that the memory of picking up the spear in Janus' flat was beginning to rumble my digestive system, and although denial had always been a go to in my defensive armoury, it didn't seem to be offering a whole lot of protection given the current context.

Filippo said something, but I missed what. My attention was stuck on the feeling of that spear on my hand. I'd suppressed the weight of it as I'd thrust it back onto the bed, but I could still feel it, wet and sticky with blood, 'though there'd been no blood to feel.

Help me now, if you can. How exactly was I supposed to disassociate that feeling from the dream sitting fresh in my head? Nothing to offer? No, neither did I. I felt a bit sick and thought that I'd better open a window rather than puke across the dashboard with almost three hundred miles still to go. A cold breeze cut across my face and Filippo phased back in.

'You know, Loman, it doesn't matter that much whether my theory is correct or not. The fact is that all the samples came from the right time period from a middle eastern location and have likely come from the same person. The source material has been revered as remnants from Christ for centuries. The samples contained blood with active elements that have never been recorded previously, and all of them have some type of healing quality. At this point it must seem unlikely, even to you, that the blood *hasn't* come from Jesus? Could you offer a more likely scenario? I certainly can't. Whether or not there's some nuance tacked onto all of that really isn't that important to me. *I* believe that what we hauled through Europe in the back of this car was the blood of Jesus Christ. I *believe* it.'

Maybe I got caught up in Filippo's conviction. Or, maybe I'd been affected by my 'vision' – His head bowed and his body sagging toward me. The mere thought of it made my guts churn a whole revelation faster. At least my response made Filippo happy.

'I believe it too.'

***

The remainder of the journey was weird, but not because of my contemplations. You'd think that a priest, basking in the glow of a revelation as deep as real, tangible proof of the existence of Jesus Christ, would have thrown up an avalanche of praise ranging from 'Abide With Me' to Cliff Richard's Millenium Prayer - actually, no, maybe not that one. Anyway, he didn't. If anything, Filippo had taken this deep affirmation of his faith as a sign that going home while Hettie was still stuck in a laboratory in Madrid was fundamentally wrong, regardless of the multitude of tasks that would lapse in his absence. I found this out as we drove up to the church of St. Francis to see Ginger treading sheepishly around the vestibule with a scooper and a wet cloth, both covered in a material which didn't look hygienic.

'We have to go back.'

'What? Fuck Filippo, we've just driven twenty hours. What for?'

'I don't know, exactly. But we have to go back. For Hettie.'

Ginger approached the car, utensils in hand, and beckoned us into the building.

'You'd better see.' he said, nodding from Filippo to the vestibule door.

'Fuck. What now?'

Shepherd came first. The fur had been shaved from his body and his pencil topper head twisted around narrow shoulders as Filippo entered the room. His eye had already cleared, and his tail buffeted the floor in an enthusiastic celebration of fading discomfort. He still looked a state, but he didn't know that, and smiled as Filippo approached. Dogs, it appeared, regained their trust with amazing grace.

Behind Shepherd, peering between the blankets which covered the vestry table, were two mongrels. Their shape would have suggested Retriever in their lineage, but they were entwined in a nervous embrace which made it impossible to determine their form.

'What the fuck Ginger? What are these dogs doing here?

'They're mine.'

Filippo stared at the pitiful trio. He'd driven back on a wave of rapture overshadowed with a cloud of Delgado's deceit. The drive alone would have been enough to send most people straight to their bed. I was used to watching Filippo battle though his tiredness, but nothing about this situation was usual, and I swear I saw him sway as he contemplated the scene.

I didn't know it, but Filippo had just stopped himself from trawling out the same diatribe about church insurance and hostel protocol, the one that he'd given to Hettie just before she left. I suppose something had changed.

'Where did you get them Ginger?'

'From the street. They were hurting.'

'And you decided to help them?'

'Yes.'

'Alright then. I want to go back to Madrid, to see Hettie again. Are you still able to keep the hostel open?'

'Yes'

'And you'll keep the dogs separate from the people?'

'Yes.'

'Ok, Ginger, they can stay. Are you sure that you can still help me, to keep the place going, I mean? It may be a few more days yet.'

'Yes.'

And that was it. On the way out, Filippo reached into his cabinet of angels and deposited a wad of notes inside his little ossuary.

'That should cover it.'

Ginger watched from the door as I put Angus back into the car. 'Sorry boy' I whispered, hoping that Filippo wouldn't hear. Ginger's dogs had followed him, and all three sat behind his legs. I'd watched him come and go to the hostel for almost as long as I had. I never had really seen much beyond his snoring. I suppose I never really looked.

'Why are you helping them, Ginger?' I asked.

'Because they're us, only better.'

***

The car sparked into life and settled comfortably to a steady rumble. I'd taken the driver's seat without asking, and Filippo had flopped into the seat next to me, slumping it back to a mild recline. Neither of us expected the minor skip in the car's idle and we locked eyes over the gear stick.

'Will it be ok?' I asked.

'Yes. It will.'

I pushed the car into first, and half engaged the clutch before Filippo cut in.

'Hang on. I need to ring the bishop. And get a copy of the report to him. The right report.'

'Can't it wait?'

'No.'

The call took twenty minutes. The bishop shouted down the 'phone in old person. I still couldn't quite catch what he was saying, but his squeals told me enough. 'Ok.' Said Filippo as the 'phone went dead, and I reached for first again. We were almost away when Filippo placed a hand on my arm and pulled my gaze from the road ahead. I expected something profound. It had been that sort of day.

'Hang on, I need to pee.'

Chapter 36

Under wraps

Beatrice had spent decades varnishing her past to invisibility, but here it was, laid across Enzo's desk. The final act of her turgid existence, swimming in shit. What the fuck was he supposed to do with her now?

Enzo had already eased through whatever shock he'd felt, and although grief had troubled him for a moment, he'd determined it a cultural embedment rather than any genuine remorse for his aunt's passing. Her absence from his life should actually make it several strides easier, but her body brought complications.

When someone dies, the decomposition process begins immediately. The smell of death has been described as 'rotting meat with fruity undertones', a phrase frighteningly close in intonation to the adjectives applied to merlot. What connoisseurs may appreciate less is the stench of rotten eggs, as methanethiol leaks from the blood and brains of the deceased.

Beatrice's body was arched and stiff. Her back vaulted from the table in a macabre pretence at rising. 'Maybe twenty-four hours, no more than thirty-six,' thought Enzo. Her eyes still followed him through their milky haze - engorged pupils overseeing his thoughts from their infernal purgatory. 'Fuck off' he told them, but they still followed him 'round the room as he paced through his options.

One. He could call the authorities. Police and ambulances bumbling around his laboratory in their size elevens. There was a likelihood that they'd recognise her demise as misadventure – a clumsy attempt at self- medication with tragic consequences. Whether they did or didn't, the verdict was still accompanied by the probability that his research would be uncovered, compromised, or worst of all, stopped. Hanging from that particular branch was also the possibility of a state autopsy. That meant investigation by the AIFA – The Italian Medicines Agency, and at least a dozen civil cases for fraud – including the report prepared for Janus *and* the earlier assessment of the shroud for the Catholic Church. And of course there was Gamma. The miraculous but unregulated creation of a human clone.

Two. He could dispose of the body. A task that was well beyond the scope of his experience. He could and would be prepared to execute the *physical* undertaking. In fact, he wouldn't entrust it to anyone else. Almost forty kilos of new flesh to determine the effects of *whatever* Beatrice had affected upon herself. God, he could almost salivate. But the wider implications – her absence from the management structure, where she had gone, so quickly, and why, were a challenge which sensibly should be met with the support of those with the correct expertise. And that meant Santo.

Enzo detested the man. Even Ollie, that short, fat escapee from Beryl Cook's imaginings was more bearable. At least he had the diffident reserve to fade his persona into the woodwork. Santo was no such shrinking violet. He wore his arrogant indifference to the grimness of his role like a halo. In fact, he revelled in its nastiness. But - how do you write a job description to replace a man with such disreputable talents? And where would you advertise once you had?

Of course, it would always have been option two. Even without the interjection which jolted through his plotting.

'My God, Enzo. Who is that woman? What's happened to her?'

It was Hettie. Standing in the doorway with Gamma in her arms.

***

Santo leant against the wall of Gamma's room, and observed the child and his mother through the observation window. Hettie was finally sitting quietly with the boy after twenty objectionable minutes shouting through the door and peering threateningly through the one-way glass. Santo had enjoyed the heave in her chest as she'd presented a deluge of impotent anger to the mirrored surface.

'You have a problem, Signor. But it's one that we can help you with.'

'That's why you're here.'

'Of course, of course. But we do need to agree on the details.'

'What do you suggest?'

'Well, Signor, I'm not sure that's for me to say,' Santo replied under a half-grown Dali moustache, 'though he was pretty sure that it was.

'I can offer an option for your consideration?'

'Please do.' Enzo snarled his abhorrence.

'You want to keep the girl, yes? Well from what you've told me that's entirely possible. The police already see her as deranged. And all that she's actually observed is a mournful nephew spending a few quiet moments after the shock of discovering his poor dead aunt. What could she tell them that isn't true?

Now, you have documentation confirming her wish to reside at this facility? Then why not just restrict her movements – make sure that she doesn't drift off and hurt herself, if you will. For her own benefit, of course. Until she's had the opportunity to calm herself. She's been terribly erratic since the moment she came here, I believe. And the poor thing's just seen a dead body – horrible for the most balanced of people. As her friend, and a responsible medical professional, it would seem like the right thing for you to do.'

'And how do you propose that we 'restrict her movements?'

'Myself and Ollie will stay to assist you.'

'And what about my aunt?'

'Easier still. She is a member of your family and deserves a memorial. She is dead, let's just keep her that way – the dead don't need to disappear, they just need to be buried. Her death certificate can circumvent the need for an autopsy. I know a man.' Santo smiled.

'You sound very confident.'

'Ha. Prison does not hold the same fear for me as it should for a man of your own exquisite tastes, Signor, but I still value the pleasures of freedom as much as yourself.'

'Alright. But I don't want her buried, or cremated. I need to keep the body.'

Santo's eyebrows arched.

'As I say, exquisite tastes. But she deserves a funeral, yes? She is a member of your family, and such a thing will be expected. It really doesn't matter whether she herself is in attendance. I can arrange it all.'

He smirked, and the pointy moustache tilted skyward.

Enzo felt sick. It could have been the situation, or the fear of its consequence, but it wasn't. It was Santo. He really was a cunt.

'Arrange it.'

'Of course, Signor. But first, we should agree on my expenses for the task.'

Chapter 37
Babysitting

'It's called false imprisonment. We're not just stealing a fucking rucksack anymore.'

Ollie's face bloated, and he panted his discomfort from his seat, one of four forming a makeshift 'waiting area' outside Gamma's door. A passer-bye could have been forgiven for looking for the vending machine.

'Don't be so dramatic. We're just babysitters. Caring individuals tasked with the safety and security of a needful girl who is struggling through the trauma of poor mental health.'

Santo stood at the window as Hettie paced. She bobbed and weaved with the edgy expectancy of death row - an adrenalized mess of bodeful anticipation. Santo snorted and dropped into the chair next to Ollie. All four chairs scratched along the corridor and the round man blobbed with the invasion of his personal space. He dropped his copy of Max magazine onto the side table next to him. It was ten years old and one of a dozen ancient books that he'd added to the subterfuge at Santo's request.

'Fuck Santo, couldn't you just sit over there?' He pointed to the chair on the opposite end of the row. The one furthest from him.

'Better get used to it, compadre, space is tight in a prison cell.'

'Funny.'

'I thought so. Ha.' He nodded satisfaction at his mirthful exchange.

'You know, you should have seen old Enzo squirm. That was also funny.'

Ollie sidled to the edge of his seat and said nothing. Santo kept pushing.

'If there were more of us, we could be Ocean's Eleven. I'd be Danny, and you can be Mushy.'

'Who'd be the girl?'

'Mrs Ocean? Good point. Our little attendee? She'd work. I like them spunky.'

Ollie rolled his magazine and tapped it on his leg. God, he was bored, and the chairs were hard and tiny. It hadn't even been two days and he swore his ass was permanently imprinted with a twelve-inch wedge where the seat cut into his flesh. If his companion had been less boorish, he'd have made an effort at conversation, but the words came thick and fast enough with zero input from him.

'You know, I don't think you'd suit prison. Too soft.'

'We can't all be as hard as you, Santo.'

'Ha. You think that's funny? I never did tell you about 'Gordo' Diaz, did I? He was a fat man, very much like you. Until I ended him.'

'Of course you did. I always had you down as Mafioso.'

'You doubt me, gilipollas? Shall I tell you what I did to him?'

'Why not, I can't get any more bored.'

'Ok, but listen up, it's just for us, yes? If you share it with anyone else, I won't be happy.' Santo ran a finger over his throat. Ollie's expression spelled 'prick' but Santo's attention was already autobiographical. His very favourite topic.

'So, Estremera Prison, not the most comfortable of establishments, but not the worst. I had already gained notoriety for passing Covid to a guard by coughing in his face. He was a boole, and deserved it, and I received kudos from my block mates in appreciation of my work.

Unfortunately, some of these 'kudos' had been commandeered from Gordo Diaz. Now, 'Gordo' – not his real name you understand – had been picked on since his arrival. Weak, fat men aren't built to prosper in the penal system. Plus, he'd been targeted as a spinner – someone who is loco and not to be trusted. It was a poor combination to engender friendship anywhere, but in a community where you can't walk away, well.... Anyway, when he found out that I was walking around with an ipod just like the one he was missing, he went full chalado in the prison library with a hole punch. Not a small hole punch you understand, but one of those that'd punch through War and Peace. It had a handle longer than your arm and must have weighed five kilos. Apparently, he bashed through half the new plasterboard that had just been added to the library walls before they brought him down. They'd only painted it the previous week and it looked like a state school changing room. The prisoners were told it was to help keep the space quiet for 'our benefit' but I heard that a fire audit would have condemned the whole building without it.

Anyway, I'd been warned that Gordo had decided that he wasn't content with half the wing thinking he was batshit crazy, and that he'd decided to embellish his rep. That was *before* I'd gotten his gear. The word now was that he'd been stockpiling sugar in his cell – a sure sign of intent to napalm. Gordo, fat bastard, could actually have been planning for his birthday, but there was a chance that he'd come for me, and look at me, amigo - you don't risk looks like these.

In case you *do* ever get to be accommodated by the regimen ordinario, Ollie, you should know that it's not so easy to find 'shanks' as the films would have you believe. I worked in the sewing shop. Try protecting yourself with a fucking quilting needle. Plus, everything's made of cardboard, and razor blades are banned. It's all electric now, even at his majesty's pleasure, so where do you actually find a weapon? Well, I'll tell you.

Occasionally, things happen within the establishment which present opportunity, and most inmates eventually turn part cuckoo. Not loopy, you understand, not in this context any way. No, they just start to collect – and conceal – all manner of useless shit. It just so happens that some of this shit *can* be useful, at least for those of us with imagination. Remember I said that the library walls had been smashed up? Well, the builders had repaired them almost immediately, and what do builders use? Tools, of course. But also building materials.

Now, it would have been pointless trying to steal anything obvious – the guards counted the hammers and blades, even the drill bits, and sometimes even the nails. But sheet materials, timber, other consumables – they're more difficult to count, and someone snatched two cans of expanding foam that a carpenter had left on the floor beside a stack of wallboard. Most people wouldn't think to use spray foam for protection, but as you know, I'm not most people, and a vision formed in my head.

That evening, a half hour before the dinner bell sounded, Gordo was laid out in his cell, lounging on his bunk asleep. Of course he was – what else was there for a fat fuck with no ipod to do? So, I dropped the cannister into my trousers and strolled casually toward him. The guards were already milling toward the canteen, and there was no interest from the other prisoners. They knew my rep. Half of them were probably already imagining dessert disappearing down their necks, ha.

Gordo really was fat. God knows where he found that many calories in prison. Bad metabolism, I guess. He makes *you* look like fucking Olive Oil. Anyway, he was on his back and his belly ballooned as he breathed. Up and down like a fucking dumb waiter. I stood over him for a second, to make sure he hadn't heard me, then screwed the applicator nozzle onto the can and held it under his nose. He sniffed away at the plastic tube like it was bacon, and opened his eyes.

Really, you should have seen the look on his face. I thought he'd end up like poor old Beatrice did, covered in his own shit, but he grabbed at the can.

Have you ever seen a turtle on its back, Ollie? Strange sight. It can't thrash, its legs aren't long enough. It just rocks, like you see those saddos in an asylum do, desperately seeking comfort that isn't there. That was Gordo. His arms were too chubby to reach 'round his body, and his fat hands were feeble. I just pushed the nozzle down his throat and pressed.

Christ, it was gross. At first I didn't think it was working, but then he coughed, and I saw something white and sticky squeeze out of his nose. He started gasping and let go of the can to reach down his throat. He stuck his fingers down there and scrabbled around like he'd lost his keys down a drain. Fuck knows what he thought he was going to do. The foam was swelling, and two streams erupted from his nostrils while his mouth stretched wide as the stuff pushed at his cheeks. It bilged past his lips like rising dough and his eyes began to bulge. I guess the pressure must have built behind his nasal cavity because gummy froth leaked from his eye holes until I swear one eye popped out, right onto his forehead. It hung from its stalk and rolled between his eyebrows as the fat fucker writhed in his sack. I've always wondered whether the last thing he saw was the top of his head. Ha.'

'Jesus Santo.'

'I know. Prison life. What can I say? Better not get caught, Ollie.' He grinned.

Ollie heaved from his seat to watch Hettie. Nothing that Santo said was ever guaranteed to be true, but even the slightest chance would have been more than enough to make him wish that he'd stayed in Greg café watching the fountain and drinking flat whites.

Chapter 38

The door

Sara frowned and moved the hair from her vision. She'd face planted against the staircase door - which was locked for the first time ever - and two plastic cups of hot latte spilled around her Reeboks. Her card swipe hadn't worked. She cursed it and strode to the lavatories, returning to the scene with an armful of paper towels. The door nearly got her again as Enzo strode through the opening with a tut at the mess and a general air of irritation.

'Sorry Sir, I didn't know the door would be locked.'

'Don't worry. You're Sara, aren't you? Where were you going? I thought you worked in Beatrice's labs?'

'Yes. I do. I was looking for Hettie. Hettie Eddy. I haven't seen her for a couple of days.'

Enzo's eyes narrowed.

'No, you won't have. Hettie's been a bit under the weather.'

'Is she ok?'

'Yes. It's nothing serious.'

'Could I see her? I brought her some coffee.' Sara looked at the liquid still pooling 'round her feet, then back at Enzo.

'No. She's not quite well enough yet. Are you working today, Sara? What are you working on?'

'Umm. It's a paternity test. For a child called Beradi. Senora Delgado gave it to me last week.'

'Last week?'

'Yes. Sorry. It's been busy. And Senora Delgado's not been in for a few days.'

'No, that's right.' The coffee trickled its way toward Enzo's shoes. They looked a little more expensive than Reeboks.

'Should I clean this up?'

'No. Ring the caretaker when you get back to your office.'

'Ok.' Sara swivelled, and saw the key card in Enzo's hand as she turned. What the fuck was going on now? She'd never tried to drop down to Gamma's floor, except that one visit with Gabriel – it hadn't been necessary – but the door that had so offended her face accessed the stair to the floor above it. The only thing out of bounds on that level was Enzo's personal office and laboratory, and he was in most of the time anyway, so even that was never locked down. Really, what the fuck?

'Oh, Sara.' She swivelled back, not sure which way her feet were turning. 'I'll let Hettie know you asked after her. I'm sure she'll be grateful. Thank you.'

***

'What the fuck?' Sara repeated, rubbing coffee from her boot into the office carpet as she dropped the unused wads of paper onto her desk. It still seemed like a reasonable question.

She'd seen Hettie virtually every day since they'd met in Gabriel's office. In truth, Hettie was probably the reason why poor Ninos Beradi was still unsure who his daddy was. She'd 'pop upstairs' three or four times a day, most days, and chat briefly about nothing before returning to Gamma in their subterranean lodgings. It hadn't even registered that Hettie had no 'phone. They didn't seem to need one, she was there that often. For the last two days though, there'd been nothing.

One day without her new friend hadn't bothered her. She'd actually been grateful for the time to catch up on her work - it was just as well that Beatrice *had* fucked off somewhere - but by the end of day two the cogs in her head had turned toward bleaker possibilities. She couldn't actually say that something even more untoward was happening, things had been 'untoward' from the moment she'd picked up commission RCA1001-6J. No, it was a sense of uncomfortable foreboding. Like things were coming to a head. Starting with that fucking door, she thought, gently fingering the lump on her scalp.

So, what was she going to do about it? Nothing, her erstwhile preference, had already been picked to the bone in little gristly chunks, and she still felt like shit. Even offloading to Father Filippo hadn't really changed her mood. And laying back on the deep pile with Boris nibbling at her sleeve while the world moved past her wasn't changing anything for anybody. So, options. What, exactly, was she supposed to do? Police? No. Enzo? Fuck, no. She'd rather face Beatrice's bony digits – if she ever turned up. So it looked like it would have to be Filippo - again. He had a legitimate reason for visiting Beatrice, maybe even Enzo, and of course he would want to see Hettie on his next visit even if she *wasn't* feeling one hundred percent. She'd only met him once, but he'd reminded her of a stout Gandalf. She imagined him, staff in hand, battering at the door with his magical stick, and determined that it was almost time for bed. She'd reach out in the morning.

If only she'd thought to take his 'phone number.

***

'Hi. Is that St. Francis? I'm trying to get hold of Father Filippo.'

Sara had looked him up on the internet and found the number for his parish. His picture looked great – trimmed, demure and eminently approachable - you'd never have suspected the filth that came out of his mouth.

'Hello?' Ginger picked up the 'phone as if he were handling a snake, with a telephone manner which suggested that it may be poisonous.

'Hello. My name is Sara. I'm trying to reach Father Filippo. Is this the right number for him please?'

'He isn't here.'

'Oh. Do you know when he'll be back?'

'No.'

'Sorry, could I ask who I'm speaking to please? Is there someone there who may be able to help?'

'No. It's just me.' Ginger raised his voice over the barking that was waxing from the vestry. Shepherd was feeling better, and his ball came shooting through the doorway with the little dog cascading after it. The growing menagerie that Ginger was accumulating gave voice to the excitement of the chase.

'Hello?'

'Hello?'

'My name's Sara. I'm trying to speak to Father Filippo.'

'He isn't here.'

'Do you have a number that I can reach him on?'

Crash! Something broke, and Shepherd appeared between Gingers legs whining like a windsock. At least three canines emerged from the pack to chase down the contents of the fallen cabinet as a host of heavenly angels skipped and bounced along the floor of the hostel.

'I have to go.'

The 'phone went dead.

***

Ring! The phone resurrected almost as soon as she'd put it down. For the briefest instant she assumed that it was St. Francis calling back, but Enzo's voice fluttered down the line. He was meticulously casual, and she imagined a jobbing actor in bed with a naive debutante that he'd met at first rehearsal no more than two days previously.

'Sara? Good, I'd like to see you. Please meet me in meeting room one on the first floor. It's the large one overlooking reception.'

'I know it.'

'Good. Could you come now please. And bring your laptop.'

***

Sara knocked gently at the door from the gallery hallway. *The Delgado Legacy* had been stencilled on the wall of the room below, and peeked accusingly at her trainers. It sat above a pair of screens, several magazines and books, and a display case containing photos and old apparatus. It shouted accusations from no more than twenty inches below her feet.

'Come.' Sara pushed against the heavy door and emerged into the room with a lurch.

'Sit down please, Sara.'

Enzo took court at the head of the table, and Sara scanned the dozen chairs which flanked each side. She selected one, two chairs from her boss, and set her computer on the surface in front of her.

'I'd like to see the Beradi report please. Could you show it to me.' Enzo nodded toward the laptop, and Sara flinched at the sticker that

Gabriel had glued to its shell. '*Vive rapido, muere jovin*' – 'Live fast, die young.' He'd slammed it shut and slapped the sticker on in response to some refused lunch invitation over six months ago, and there it remained, half picked around the edges, but with the words still ringing in red, black and gold.

'The Beradi report? But it's not finished. We discussed it in the corridor. It's almost there. If you could give me a few hours I could ...... '

'When did my aunt first give you the commission, Sara?'

'Well, maybe seven of eight days ago. But it's been busy, with her being away. I told you.'

'I see. Did you feel that you needed Senora Delgado's input to complete this piece of work, Sara?'

'Well, no, but I .... '

'No. It's a commission which should fall well within the capabilities of someone employed at your grade. Would you agree?'

'Yes.'

Enzo looked pointedly at the sticker and sighed, and fixed Sara with a gaze. If he'd meant to intimidate, he got his wish, and she dropped her eyes to the worksurface. She wasn't sure, but it looked like 'Light Sorano Oak'. She'd once considered buying a cutting board which looked similar, but her salary wouldn't stretch to such luxury, and she'd settle for a plastic one with a picture of a plate and some celery.

'I'm sorry, Sara, but commissions like this are the lifeblood of our organisation. They fund research that benefits the whole medical community, without which many people would continue to suffer and even die. We need people here who are alive to this obligation and willing to contribute effectively.' He raised a finger and beckoned to the glass behind Sara's head, and she heard the door creak open.

'This is Santo. He'll escort you back to your desk to pick up your personal effects. I'll have your outstanding salary made up to the end of the month and paid into your account. I'm sorry that things haven't worked out for you here, but wish you good luck for the future. You'll receive all the necessary paperwork within the next week. You can leave your laptop on the desk.'

Santo loomed and Sara looked up. He was smiling. Sara considered objecting, even pleading, but Enzo stared blankly through the windowed wall to the reception desk, where the employees of the Delgado Research Establishment were still answering 'phones and taking visitors.

***

Sara stared at the numbers on her 'phone. Six hundred and twenty-one euros, and a few cents. Enough to pay her rent for another month or two, assuming that Enzo paid her the full month that he'd promised. She should probably look at the vacancies, or consult an employment specialist, or a half dozen other things that her mind wouldn't settle to, but Hettie still picked at her conscience. Alongside everything else, she felt a prickly apprehension that Santo had followed her home.

Boris snuggled onto her lap and whirlpooled like a cat before settling with his bum between her legs. His head rested neatly on her thigh while his eyes continued to orbit, swivelling around the room while his ferret ears twitched in a wide circle, halting at odd points to flag up sounds that Sara didn't hear. She stroked them down, watching them flick erect as her hand massaged past them.

Sara sighed, and Boris raised his head in response. He looked irritated, and she slipped her hands under his body and dropped him gently to the rug to tramp to the kitchen for a handful of raisins and a tug rope.

She heard the footsteps from the hallway with her head in the cupboard, and snuck back to the room with the rope dangling loosely from twitchy fingers. Boris was behind the sofa. He eyed her nervously and arched his back before backing out of sight.

Bang! -Bang! -Bang! thumped against the door.

Chapter 39

Pieces

Beatrice had been dead for four days, but groaned like an old hinge when Santo dragged her onto the autopsy table he'd carted to Enzo's lab under a sheet. Enzo knew it was just the gas escaping from her guts, but still started as if he'd heard the devil himself touting evils through her lips.

Putrification is the fifth stage of death, following pallor mortice, livor mortice, algor mortice and rigor mortice. In broad terms it can be viewed as the decomposition of proteins, the eventual breakdown of the cohesiveness between tissues and the liquification of organs. For Beatrice it meant an oddly green discolouration of her lower body and the beginnings of bloat to her emaciated abdomen. In a singular and highly morbid way, it almost made her look healthier.

Enzo knew that he'd need to begin the process of dissection soon, before her skin blistered and turned black, but the finality of cutting into her felt far too personal and oddly obscene. He knew that without the pumping of her heart she wouldn't bleed. Any blood would simply ooze from the wounds in an elongated drip, unfettered by clotting or any of the other bodily functions that seek to preserve us. But for all his embedded dislike of his aunt, it was still *her*. Her lack of circulation was no more than he'd suspected of her when she'd been alive, and the process of preparing her body smudged around his head like gum. Even so, it needed doing.

The initial dismemberment would be first. The removal of extremities. Arms and legs set to one side and stripped of muscle and fat, and the head cracked open to remove tongue, palate, bone and skin before accessing the lobes of the brain. Then the first cut of the autopsy, down the full length of the body to the pubic bone, followed by a choice of secondary incision. His preference would likely be a long Y, starting at the top of each shoulder and running down the front of the chest to meet at the lower point of the sternum. Finally, dissection of the torso. The extraction of organs and fat and gristle and meat, all catalogued and stored for future study. His aunts best and most valuable contribution to the Delgado legacy. It still turned his stomach.

He inspected the tools laid out around her. Scalpels, scissors, forceps and scapula. Then the more elemental of the options. Saws and prongs and a long surgical chain and hook. It would be brutal, and twanged a misplaced chord in his heart as much as it rumbled his guts.

'Tomorrow.' He thought, turned away and aimed himself downstairs at Hettie. Santo was waiting at the door.

'Come with me please.' An indiscernible misstep stumbled from his voice as he instructed the henchman, who locked the door behind them and followed, extending his stride to match Enzo's unexpected pace.

***

'You followed her? All the way home?'

'Yes.'

'And she didn't stop, or talk to anyone? Not even on the 'phone?'

'No senor. No-one at all.'

‘Good.’

Enzo questioned his employee as they surveyed Hettie at the corridor window.

'And this one. What will you do with her?'

'What do you mean?'

It’s been two days, senor. That’s fine, but you can't keep her here forever. So, what will you do? When it's time to make a decision?'

'Nothing. I'll talk her ‘round before then.'

'You think? Good luck with that. Ha.'

Unbelievably, Santo’s confidence had grown to dwarf its formerly expansive girth. The occasional disrespect, that he’d at least tried to temper, now oozed from his persona with irritating regularity. He’d slithered under Enzo’s guard, and now fed from his world like a weevil in his pantry. Enzo abhorred him, but he was just an opportunist, and not very bright - a bridge to be crossed not long from now. But a short one, with shallow waters. For now, all Enzo wanted was a pleasant conversation with no undertones and no subtext. Why he thought he could still procure one from Hettie was a mystery known only to him.

‘Hi Hettie. How’re you both doing?’

‘Are you serious? Why don’t you just go and fuck yourself, Enzo?’

Hettie laid the babe on his bed and faced off with her 'benefactor.' As always, he was immaculately presented, and slid a smile from somewhere beneath his countenance. It gave him the predatory air of a weasel.

‘There’s no need to be like that. Why don’t you sit while I give Gamma his blood test? We can chat.’

‘I don’t *want* to sit, and I certainly don’t want to *chat.* And there aren’t going to be any more tests. No needles, no blood, nothing. On Gamma *or* on me. I’m taking him somewhere safe. And that means somewhere away from you, you fucking quack. Now, open that fucking door and let me out.'

Enzo's lips tensed at the word 'quack.'

'I don't think you're ready for that Hettie. You're obviously still upset.'

'Really Enzo? What could possibly give you that idea? Is it the fact that you've locked me up here in this fucking basement, or the fact that I caught you standing over your dead Aunt?'

'Aunt Beatrice. I can understand how confusing that must have been. It's been awful for everyone. Hopefully we can all start to relax once we've had the funeral. That's what they say isn't it? Santo's arranging it now. It shouldn't be more than a couple of days, then we can all start to get back to normal. Maybe you'll be well enough to go into town.'

The word 'flabbergasted' is infrequently used. Hettie was flabbergasted, and the multitude of things she could have said log-jammed on the way to her mouth. No doubt she'd think up a clever response in a few hours and spend the next week wishing she'd said that. Instead, she ended up saying nothing. Enzo, however, had the knack of stepping in with answers to questions that he hadn't been asked.

'Poor Beatrice. Misadventure they said. Apparently, she was self-administering her treatment. Got everything spot on except the flow rate for the IV. Tragic really. If only she'd have let me help her.'

Enzo reached for her. An algid hand brushed Hettie's arm and her whole trunk convulsed, springing her against Gamma's bed. It rocked once onto two legs and righted itself as the boy released a tide of tears.

'Get off me you sick fuck. Are you fucking kidding?'

Enzo sighed. He'd known that today wasn't really the day for masquerades and to be fair, he'd made a pretty poor fist of it. He allowed the remnants of the mask to slip from his face and tapped at the mirrored surface before wafting the two henchmen into the room.

'Hold her still' he said and took blood from her arm before stripping the baby and completing his examination. Santo loomed like a cliff edge, threatening and wildly impulsive and too unstable to be trusted near a child. She flared her nostrils but sat quietly on the chair where they'd placed her.

'You're a cunt Enzo.' She said as the three retreated to the door. Hettie rubbed her arm in revulsion, and Enzo noted that she'd chosen the area he'd touched over the entry point of the needle.

'Yes.' He said simply, before heading back to his laboratory and the task which awaited him.

Chapter 40

Pistol

Madrid is a safe city. A multitude of international studies affirm that the capital of Spain is one of the safest cities in the world. For visitors who wish to enjoy its most celebrated attractions, the areas within the curtilage of the M-30 ring road offer little threat bar the occasional stray hand of a pickpocket.

For the Santos of the world, an excursion to more shady territories are necessary if specialist goods and services are to be procured, and he headed out toward the southeastern regions of the capital.

Villaverde accommodates a community which has historically grappled with significant socioeconomic challenges. High unemployment rates, prevalent criminal activity, small-scale drug dealing, and gangland culture have all contributed to its disadvantaged status. Santo and his associates also did their bit.

Madrid does not have a right to bear arms. The only firearms available to the Spanish public are shotguns intended for hunting and farm work, and the only individuals who can be licensed for handguns are government agencies and security employees. But – of course - Santo knew a man.

'Why Santo? I have a dozen options available, to cover all situations and undertakings. Why is it so important to you?'

'Look at me Daniel. Do I look like a man who will settle? The Smith and Wesson model 10 was the firearm of choice for Capone himself. When I am seen using it, people will know who I am.'

'You know that Capone died in prison?'

'No. He did not die in prison. He was granted parole in 1939 and lived free for another eight years.'

'Fuck. You're really not going to take anything else, are you?'

'Ha. It shall deliver my will like an eleventh commandment.'

'Jesus, Santo. How the fuck were you never garrotted in prison?'

'I never let anyone behind me.'

Daniel guided Santo to a large Ford. It was a Gran Torino sedan, and its onyx paintwork gleamed more brightly than the chrome on its bumpers. Gold coloured wheels accentuated its muscular stance.

'Which one of us is Starsky?' asked Santo, a cultural reference lost on a thirty-something member of the Calabrian mafia.

'Get in. We'll need to travel to get you what you want. You'd better be able to afford it.'

They drove for an hour before reaching Esquivius. Santo had never visited before and was disappointed at the lack of bullet holes in its boundary signage. It was a small town, in the province of Toledo, and home to an old couple that Santo assumed must be Daniel's grandparents, 'though there were no introductions as he marched his customer through an enclosed garden to a block built shed. It was surrounded by an explosion of lilac jacarandas on a bed of red carnations, the national flower of Spain.

'Wait here'

Santo waited at the door of the convivial building. He'd pictured it lined with rows of compost, with garden tools hanging neatly from the walls. Instead, he stood upon a dirt floor with a table set over a wooden hatch which led down to an area that he could barely glimpse, despite the wall light which illuminated its steps as Daniel penetrated the depths. It would have slotted into any spaghetti western, and he grinned from ear to ear at the theatre which bloomed in his presence.

When Daniel ascended, he brought with him a 2012 model 10, version 14, six shot revolver with double action trigger system. It had a snub nose, favoured by members of the American CID, and looked just like the one that Santo had seen in a black and white promo for the film 'Scarface.'

'Well?'

'It is perfect, Senor.'

'Yes. It's also three grand including a dozen rounds. The serial numbers have been filed clean and the frame re-finished. You'd never know it wasn't made that way. It *is* perfect.'

Santo grinned again. He would have paid double.

The car, the gun, and Santo in his element drove through Esquivius. He fingered his new toy as they pervaded the parochial streets, cruising to pick up the R4 motorway back to the city. Daniel revved his vehicle as they pulled alongside a quaint café with a striped awning and a handful of street tables edging onto the road.

'Hey!' A petite girl with freckles and a pram shouted her complaint. Daniel revved harder and fumes shot from his exhaust, reinforcing the din and obscuring the woman from sight and earshot.

'HEY! My baby's asleep!'

'Fuck that lady. Ha. It's not my DNA!' Santo shouted, and felt like a bandit.

Chapter 41

Through the motions

Sara hugged me. She'd taken minutes to finish with Filippo and I'd assumed that it would sate her, but she grabbed me and pulled me in like a lover, unseen for twenty years. It was the first time that I remembered feeling loved. By a human being anyway.

It had taken almost ten minutes of increasingly vigorous shouting through the woodwork before she'd even answered the door. I swear it was only Filippo's cursing that finally persuaded her to open it. God only knows what the neighbours must have thought.

Angus and Boris faced off. I found the consistency mildly comforting, given the info that Sara related. Poor Hettie. Maybe someone *was* pulling our strings when we'd piled back into that groaning Fiat to 'rescue' her, but if that were truly the case, I couldn't see the logic in bringing us to a grinding halt on the outskirts of Monaco's Fontvieille sea front. The cost of accommodation was eye-watering, even for a tiny double room with no en-suite and a view of a backstreet bin store. The mechanic spoke broken Italian through a French accent, and we caught the gist of 'You had all of this laid out for you and did nothing?' as he reviewed Luis' diagnostics. He tutted like a flouted primary teacher, but at least he smiled when we paid. His bill didn't help the finances. By the time we reached Madrid Sara's couch seemed like a sensibly frugal, if rather intrusive option. 'Let's risk it' said Filippo through a beard which twitched. He was clearly reticent but checked his wallet and found vacancies in each compartment except the one holding the parish credit card. He didn't often look embarrassed, despite the fifty odd calories that were often spread through his facial hair. On this occasion, the glow in his cheeks looked like a cheap Christmas.

'What should we do?'

Sara's inflection indicated clearly that she hoped that 'we' would end up being Filippo and me. She'd already visualised 'Gandalf' stepping in to save the day, sweeping away the demonic Enzo with a mystical casting which would absolve her of further responsibility. Maybe being down to her last six hundred and twenty-one euros had messed up her resilience. She'd certainly relinquished her determination of a half dozen hours ago.

'Fuck it. It *has* to be the police.' Resolved Filippo, not yet Gandalf the white. 'At the very least they'll record our concerns. Hopefully they'll feel obligated to investigate – go and have a look around. They may even march straight in and drag her out.' Maybe Filippo was feeling the weight of reality too.

'What? Into the *Delgado Corporation*?'

Sara's observation didn't need embellishment. She embellished anyway.

'Why the fuck would they do that? And what are we supposed to tell them? That I haven't heard from a girl I met in a colleague's office a week ago? Or that I'm worried that my boss has been off sick for three days? No-one's actually 'missing' are they? Christ, even I'd tell myself to fuck off.'

Sara was right. The fact that we were worried meant Jack Shit to anyone else. Of course, it was 'concerning' that our friend was unhappy. That she was struggling with life in a new environment away from the streets, and that she thought her benefactor was mean. Not really enough to unleash operation 'Get Hettie' was it? But we did have something else. Something that may begin to evidence the true nature of Enzo Delgado.

'We can show them this. Assuming that you still have your alternative copies.' Filippo pulled out a folded photocopy of Janus's report from his inside pocket and placed it on the table.

'Would they care? I'm not even sure that this type of fraud is criminal. They may not be interested.'

'Well, we won't know unless we ask, will we?'

***

'Please come in officers. I've instructions to take you directly to see Senor Delgado.'

Two burly plods followed behind the receptionist. Plod one was a sub-inspector and had been with the Policia Nacional for almost twenty years, but still couldn't wrap his head 'round why his colleagues avoided him at the drinks machine.

'You're sure you've got what I told you, Gomez?'

'Yes, Inspector Perez, I'm sure.'

'Say it back to me.'

Gomez sighed internally. There were over forty officers covering the Tetuan district of Madrid, but he'd been allocated to 'Poota' Perez, the shortest of straws. His six months alongside him had been the least productive of his career, unless you were seeking an education in apathy. The man didn't even talk the talk, he just talked. And he couldn't even do that nicely.

'You've spoken with Enzo Delgado. You've outlined the nature of the complaint against him. He's invited us to visit him at the location of the alleged wrongdoing. He's done so of his own volition.'

'And we're grateful for his co-operation. Delgado's company employs over two hundred people. And he has zero felonies against his name, and even less misdemeanours.'

Gomez didn't bother to comment, let alone correct. Perez had actually told Delgado the name of the complainant – one of them anyway. Sara. He was mildly surprised that his 'superior' had the professionalism to omit Father Filippo's name from his discussions with the man. He'd probably just forgotten.

Dalgado was waiting for them as they hit the top step, and opened the door to meeting room one. Coffee and scalded milk was already laid out on the table, alongside a range of soft drinks, water and a plate of Fontaneda biscuits.

'You have café con leche!' Exclaimed Perez, and Enzo prepared the cups while the two officials took their seats.

'I hope you don't mind, but I took the liberty of extracting a few documents for you to see before you arrived. I thought it may save you some time, but I'm more than happy to follow your lead, of course, officers.'

Enzo watched Perez grab at the chocolate biscuits and deduced that he'd already taken the lead for himself. He wasn't so sure about Gomez, but the younger man held a junior rank, and he directed discussions toward the insignia.

'There are copies on the table in front of you, and the originals are here if you'd like to see those?'

'No, no Senor, the copies will do for now.'

'Excellent, thank you. Would you like me to talk you through them?'

'Yes. Please proceed.'

Enzo opened his copy of the files. The first related to Sara.

'The complaint has come from Sara, yes? Unfortunately, I had to dismiss her yesterday – the first letter is a copy of her severance letter. You can see that I haven't stated the full reasons for letting her go - I didn't want to undermine her chances of future employment. But I can share with you gentlemen that her performance and her conduct have been unacceptable for some time. It's really no surprised that she'd feel bitter about her situation, but I am disappointed with how she's responded to it.'

Perez nodded his agreement, adopting an expression of sympathetic resignation.

'Could you explain her conduct in greater detail Senor Delgado?' Gomez commandeered the conversation.

'Of course, constable. More recently it's been more about performance. She's been late with important commissions and uncooperative when questioned, but behavioural issues actually began some months ago. She'd make mistakes – we all do – but rather than let us know, so that we could rectify them together, she tried to break into our systems to cover up her errors. I considered parting ways with her at that point but decided that I should give her the chance to learn. Seems like I made a mistake.... I have several colleagues who could corroborate, if that would be useful?' Gomez ignored the offer.

'I'd like to discuss your Aunt, Beatrice Delgado. We'd been told that she was missing from the office for several days but have found since that she's actually passed away. Is that correct?'

'Yes, I'm afraid it is.'

'I'm sorry for your loss, Senor, but I'm struggling with the dates. The death certificate is dated two days prior to your termination of

Sara's employment, but she wasn't aware of her death. Did you decide to withhold the information from Sara's team?'

Enzo sighed mournfully, and Perez adjusted his expression accordingly.

'Yes, yes, you're right, of course. I should explain. My aunt has endured the symptoms of hepatitis for many years. If you understand the virus, you'll know that it can be a particularly debilitating disease. She'd become somewhat muddled of late. I'm afraid that I found her in my office after she'd tried to self-medicate. I can only speculate, but it looked as though she got confused when setting up the IV. That's what killed her. After you raised the issue, I made sure to include her death certificate, but I needed a couple of days before telling everyone what had happened. I needed that time, you know, so that I could ensure that I would remain professional while informing her staff. I didn't think that an e-mail would be appropriate. I wanted to tell people myself.' Enzo re-directed toward Perez. 'If you'd like to turn a couple of pages, you'll see the certificate within your paperwork'.

Perez flicked and fingered while Gomez read. Sure enough, cause of death was recorded as 'misadventure' while the detailed notes confirmed Enzo's remarks. The document was stamped by the Ministerio de Justicia and signed by an MD. He made a mental note to review the doctor's registration later, but there was no indication of anything untoward. He noticed that Enzo had identified the body himself and considered whether he'd be justified in asking to see the deceased before her cremation, but without real cause, it would just be cruel.

Gomez remembered the first time he'd seen a dead body. Grey and absent, with their mouths gaping. Seeing someone you'd loved, so 'missing' - that would be heart-breaking.

'I really am sorry for your loss Senor. I know it's difficult, but do you mind if we continue? It may save time later.'

'Of course. Anything to help.'

Gomez produced a sketchy print of a report with the Delgado crest emblazoned across its cover. It looked as though it had been run off an eighties dot matrix, but Enzo recognised it instantly. He didn't even flinch.

'May I?' he asked, and Gomez passed him the document. He poured attention upon it as Perez finished off the biscuits. Finally, 'It may be helpful if I send down for some more information. It's entirely relevant, I promise you. Would you mind?'

'No. Please do.'

Ten minutes later Gabriel stuck his head 'round the meeting room door and passed a copy of the Janus report into Enzo's hands. His frequent stench of fusty booze was thankfully thin, but he still saw the hard glint in his director's eye as he withdrew.

'I don't know what Sara's been producing, but here's a copy of the actual commission that we completed for the church. You'll see that it's quite different from Sara's version.' Enzo handed the papers to Perez, who flicked quickly through the pages. Gomez watched him leave a diminishing chocolate thumbprint across three leaves. Perez didn't notice.

'It is *different*, isn't it?'

'It is.' affirmed Enzo. 'Once again, I can only speculate, but it would seem that Sara is attempting to undermine the reputation of the company. I do understand that employees can feel disgruntled when things don't work out between us, but I can't accept fraudulent versions of confidential commissions being released into a public forum. This (he waved Sara's version through a disgruntled semi-circle) could cause irreparable damage to our reputation. Especially given the ridiculous statements contained within it. We don't deal with the occult in science, officers. I'm afraid that it really is unacceptable.'

'Of course it is, Senor Delgado. Don't worry. We'll have words.'

'Thank you so much, gentlemen. I'd certainly appreciate it. I wouldn't want Sara to get herself into further trouble. It would be good of you to help her.'

Enzo inflected his assumption that the conversation had finished and sat back in his chair with fingers interlocked across his chest. A flutter of surprise as Gomez failed to rise was the solitary chink in what was otherwise another exemplary performance.

'We do need to ask you about Hettie, Senor. And about her baby, Gamma.'

Enzo exhibited his first sign of stage fright.

'*Her* baby? I'm not sure what you mean.'

'Ok, senor. Let's start at the beginning. Heather Eddy. Hettie. She's been staying at this establishment. Is that correct?'

'It was, yes.'

'It *was*? Isn't it now?'

'No, she left some time ago.'

'She did? Our understanding was that she'd been seen here within the last few days. Is that incorrect?'

'No, that's right. She stayed here while she was undergoing testing – she's part of a sample group for a new drug we've been trialling, but she left once the trials were complete. She comes in sometimes for follow-up appointments. She's had a few over the last few weeks.'

'So, you know her well?'

'Yes, I suppose so. I was heavily involved with that particular sequence of trials. I'd only caveat that by saying that it's difficult to really know any person with Hettie's difficulties. You're aware of her background, I presume?'

'We are. You sounded surprised when we referred to Gamma as Hettie's child. Why is that?'

Enzo adjusted his expression. A gambler's front which elevated the terseness on his tone to gently threatening.

'Gentlemen, I am more than happy to help in whatever way I can, but I am starting to feel concerned. Am I actually under suspicion of anything? And if I am, could you tell me the basis of those suspicions?'

Perez stepped in.

'You're not under suspicion Senor. We just need to ask certain questions to ensure that our enquiries can be concluded. We could return at a later date if we're inconveniencing you, but we will need you to answer our questions at some point. I'm very sorry.'

'Of course, I understand, Senor. *I'm* sorry. I just get defensive when it comes to my child. I'm sure you understand. Do you have children, Inspector?'

'*You're* child?' Gomez returned. 'I thought Gamma was Hettie's child.'

'No, Senor. Gamma is my child. I adopted him within days of his birth. I am all he's known. He is my *child*. What more can say? I can access his adoption papers for you right now, if you need to see them?'

'So, Hettie isn't his mother?'

'No. I'm aware that Hettie had a child. I arranged her surrogacy. But Hettie's child was adopted by a couple in France, I believe. I don't have access to that information unfortunately. You'd need to ask Hettie for the details. She held Gamma a few times when she was here, under my supervision of course. Perhaps she got confused - she wasn't always entirely tuned in to the world. But I can't have her questioning my relationship with Gamma. You understand that, surely officers?'

'*You* arranged her surrogacy?'

'Yes. She asked me to, to resolve her debts. You should be aware that I tried to help her in several ways. It is important to me personally - and to the reputation of my company - that we do our bit for those less fortunate, but you can only do so much, and sometimes we get it wrong. I understand that I occasionally act beyond convention but never illegally. The Hetties of the world are difficult people to rescue. You know that, given your own professional calling.'

Gomez looked perturbed. The 'half an hour, tops' assurance that Perez had given to Enzo had already wheeled past, and he needed time to re-assess. He looked at his inspector, who was still rubbing confectionary from his trousers. He didn't personally have the authority to pull the man to the station regardless of the dubious direction his story was taking - not this man anyway - and Perez was too distracted by his fucking chocolate dick.

'Do you know how we could find Hettie, Senor? An address, or a telephone number perhaps?'

'No. I'm sorry, I don't have anything.'

'Thank you, Senor. Would you mind if we take these with us?' he lifted the papers that Enzo had provided from the worksurface.

'No, gentlemen, not at all. They are for you.'

'Thank you.'

Enzo rose, followed by Gomez, then Perez.

'You will speak with Sara? I can't allow the company to suffer out of spite. You understand?'

'We understand.'

On their way through reception, Gomez looked for a door to a lower staircase. Perez had denied him access to specifics, saying that it wasn't necessary. In all likelihood he just couldn't be bothered to brief him properly. Whichever, the results were the same. He had, however, gleaned that Sara'd referred to her friend as 'down'. If he'd had any other partner he may have asked to look around 'while they were there,' but couldn't be sure that Perez wouldn't close that door for good with some ill-conceived interjection. There was still a litany of questions to be asked. Perhaps, if he took the legwork upon himself, the inspector would accede to just a little more digging. Maybe he'd buy him some chocolate before he asked.

He glanced behind him as they exited the lobby to the car park. You'd barely know that the Delgado's existed from the featureless grey of the structure. Even the fucking building screamed subterfuge.

Upstairs, Enzo watched the officers depart the car park. 'Cunts.' He strode to the lift, prodding the buttons on his phone so hard it hurt. There were maybe a dozen e-mails to review, but for now, 'Santo? Go and get Hettie's laptop. Do it now.'

Santo did it now, and handed the article to his paymaster. It was supplemented with advice.

'We have a problem, Senor.'

'We have several problems.'

'Yes. But one will soon begin to smell. People will notice.'

'Could we move that problem? To a more discreet location?'

'You do not move a body with the polizzi at your door Senor. Could we not simply dispose of it?'

'What do you mean?'

'You have the necessary chemicals, yes?'

'No. That won't be happening. I'll deal with it.'

'Your call. But do it quickly, Senor Delgado. It is not wise to sit and wait once the dogs have your scent.'

Chapter 42

Apathy

'There's no evidence.'

'Aren't you in the slightest bit suspicious? Couldn't we at least take a look around the lower floors?

'Not without evidence. We'd need a warrant, and we've no justifiable reason to be granted one.'

'Or we could just ask Delgado. He's been pretty co-operative up 'til now. At least we'd be able to observe his reaction.'

'Precisely. He's been co-operative. And he's a renowned businessman with a professional background and a fucking *reputation*. And you want us to invade his privacy – and insult him by questioning his word – without anything other than a fucking hunch that he's abducted a woman off the streets. Why would he do that, Gomez? Why would he fucking need to? You'll just get yourself into shit. You'll get *me* into the shit.'

'But you must have seen him? How shifty he got just before we left? Don't you think we should at least try to find the girl? I'd be happy to ....'

'Just wrap it up, man. The answer's no. Who do you think you are, Gomez, fucking Pepe Carvalho? I'd have been more likely to ask for a 'look around' if you hadn't already pissed the man off. No, we've asked the right questions and he's answered all of them, complete with

EVIDENCE!' Perez held up the file of photocopies that each of them had received.

'Now, I'm going to ring the priest and Sara and tell them that their suspicions are unfounded. Then I'm going to tell Sara to pull her fucking neck in before she gets herself and her friends into trouble. And that'll be the end of it. Now, go and find a fucking jaywalker to prosecute, and ask yourself if that's *all* you want to be doing for the next twelve months.'

***

Sara's thumb hurt. Her mobile had already disconnected but she was still trying to push the little red button through the back of the case. She only stopped when she remembered that she had no money to replace it.

'What a cunt.'

'What did he say?'

Filippo suspected that he already knew. He also suspected that Sara was about to launch into a run of expletives that even he hadn't heard before. But he was wrong.

Remember Clint Eastwood? The steely grey which shafted from his gaze in every movie he made? He'd never shout, he'd just ask 'Five bullets or six, punk?' just before he blew the head off the bad guys.

'Fuck them. We'll get her ourselves.'

I wasn't sure whether Sara could carry off a Stetson. I certainly couldn't visualise her and Filippo in dusty ponchos riding in to save the day. Maybe Filippo could.

'I agree. Let's do it.'

There's a certain sting which accompanies reality when you've experienced life as a destitute. Optimism invariably shrinks away to leave a somewhat skewed internal risk appraisal. I didn't *want* to piss on their bonfire, but I also didn't want to run headlong into the fire without at least a bucket to douse the flames.

'*How* do we do it?' I asked.

How many spoof versions of James Bond are there? I like the one where the guy comes back from the sixties. Given my contexts, it feels kind of thematic. Anyway, it reminded me of us. None of us was heavy with spy experience. I doubt that we'd have made the interview, never mind got the job, so discerning a viable plan from bombastic enthusiasm was always likely to be problematic. After an hour, the conversation had slowed sufficiently for us to agree to sleep on it. Who knows, maybe divine intervention would turn out to be a real thing. But if that was what we were relying on, I guess that Filippo slept better than I did.

Chapter 43
The Macintosh

Bang. Bang. Bang.

After years of waking from storied episodes of a ragged mile that may or may not have been mine, I wasn't always sure which noises came from the world, and which were quietly exploding from my head.

Subconscious meanderings in which I seemed quietly pulled along an endless road of zemblanity often invaded those moments where you're no longer asleep, but not quite awake. In simple terms, 'zemblanity' means being subject to bad luck and unhappiness, but it'd be more accurate to say that it's the opposite of serendipity. I'd learned the word from Filippo. He'd been writing the story of Job and looking for a word to describe his troubles. In the end neither zemblanity nor serendipity made the cut for that Sunday morning, but 'zemblanity' struck a chord with my understanding of my mental state. If it hadn't been for this episode, I may simply have said that my dreams sometimes woke me up. Maybe I should have just stuck with that.

The *volume* of nocturnal sounds didn't disturb me as much as the timbre. The 'Bang. Bang. Bang.' of a rap at the door was a regular interlude through nights at a drop in shelter, and Ginger's nasal passages would compete quite comfortably with the racket unless the visitor was particularly voracious.

It was '*Bang. Bang. Thud'* that finally got my attention.

Sara had already risen and slumbered into the living room with a dressing gown tied loosely' round her waist. It held together with luck, and I barely managed to avert my gaze while keeping eyes on the door. 'It's alright. I know who it is.' she said, holding her mobile aloft in confirmation before proceeding to unbolt the locks.

Gabriel flopped to the floor in a graceless swamp of vomit and Jack. The more discerning may have smelt Cava in the mix, but there were a multitude of aromas to choose from. 'I want to fuck you Sara' he slurred as she helped him to a chair.

'Let's just start with keeping our puke to ourselves.' The phrase sprang easily into existence. I guessed they were words that she'd uttered before.

Gabriel didn't make much sense to me, even after two cups of coffee, but it seemed that Sara could interpret his meanderings. She addressed him in an exaggerated whisper before explaining his slur as we muddled together in the centre of the room. Father Filippo's cheeks puffed as he fought down the urge *to* urge at Gabriel's adjacent proximity. Sara seemed immune.

'Enzo. He's lying through his teeth. But he's doing it in a way that even *I* might believe him.'

'What else did he say, Gabriel?' but by now, Gabriel had reverted to his own thoughts.

'You're not just my friend Sara. I'm sorry I'm such a dick.' Gabriel's parting words. For that night, at least.

It could have taken two grown men to trawl Gabriel onto Sara's bed. Instead, she snapped into action like a squaddie at drill. She laid a macintosh where his ass would land and dropped him down. He slapped onto the coat like a wet fish. His head lolled off the pillow and she slipped it gently back behind his neck before throwing cushions onto the wooden side chair that lived beside her wardrobe. It would be a long night, but she couldn't risk him spewing and drowning in his own puke. He whispered something through crusty lips, and she leant in, but his words got lost in the stench.

'Uugh. Rancid.'

Spittle bubbled with his breath, and she sat back into the seat with a gingham blanket draped around her shoulders. 'If all your girls could see you like this,' she thought before grabbing a book from her night table. 'Wuthering Heights'. She'd always intended to read it, but it had sat by her bed for six months behind a procession of more than fifty shades of grey. She'd known Gabriel for over a year and surfed above his crude advances with such regularity that now she barely noticed them. He was the same with every woman between the ages of eighteen and forty-five - and the thought of every other night doing this – and every other morning throwing her mac back into the washing machine – wasn't a life she intended to live. She opened the book to page one and glanced again at her friend, stinking with fluids and heaving his chest through a marathon of effort. 'Fuck. You really are a dick.' she sighed, before settling into '1801 – I have just returned from a visit to my landlord – the solitary neighbour that I shall be troubled with.'

On page two hundred and forty, Gabriel shifted his head and Sara shifted her backside. She'd bobbed across the cushions looking for comfort for half the night while Gabriel had limited his movements to little more than a putrid guttural snore. She rose to check on her friend. His lanyard had plopped off his chest and was draped across his neck with his key card dangling under one armpit. Sara returned him to his previous comfort and slipped the cord from his person. 'Can't have that pretty face garrotted' she whispered before dropping back onto her constricted pedestal. Gabriel's picture glowed from his security card. He'd dressed for the camera and looked polished, if a little drawn around the eyes. She knew he'd be awake in a few hours, and any risk of him choking in the night had passed around page one hundred and fifty. And it was still two hours before dawn.

'Filippo. Loman. Wake up.'

Sara hadn't actually woken anybody. Have you ever tried to sleep between a hairy collie dog and a hairier priest? Both of whom twisted and groaned and barked – yes, barked – in your earhole as they squirmed in search of slumber? Nobody slept, and I think we were all relieved when Sara disturbed the attempt with a flash of Filippo's card.

'We can use this to get in.'

'What is it?'

'It's Gabriel's security card. It's access all areas, he told me.'

'Won't he get into trouble?'

'Not as much trouble as Hettie's in. Maybe I can make it up to him if he does. Loman, you can stay here if you want.'

Maybe Sara was trying to be generous, but I was mildly insulted. I was also still aware that our plans hadn't advanced one iota beyond that little piece of plastic in Sara's possession. Perhaps *that* was all the divine intervention that we'd get.

'No. I want to come.'

'Alright. But you'll have to bring Angus. He can't stay here with Boris on his own.'

Less than ten minutes later we were kicking Filippo's Fiat back to life.

Chapter 44

Not breaking and entering

God, we are told, resides. That is the nature of omnipotence. He resides everywhere, in all things, at all times. In me, in you, in all people and all things. It doesn't matter if you believe that He resides, or whether you want him to. He just is. Whether *He* would want to be here, however, in this place where humankind prods and pokes at his creation? Perhaps that's a matter of faith.

Sara hesitated and rubbed the bruise on her head. She could see it, brown and yellow, as her reflection stared from the vision panel of the offending doorway. She looked at Filippo and whispered for a prayer that the thing would just open.

Gabriel's card had accessed the entrance, reception, and the heart of the building. No alarms had sounded. No security had challenged them. Only the glow from a conceited sign, high up on the wall of the reception area, had been alive to their passage. 'The Delgado Legacy,' it screamed.

'Shall I try it?'

'No. Let's just stand here all fucking day.' Filippo's words were unbecoming of a man with a dog collar but did at least reinforce the urgency of the undertaking. Sara still found time for a middle finger.

She swiped the card through the lock, and the doors parted. I felt like Moses at the red sea. They even opened by themselves, courtesy of overhead closers.

'Thank you, Jesus.'

Angus looked up. I guess he was as keen to get on with it as I was. I would have left him in the car but for the noxious stink that had returned from the engine bay. So much for Monaco mechanics. Maybe the grand prix takes all the best ones. He'd barked like a sergeant major through the open window and I hurriedly retrieved him with a look that said 'behave'. He stared back with a look which said 'maybe.'

Sara led the way. Two floors down toward Gabriel's illicit store cupboard. Except we didn't get that far. Just past the landing to the lower ground floor we heard a groan. *Groan* didn't really do it justice. It exuded like an inarticulate expression of grief so mournful that it could have filled a graveyard, and resonated up the stairwell causing Angus to swirl behind my legs with a stifled whine. All of us stopped. I froze with my feet between steps, poised at a downward angle only slightly more erect than an athlete at the starting blocks. If I'd have been that athlete, and not me, I may have shimmied to view the gap down through the stairwell, to catch a glimpse of our would-be assailant. Instead, it took Filippo's urging nudge for me to peer between the flights.

It may have sounded like Frankenstein reborn but was actually a rather rotund character, red-faced in his struggle to negotiate the flight. He braced against his knees with every step, pushing and panting to ease his ascent. Fortunately, the knee thing drew his eyes firmly toward the floor, and he groaned up one more step oblivious to our presence. It may have been my paranoia alone that saw him kink his eyeline slightly upward.

I widened my arms and guided the troops back to the landing. I half strangled poor Sara when I grabbed her keycard and ran it through the slot, and she gasped behind me as I led us down the corridor. The first room along was a toilet. At least Filippo would feel comfortable.

I was heading in, away from discovery and disaster, kinked or otherwise, but Sara pushed us on to a room with a bronzed plaque glaring at eye-level from the door. 'Enzo Delgado – Research Director.' It didn't sound particularly relieving, but we piled into the darkness and eased it closed behind us.

Enzo's room had no windows. How could it? He'd secreted his activities twelve feet underground. The only natural luminance came from a light tube which descended through the ceiling directly above his desk. A thin fragment of moonlight shone across its surface and tempted our eyes to adjustment. It took a couple of minutes, which wasn't nearly long enough to prepare me for the sight spread out before me.

I didn't know that it was Beatrice. It could have been the meat counter at an international mini mart. The remnants of her corpse were laid across the trolley in ordered atrocity. Chops and joints and shanks all cured in sterile displays. She'd been covered in plastic, but the vague translucence couldn't obscure the savagery. Arms and legs and the top of her head had been removed. Worse, her face had been split, and one half sagged towards us in hopeless resignation. The eye may have stared, had it been present. Instead, a reddened void watched in fathomless blackness, longing for restitution. I heard Filippo turn to God for guidance, but if He spoke, we could not hear him in this place.

'Christ. It's her. Beatrice Delgado.' Sara filled the void.

'Jesus, Sara. How can you tell?'

'She used to look at me like that when she was alive.'

Filippo shuddered.

'Oh, my God, Sara, that's gross.'

'Yes, it is.' She gagged and turned away.

***

'This is it, isn't it? We can just ring the police, right now.'

'Yes, let's do it right now.' I offered. 'They won't bat an eyelid at the three of us sharing company with the desecrated corpse of Sara's ex-boss. The one that she's openly hated for the term of her employment.'

I didn't feel entirely comfortable objecting to Filippo's suggestion, but sometimes he placed his faith in the wrong places. I still flinched at my own nastiness, despite the heavy distraction of our situation, and was grateful that Sara interjected with an alternate option.

'Wait. Look at this.' A little green light was blinking from Enzo's desk.

Sara sat and opened the laptop. Its screen illuminated the room, and I tried not to look at Beatrice. The light shouted Delgado through an embellished reproduction of the sign from reception. Enzo's screensaver.

'It's on.' Said Sara simply.

She stretched her fingers and hovered above the keys, glancing behind her before descending upon them. Despite my best efforts I glanced behind too. Beatrice looked on with the rest of us.

'Windows key / E' she spoke aloud. The screen turned white, and a list of file names scrolled down its length. 'Fuck. It's *on*.'

Chapter 45

Intervention

Sara was absent. She'd been gone for fifteen minutes without a word or a movement other than her hands blurring across the keyboard and the constant flicker from a series of evolving displays.

'I'm ringing the police.' Filippo was finished waiting.

'No. Don't. I need to do this first.'

I've never seen a qualified typist in full flow, not even in my dreams, but I couldn't believe that any of them would move like Sara did. Her fingers hazed through the darkness so fast that my eyes couldn't have kept up even under the Saharan sun I'd shared with Guardian. And it wasn't just her movement. Her whole essence had changed. I'd barely noticed at first, but it felt as though she was filling the room.

Now, I'm getting carried away, and I suppose that last phrase needs explanation. Sara didn't 'expand', not even in a mystical sense. But you know that thing people say about fifties film stars – that they 'owned the room'? I suppose it was like that. She wasn't just *there* anymore; I was *in* her presence. As if her aura had passed through and enveloped me, and I was content to just watch, to understand what 'I need to do this first' actually meant.

It took another ten minutes to realise that Sara wasn't going to move, and that whatever she was doing, we were still stuck in a darkened laboratory with a dead body and the morning's throng getting ever closer.

'What about Hettie?' I found my voice.

***

The corridors were still lit by the understated glow from the fire exits. Understated it was, but still more than bright enough to see a target as large as our stout interloper, if he'd still been present. It had been almost half an hour and the silence hung like art - the type that Francisco de Goya may have painted – and we ventured nervously toward the staircase in silent subterfuge.

We'd left Sara and Angus inside Enzo's lab with the door ajar. A stripe of luminescence squinted through the crack, but we needed the key card and weren't sure that Sara could open the closed door without it. I could see Angus's shadow standing guard within the room as she worked.

Traversing the twenty odd feet to the lobby felt like a mile. I knew that it was my gurgling gut indelicately undermining my perception, but still never questioned whether my feeling toward Sara was similarly skewed. That had been different. Considering that we'd only spent a handful of hours together, it already felt as though we'd been teammates for years. Like when the full back for Real pinpoints a through ball for his wide man without ever needing to see his run. I hadn't asked Filippo whether he felt the same but hadn't really needed to. That night we all just felt different, and we all knew that we knew it. Even Angus.

I still wondered whether my boy jumped as high as I did when I heard the cistern flush as we crept past the toilet door.

Fuck knows what he'd done in there for thirty minutes, but the fat man chose that moment to push onto the corridor and into our faces.

There was no way that he'd washed his hands. He was still pulling his zip and froze halfway up, a Mexican standoff with olive green underpants. Twenty seconds later the zip was abandoned, and I was pinned against the wall with flubbery lips shouting at my face.

'Who the fuck are you?'

My mind always did strange things when I was scared. Sometimes it just shut down, like a rabbit in the headlights. Other times it would deflect me away to a different place deep within my head, with no real relevance to my current situation.

I'm not sure why my thoughts turned to his hands. One had my shirt scrunched into my neck while the other flapped at the end of an arm which pushed against my chest. Maybe I could have broken free had the thought crossed my mind, but I'd fixated on the notion of his pee-stained digits all over my tee shirt, and I gurgled a response that neither of us understood.

Filippo was being as useful as I was. He'd adopted the role of spectator at a wrestling match. At least at Madison Square Garden they'd shout at the butchery unfolding before them, spouting derisory objection as the bad guy held his victim's head before unleashing an elbow at its crown. Filippo's effort was tepid, to say the least.

'Stop it!'

I only saw my hero from the corner of my eye. A swathe of black and white snarling through the laboratory door. He bounded toward us, teeth bared and hackles raised. He was at us in an instant, and I heard the fat man howl. I still don't know which came first, the flash from the stairwell or the resounding thunder. I just remember the thud as my baby dropped to the floor.

We've all read articles about episodes of superhuman strength. Little miracles where a child lifts their dad's car to release him from underneath, or giant boulders rolled to access those injured in a landslide.

Ollie's hands slid from me in a swat. I grabbed his bulbous head and squeezed. His face contorted under my grip, and he began to squeal. I knew. Knew with utter certainty, that he would die. My mind saw his features collapse even before my hands tightened. There was no remorse, or pity, or doubt. My boy was shot, and Ollie was dead. It was fortunate for all of us that the butt of Santos gun hit my skull before the thought reached my hands.

I blacked out. A swirling maelstrom of nausea drew me down and I hit the floor.

The next moments happened around me. A scrabble followed a second gunshot. A crash, a bump and a crumpling of bodies before another pop and a dull thud as something soft clunked against a wall.

A chink of light reached my eye, and I could have risen, but I felt Angus lain against me. His side heaved slowly, and I laid my hand upon him. I heard his whimper and felt him push his body to me, and I turned to accept him. He was leaving. I whispered quietly amongst the tumult, and he heaved again. I felt his love, and then I felt his absence. The world raged on about me, but they could have cast the heavens down - I would not have moved. I knew it when he went, I felt him leave me, and a desert of nothing took his place.

***

'Loman. LOMAN! Are you alright?'

I rolled onto my back. Sara was speaking. She reached down and placed her hand on my shoulder. In the other she held an old-style Smith and Wesson, aimed unerringly toward a greasy looking spiv with Giorgio Armani jeans and cowboy boots. He was propped against a wall and crimson spilled to the floor from a wound in his knee. Something white peered through the red. I guessed that it was cartilage, since it frayed and flopped in a way that didn't seem like bone. He spoke contempt through expression, despite the pain which must have seared his nerves.

The fat man, Ollie, lay as flat to the floor as his form would allow. He rocked with his breath, but had no injuries that I could see. His unconscious rasp underscored the scene.

I looked for Filippo. He was knelt behind Sara. He smiled at me, and I didn't see the hole in him 'til I picked myself from the floor. A stain spread from his gut. I couldn't tell how far against the black of his robes, but his skin matched the grey of his beard, and his voice came in faltering gasps.

'I'm... so sorry... Loman.' He looked toward Angus.

Some people say that grief is a lonely emotion. What a pitiful understatement for the end of love. Their death rattles the foundations of existence. You writhe in obsession. Trapped in an endless loop of thoughts and memories, replaying images of your beloved in a hopeless attempt to keep them close. Praying that your run of imaginings can somehow keep them alive. Less than this would be betrayal - an acceptance and agreement to their end.

Such thoughts survive within a context of denial, and pain and yearning. Competing waves which crash against your heart in hateful resentment. It can take years to resolve such emotions. Some never do.

'Give me the gun.'

'What? What for?'

'Give me the fucking gun, Sara.'

I would have. I would have done it. If it had just been me and her, I would have had it from her and shoved it through their spines before pulling the trigger. But it wasn't just me and Sara, not quite yet.

'Loman. Don't. You need to help Hettie.' Filippo breathed the words, then closed his eyes.

I looked at Sara. 'We need an ambulance.'

'We need to help Hettie. It's what we came for. I can't do it, and neither can Filippo. It's down to you.'

'He's dying. We can't leave him.'

'*We* can't. *You* can.' Sara glanced back up the corridor. Light still shone from within its void. 'I think I know a way.'

Chapter 46

Trust

'Am I in trouble?' asked Angus, filled with worry and guilt. The first time he had hurt anyone, or anything for that matter. His contrition was absolute.

'No boy' replied God, 'I know that you didn't mean to hurt him. And Loman would have been hurt much, much more badly if you hadn't been so brave.'

Angus was relieved, but curious.

'Why do people hurt each other all the time?'

'Because people are not so wise as you, and always want more, even when they have enough.'

'But what's the point of that?'

'Exactly.' said God 'What's the point of that? You are a clever dog'.

Angus didn't understand exactly what God had meant, but trusted Him and knew that He would always make sure that he understood what was important. He had seen that people wanted more, craving the world as if they would starve without it. They never starved, not for that reason anyway, but never seemed to be happy. He was glad that he was a dog. God always answered dogs, because they always listened.

And with that, Angus sighed and stretched, and settled down to sleep, grateful for God's company, and the warmth of Loman's hand where it had come to rest gently upon his side.

Chapter 47
Advent

My head hurt like fuck. I could already feel my skin stretched around an expanding lump which throbbed in my scalp like a second heartbeat. I wanted nothing more than to drop onto the cold hard floor and succumb to grief, but it was my time to do something useful, and that hadn't come 'round for a long, long time.

Hettie and Gamma were no more than a staircase away. It was just two floors underground but felt like hell's seventh circle to my burgeoning headache. It had the odour of recycled air, and the hum of ventilation dampened my descent – down the staircase and into the synthesised fluorescence of a single corridor no more than ten metres long. Its aspect was stifling, and made worse by a thrusting artificial luminance which cast shadows down its length. The wall to my right was fitted with a row of three windows, each around one metre square. I reached the first and gawped inside.

Hettie faced inward. Her dreadlocks swept the glass as she cooed and gestured to her child. Her hands threw shapes, which transformed to an ill formed rabbit where the light rested upon the wall to her left. Gamma sat intrigued, upright and gurgly on a floor lined with foam squares and toys. A stuffed pink pig, sodden in drool, looked to the ceiling in silent resignation.

If you ever find yourself in an interrogation cell at the local police station, I've heard that there's a 'finger test' to check for the artifice of one-way glass. If you place your fingernail directly against the surface, there should be a gap of a few millimetres between it and its reflection. This indicates that the outer surface is painted with material which is opaque. If there isn't a gap, and your nail touches itself, chances are you're being watched by a bored junior officer from behind a copy of poliiziotto monthly. In this instance, the glass saw me coming and gave itself up with the words 'mirrored on opposite' etched along a bottom corner. It didn't even put up a fight.

There wasn't a cat in hell's chance that Gamma could have seen – or heard - me through that glass. He still raised his head and turned his gaze toward me, and when he did, I saw his eyes. They were not the eyes of innocence. They were brown and deep and filled with time, and I could have drowned in the history of them. They knew me. I felt that they'd followed me since before my birth and understood me with the wisdom of forever. It was a hundred lifetimes ago, but I saw Him through a millennia of dreaming, and had no doubt.

I looked, and there before me was a white cloud, and seated on the cloud was one like a son of man with a crown of gold on his head and a sharp sickle in his hand (Revelation 14:14).

I pushed at the door, barely three steps from my revelation. I'd thought that I would swoop the babe away, away from this place while grasping Hettie to pull her with us, but as I peered inside, the babe was gone, and so was she.

***

There, in the corner of the room, a slight figure leant against the surgical harshness of the marbled wall. The room enveloped Him, like He'd been swallowed by its impropriety. He didn't belong here, and the little pig looked bemused at His presence. He sagged heavily, as if the whole of the world weighed on His shoulders, and I thought to approach Him, but my conscience gripped me, for what I had done to Him.

He may have heard the door open, or my footsteps advance, but my decision to elude His gaze was lost as he rose and turned. His eyes were brown and full, and wet with sadness. They ached with knowledge, the fulfilment of betrayal, known and raking, and his body swayed. Emaciated. Bloodied. Exhausted. He was broken. Worse than I had left Him on the cross. My eyes fell to the tear in His side. It was ragged, and I wished that I had sharpened my spear. *I* had done this, and I reached for Him, but my guilt weighted me. I was frozen, frigid, but He touched my face, and slid His arms behind me. I held His weight, and we moved together, out and up toward the waiting stairs. And then he breathed.

He inhaled - slow and deep and endless – and I felt His shudder, as if He breathed the sins of humanity into Him. He stared upward, toward the world, and I felt Him pull me on. We stepped up, tread upon tread, and His weight eased from my shoulders as his muscles tightened - 'though He did not release me.

He breathed again - a ceaseless, unfathomable consumption, and I felt the earth breath with him. His legs straightened and I realised that I no longer carried him.

We passed the landing and continued to rise. Past Sara. Past Filippo. Past my Angus. An eternity of waiting condensed to seconds, until we emerged together onto the first floor of the Delgado Biomedical Research Establishment. Sun streaked through the building. Through meeting rooms and corridors, past offices and function space and alcoves with watercoolers. Even through the workspace of Beatrice Dalgado, until the dawn enveloped us, and I heard Him breathe again.

The hairs of His head were white as white wool, white as snow. His eyes were like a flame of fire, his feet were like burnished bronze, refined as in a furnace (Revelations 1:14-15).

His hair was not white, and His eyes did not burn. They were still brown, and they surveyed me with the love of a father. It was still Him, but no longer as I had seen him on the cross. He stood renewed; the Word become flesh. God had washed through Him, leaving no trace of pain. He stood as John had described him, with grace, but also power. The lion and the lamb combined. Blood stained him, but his wounds were gone. He was perfect.

I looked back toward my friends and heard a child's cry. Then the thump in my head grew louder and the world fell back to black.

Chapter 48

Resolutions

It's a common complaint. Spend the night in a hospital bed and you won't get much sleep. There's the noise, the brightness of the hallway lights, and an unending barrage of night-time interruptions. Medications, vitals checks, 'phone calls and the constant bustle of concerned carers. Essential, compassionate, but still bloody annoying. Fortunately, I was spark out, and missed the lot.

I finally opened my eyes at a change of shift. It must have been around eight AM. I felt the sun accost the bump at the base of my skull. It was a full twenty-four hours since I'd passed out on the floor of Delgado's offices.

I'd subconsciously turned to my side to take the pressure off my wound, and the heat from the morning rays was enough to prompt its stabbing throb all over again. I dropped my hand to the side of the bed, searching for a furry head or a wet nose, and the shroud of sleep slipped away.

I stilled my panic. The second coming - an ambitious storyline even for me. It really hadn't felt like a dream, but they never did. And if it had been, well, maybe other events had been too.

A face loomed around the foot of my bed. It moved in response to my shuffling ponderings.

Constable Gomez moved to my side and exhaled his exhaustion. 'Christ, Loman, it's about bloody time.'

'Where's Angus?'

Gomez placed a hospital chair quietly at the side of the bed. His face said that he was too tired for the conversation that was coming. It also told me what that conversation was going to be. Angus, my little boy, was gone. The police had found him, and 'addressed his disposal'. Gomez hadn't used those words, but I'd known what he meant. If I believed unequivocally that I could have joined him when I died, I would have left, without hesitation, in that very moment. But despite the stories I'd heard through my dreams, I still had doubts. And, of course, there was Filippo.

Filippo had survived. Just. Still, it didn't look good. The bullet had opened a tunnel through him which had grown from entry to the size of a grapefruit when it finally saw light. A nine millimetre may have offered some hope of survival, but the thirty-eight had blown his liver to pate and the shit from his intestines right through his abdomen. He'd been hooked into life support, but from what Gomez told me it was hospital etiquette rather than hope, and the word 'palliative' was written in capitals at the top of his charts. How he'd survived this long was a mystery that an over-worked medical team had little time to ponder.

Apparently, Ollie had decided that a long stretch inside Estremera Prison wasn't to his taste. He'd sung like the proverbial canary, but not until after he'd held the gun to Santo as Sara had prepared a series of injections, which she'd administered to Filippo at the scene. If leaning the barrel to his associate's throat with a cry of 'Shut the fuck up, for Christ's sake, man' was his final act of criminality, he'd certainly made the most of it, pressing down on his ruptured knee to reinforce his point. Whether it would absolve him sufficiently to earn eighteen to thirty months in a low security facility in Zaragoza remained to be seen.

Sara explained to the medics that she'd injected Filippo with painkillers and PRP – platelet rich plasma – to heal the wound. They'd looked at the hole in Filippo's back, then back at Sara with a combination of compassion and pity, before releasing her to the police. No-one checked beyond the empty bottles and syringes that Sara showed them before hurriedly bundling Filippo into the ambulance.

Senor Gaspar Escarra had 'phoned the police upon his arrival that morning. The local arm of El Pais had already taken his photograph for the paper, resplendent in his caretaker's overalls and military styled cap. They'd posed in reception under 'The Delgado Legacy', a clever twist of irony devised by the provincial journalist.

Sara was still 'helping with enquiries', but about to be released. Gomez was clear that at this point she genuinely was 'helping with enquiries' and that any thoughts of prosecution had dissipated with the dawning that everything she'd reported was actually true. Hettie had taken great delight in sharing her thoughts on Enzo, but it had taken his thumbprint on a bone saw to finally convince Perez of his involvement. The junior inspector was still explaining his approach to the station commander. Gomez wasn't being nearly so coy in articulating his dislike of Enzo or his activities. I guess he hadn't liked his biscuits.

Hettie, bless her, was for now still residing in that basement laboratory. The social worker allocated to her case had offered her accommodation at a local B & B while her case was investigated, and was appropriately embarrassed when eventually denied the funds to support a 'nondomestic'. Hettie thanked him for his efforts and explained that the world at large wasn't quite ready to open its doors to compassion. He'd bought her a 'phone from his own pay cheque.

Police forensics had taken swabs from Hettie and Gamma, and DNA tests were due back in a couple of days. Profiling was primarily to determine maternity, and fuck knew what they were going to make of the rest of the report.

Hettie returned to the lab while she waited. If the streets had once been an option, the weight of a growing Gamma slung around her shoulders dissuaded her. All corridor locks had been disabled, and only Enzo's lab remained inaccessible, locked and taped with police bunting. 'Keep out – crime scene.' It declared. No shit, Sherlock.

There was no sign of Enzo. The police had searched his home and his office and stripped both of the depravity of his ventures. His life was now logged within the local 'estacion de policia', and I imagined him a modern-day Mengele, smoking roll ups in a seaside chalet in Brazil.

For all of this information, and despite the warmth of Gomez and the depth of affection I'd developed for Sara and Hettie, it was still Fillipo that I wanted to see. Primarily, of course, I wanted some hope that he'd be ok, despite the fact that it was doubtful I'd get it. At some point, down the line, I hoped to talk to him about my episode with Gamma. How we'd climbed those stairs like a stumpy Jacob's ladder. Could all that really have emerged from a bump on my head? Hettie had been there. I guess she could tell me more.

But more than anything else, I wanted his company. To be with *him*, and to sit with someone who'd loved Angus as much as I did. I needed that most of all, and I didn't know of anyone else who could provide it.

***

El Retiro park was blooming. The pond where Angus had played was alive with budding lilies and reaching reedmace. I sat on our bench and ate Serranito Bocadillo, extracting a small piece of pork loin before devouring the final crust. I sucked tomato from it before dropping it to the ground beside me. I stayed for an hour before returning to the hospital.

Filippo was on the ground floor, in intensive care. It was tucked into a quiet corner, at the junction of two parts of a quadrangle which enclosed a covered courtyard containing a patch of grass and a ring of seats. Cyprus warblers would hop their way through drainage channels to sit inside, and empty the feeding station that the porter filled with seed and suet each morning.

'He's too ill for visitors' they'd said, but I stole scrubs from the laundry trolley outside operating room four. The legs hung around my ankles and a spotting of blood had peppered one cuff. It took less than three minutes to reach Filippo's ward, but the world gave me more validation in that walk than in the rest of my life combined.

Filippo was sleeping. There were no needles, no drips, no ventilators, just three sticky patches placed on his chest and the beep, beep, beep of a lone monitor. His hair was scraped back from his face, and he wore a blue gown below the bed covers. He looked small without his vestment.

His eyes flickered as I sat. 'How the flying fuck are you still alive, soldier?' He asked, before floundering from his sleep.

'Take Hettie home.'

It was the only thing we shared before he drifted back beyond my reach.

I tried to visit three more times. Each time I was turned away by a starched ward clerk with a penchant for protocol. On my third attempt she stopped me at the exit and informed me that his condition was 'stable'. She spoke the word with the upward lilt of a question, in the way that Australians say just about everything. From her, it sounded like surprise.

I was back on the bench at El Retiro when Hettie rang.

'Loman? It's me.'

Now, take my word for this; never bawl your eyes out in a public park as the world wonders by. It's an invitation to apathy. I suppose you can't blame people – they've been conditioned to turn away from the suffering of others by at least half the globe's politicians. The most I got was a disapproving 'tut' from a late teen in a bow tie and a costly haircut.

I wasn't sure whether it was Hettie's voice, Filippo's suffering or Angus' absence which finally turned on the taps, but unrolling the gauntness of human fellowship isn't good for the soul. Grief doesn't leave us with nothing, far from it. A thick tide of emotion overwhelms us, crashing and frothing against the void left by lost love. Except it's not actually lost, is it? It's still there – we just can't work out what we're supposed to do with it anymore. I pondered this as my fellow travellers on God's earth scrolled past with a hurried disregard, and it was only Hettie's voice shouting down the line that drew me back.

'*Loman? Are you there?*'

'Yes. I'm here.'

'Good. Do you have the keys? The keys to Filippo's car?'

I did. In fact, they'd bothered me every time I'd sat down for days. It bothered me more when I remembered them sticking in my side as I lay with Angus that last time. I must have shoved them in my pocket as I'd retrieved him from the car. I pulled them from my trousers. Their keyring was embellished with a carved wedge of yellow-heart hardwood with the phrase 'I'll always brie yours' printed over it. Filippo was a weird fucker.

'Loman? Loman, for fuck's sake, are you *there*?'

'Sorry. Yes. Sorry. I have the keys, yes.'

'Good. I'm outside Enzo's offices with Gamma. Can you pick me up?'

***

Hettie stood at the roadside with baby, a bag and a child's car seat. The seat was wrapped in clear plastic with a tag which boasted 'non-flammable – EU approved.' I suppose her Amazon card was still working. I hugged them both with a vigour which made Hettie gasp. 'Flying fuck!' she opined. Filippo's traits were catching on.

'I'll need to strap him in' she said, and crouched into the back seat with her ass in the air. After a few moments, 'Crap. Can you help with this?'

I entered from the other side and pulled the straps around the belt restraints. They clicked into place and Gamma took residence on his new throne. He gurgled and wheezed and smiled and dribbled and Hettie looked happy. The pink pig that he carried dripped down his clothing.

Hettie took the passenger seat, and I was going to ask, 'Where to Ma'am?' in my best Yankee drawl, but a strand of hair caught my throat and I coughed.

A small tuft of white fur had stuck to my shirt. I must have picked it up from the back seat. I touched it gently, then stroked it where it sat, and my fingers rubbed across my heart. The rear of the car was covered with it, pulled and moulted as my boy had milled and circled through our journeys, and I cried like a second child as Hettie held my hand.

'I want to go home' I said, blinking tears and sniffing snot back through my nose.

'Me too,' she agreed.

Chapter 49

Springtime

The public face of the Vatican Library was still open to anyone who could document their qualifications and research needs.

It was once described in 'Vatican news' as encompassing *a silence that is memory, a treasure chest of knowledge, a yearning for the infinite. This is the air one breathes in the Vatican Apostolic Library and the Vatican Apostolic Archives.* It contains 75,000 codices, 1.1 million printed books and is a research metropolis for history, law, philosophy, science and theology.

Hettie strolled through the Belvedere Courtyard on her way to the library building. It was an academic monument, erected and configured in 1589. The up-lit ceilings which oversaw the expansive wealth of knowledge were decorated with ornate frescoes depicting every topic from the birth of creation to the Tower of Babel. It was a familiar cruise, one which her graffitied boots could almost have made by themselves.

She could see her old 'study' seat from the library reception. Set atop the reception counter, a printed list was propped against a pile of check-in books, purveying admission rules in a gilt framed diatribe.

Readers admitted to the library *must*, upon arrival:

1. Present their card to the porter who will electronically record their arrival.

2. Receive from the porter the assigned electronic key number for their locker.

3. Place in the locker all personal belongings which are not pertinent to study.

4. Electronically register their arrival at the distribution desk

5. Enter their name in block capitals in the daily register, opposite their key number.

6. Choose the place where they intend to sit, according to the specific rules of the reading rooms.

7. Return to the distribution desk and enter the number of the place they have chosen next to their name.

Hettie breathed a sigh and gave thanks that her predecessor had possessed the pragmatism to allow her access, and determined that she would be just as generous when someone equally needy came to the establishment looking for help.

She took her seat at the counter and twisted her badge to expose its text to her face. It pulled at her cotton blend frock and a tiny hole appeared where the pin pierced the fabric. She knew it would run, but she didn't care. '*Hetty Eddy, Junior Archive Support.*' It could just as easily have been '*Queen of Sheba*'.

Her new job had facilitated a new home. It was tiny, and black mould infringed upon a corner of the plastic bath. The kitchen counter backed around the living room, and the hum from the freezer reverberated in competition with an ancient CRT television which had proven too heavy to move. It was all still bigger and warmer than a sleeping bag.

Hettie had spent the previous week rotating between her new flat and the Church of St. Francis. Any remnant of illness had disappeared with the laboratory, and had been replaced with a vibrant glow which suggested a fortnight on the beaches of Sardinia. The mirror told her that she could have made her living selling Vitamin D, had the Vatican not gotten to her first.

Her first paycheque was not due for a month, but Human Resources had provided an advance which covered her deposit, rent and groceries through the interim period. It was extraordinarily generous, and she suspected that a fairy Godmother was overseeing her employment. There was even enough left over for a meal at the posh restaurant with the blue awnings near the Ponte Sisto Bridge. A one-time treat to celebrate her burgeoning wealth.

***

The Tiber runs for two hundred and fifty-two miles in a southerly direction, twisting through a series of scenic gorges and broad valleys. It begins as a bubbling mountain brook on the Western slopes of the Apennine mountains before taking on a yellow hue as it clears slumps of tawny clay from the landscape. It visits Rome before entering the Tyrrhenian Sea near Ostia Antica.

Hettie selected a table overlooking the river. Hop-on cruise boats drifted placidly along its gentle motion, with a rich tapestry of creeds and cultures milled across their upper decks.

Her table was set with a white linen tablecloth whose weave shamed the green and yellow cotton in the dress she'd chosen for the day. A chunk of boot poked wilfully beneath the fabric.

The menu shone with a palate of gastronomic colour. Truffles, Arancini, Fiorentina Steak. Ossobuco, Cicchetti and Burrata. It sounded beautiful, and each dish was presented with an elaborate description of the ingredients and their source. The front page was embellished with the name of the restaurant and a white circle containing the year, two stars and the word MICHELLIN in capitals.

Hettie peeked nervously at nearby tables, seeking a glimpse of their choice. For the most part she could not discern their order. It all looked lovely, but only the steak identified itself as rivers of pink flooded the plate with a thrust from a knife.

She scanned the pages again. There were a dozen meals adorned with a little green 'V', the first obstacle overcome, at least. She'd probably eaten half the choices before, but the flowery eulogy which accompanied them may as well have been Greek. She raised her eyes and looked for the boats, but they'd disappeared past the Isola Tiberina, and she felt her heart sink. This place was for the Enzo's of the world, and she looked down at her boots and wished she'd stuck with double veggie from the pizzeria off the Via del Corso.

'Good afternoon, signorina, would you like something to drink?'

She'd wanted to treat herself. A raspberry and passion fruit martini, or a cranberry sour. Something with an umbrella. At the least a rim encrusted with salt.

'Could I just have a coke please?'

'Of course.'

The coke arrived. There was a slice of lemon poking through its surface. She'd hoped for lime.

'Are you ready to order, signorina?'

'I'm sorry. Could I have a few moments more, please?'

'Of course.'

The truffles sounded good but were beyond her budget. To be fair, almost all of the prices frightened her. She daren't even look at the wine list.

Fuck. The waiter was back.

'I'm sorry. I just don't know. I should just leave.'

In the broad context of most lives, a bad experience in a restaurant means nothing. A lost hour to shrug away with a kebab from the take-away and a bottle of Cabalie red from the supermarket. To Hettie, it felt like shit. A stretch-too-far for a single mother with a sixties frock and a fucked-up life. She was a fraud. A fraud with no rightful place in this, the *real* world.

The waiter stared.

The streets were her place. It was obvious now. At least there she was primed for people's stares. In a few days they'd find her out at the library, too, and she'd be back to begging for space at the corner table in the horology section.

'Please, signora. Just give me a moment.'

She could have left. Escaped to normality. But she owed them for the fucking coke and waited while the waiter returned. When he did, he'd brought reinforcements.

His associate wore a pristine jacket, all white and doubled at the breast. His tall white hat kinked slightly to the right, and he smiled kindly before pointing to a chair at the table.

'Excuse me, Signora. May I sit?'

She didn't *mean* to be rude, but her street defence had rolled across her, and she scowled her discomfort at his geniality.

'What for?'

He smiled again.

'Sorry.'

'That is quite alright, Signora, but I cannot allow you to leave this establishment so sad. If you will allow it, I shall describe to you the beauty of every dish available. They are all magnificent, '*but I make the ossobuco.*' The final phrase was whispered, with a wink and a touch of his fingers to his nose. He grinned with the allure of sunshine, and she noticed his eyes. They were the palest blue that she'd seen, both the same, not one of each.

'My name is Jose, and I will be your chef for the evening.'

Chapter 50
Inside

Italy does not have a bail system. The second paragraph of Article 27 of the Constitution states: 'A defendant shall be considered not guilty until a final sentence has been passed'. The accused (imputato) will only stay arrested if they were caught red-handed, or if they are at risk of fleeing, committing another crime, destroying evidence, or creating false evidence. Unfortunately for Santo, Constable Gomez had informed the judge that he was at risk of all four.

He'd been transported directly from hospital to the Alcala Meco prison, in the municipality of Alcala de Henares. Since opening in1981 it had achieved media notoriety for housing such dark characters as Mario Conde, Jose Maria Ruiz-Mateos and Mariano Rubio Jimenez. Each of these infamous individuals had been found guilty of crimes of fraud and deception from a position of high authority; Jimenez was the governor of the Bank of Spain between 1984 and 1992. It was also famous for allowing a double hitman to walk directly out of the front door over Christmas 2023 in an inexplicable lapse of security sufficiently alarming to make international news. If it hadn't been for the hole in his knee, the ineptitude would have seen Santo skipping through the entrance gates with the joyful anticipation of a cheerleading try-out.

Santo was well aware of the rules of the prison community. He'd had reason to play by them before.

'The inmate code' encapsulated the values adopted by the prison population to dictate the 'dos' and 'don'ts' of convict behaviour. At its heart was the philosophy that prisoners stand in unity against the prison guards, an approach which Santo cherished like a Texan loves his guns. Each prison has its own variation on proper behaviour, but the generics were recorded in a study carried out in New Jersey by Gresham Skyes, the American sociologist.

Never rat on an inmate, don't by nosy, don't have loose lips, do your own time, keep your promises, don't weaken or whine. All guidelines that were identified by Sykes for surviving incarceration. If Santo had been present at the point of the study, there may have been one more. Don't be an unadulterated cunt, and certainly don't be one when you're hobbling on sticks without a free hand to defend yourself. And one more thing, not so much a rule as good life advice. Never run your mouth in an environment where the whole population has twenty-four hours a day to do nothing but think up ingenious ways of fucking up your existence.

'What are you in for?'

Yet more originality from another senseless shithead. Santo had hoped for so much more. It could be six months 'til his case was heard and there wasn't even a fucking pool table. At least this cunt looked low brow enough to play with. He scraped his crutch feet forward and expanded to his full height, grinning through the pain which seared up his femur.

'I am innocent. My only crime is living freer than the establishment would wish. Ha.'

'That's not what I asked you. What are you in for?'

Santo knew that it would come at some point. He was a fish – a new prisoner – and initiations were always painful. He'd seen how inmates could be broken. Even those on crutches. Not by your more average prisoner – there was no reputation in beating on a cripple – but there were always bullies.

'I could tell you, Signore, but you have the look of FBI. Perhaps you should just go fuck yourself.'

Santo virtually shouted the letters, at least loud enough for his block mates to seek the entertainment. They gathered around like schoolboys. Joel was not impressed.

Joel *looked* like a lifer. His neck trunked from his shoulders in a mass of veiny sinew which had grown wider than his ears. His eyes held the deadened detachment of complacent violence, sunken deep within a brow which was no more than four inches below the crown of his head. Apparently, he was also a man of limited vocabulary, and stood before Santo in mute contemplation until his would-be victim had no choice but to sink back onto his sticks. Santo's legs sagged, but he'd drawn the attention of his peers, and backing down was not an option.

'What the fuck has it got to do with you?'

'Last time. What are you in for?'

'Fuck you. What're *you* in for? Looking like Frankenstein's bride? You must have got life.'

He knew that it would hurt, but pain wasn't really the point. He'd never read the Sykes report but understood that whining would underscore the remainder of his stay with disrespect and contempt. He threw a crutch to one side and held the other forward, rubber foot thrust toward Joel's face.

'Ha. Bring it, bitch.'

But Joel didn't bring it. He just turned his copious neck and looked toward a corner cell on the first landing, before meandering up the iron staircase toward the passive face which beckoned him.

***

'Well?'

'He's a prick. Wouldn't say what he's in for. If you ask me, he's a skinner.'

Joel leant against the cell door and awaited instruction. His Cappo seemed vaguely disinterested. He always did while pondering the fate of new arrivals. If they were lucky, they'd be ignored, and move straight to the treading regime of their sentence oblivious of internal politics, until they or their yard mates contravened some unwritten directive. But Cappo didn't like skinners, and had seen one slip through his fingers just two days ago.

The man was a rapist. He'd taken some teen as she'd bolted home, filled with joyous relief at her successful recital of Debussy's Syrinx. 'Grado professional', she'd finally done it, and rushed to tell her papa how she'd conquered its gestural motifs. 'He broke my flute' were her only words as he'd picked her from the street barely two minutes afterwards.

Cappo hadn't known the girl, but all men need their status – especially in prison – and what could be lower than a skinner? Cappo had planned his retribution with ruinous enthusiasm. The whole prison enjoyed such acts, and his originality, as much as his brutishness, kept the Joels in their place. Gelding was not enough, and *this* skinner would be sitting down to piss, with just two hooks to wipe the dribble from his ass.

He'd been transferred out hours before the work bell which would have seen his sentence delivered.

Cappo simmered, and Joel knew what was coming. He'd seen him take a man's fingers for nothing, just some random act that undermined his mood. The four digits had peeled from his hand as the blood lost its suction. Thunder still rolled from his gaze over an hour after the gore had been mopped from the floor. Wrong time, wrong place, wrong Cappo.

Joel liked his fingers and had no intention of losing them to the indeterminable twistings of a psychopath. Better to sate the man's needs than see them fester. And the new guy *was* a prick.

***

Living conditions within Italian prisons are 'cosy.' For the less gregarious inmate, the seconds drag by in noisy purgatory. Santo had been in several institutions. Some prisons within the European Community were designed to provide accommodation which mimics the free world. Norway offered single cells with a minimum footprint of twelve square metres, the size of a second bedroom in a four-bed detached on a Surrey high street. Perhaps he'd visit the county, once his sentence was over.

In most Italian prisons, inmates survive in communal cells designed for four to six prisoners. 'Design' in this context meant bunk beds three storeys high and makeshift cabinets made of cardboard. It wasn't unusual for each cell to house double the number of people that were originally intended. It *was* unusual, if not virtually unheard of, for a convict to find themselves in the peaceful ecstasy of their own company.

Santo propped his sticks against the frame of the bed and laid back. He could survive the months to his trial with just a few of these interludes.

He relaxed. He hadn't yet been allocated a date for his hearing, but remained hopeful. The gun was unregistered, and the handle *must* have been laden with at least three sets of fingerprints. Perhaps he'd get a year. Maybe even less, he'd only killed a dog. Then, who knew? Maybe he'd be back in that café with a view of the Trevi fountain and the pale-skinned girls in their micro dresses. They'd be yellow or pink, with a brown rope belt tightening the waist and dragging the skirt an inch too high. If he was lucky he'd have a snub-nosed Smith and Wesson tucked inside his jacket, and a Marlboro Gold swirling smoke to the ceiling above his head.

His eyelids drooped as his pain subsided. His wound was serious, but prison is prison and he'd been given paracetamol. Two tablets four times per day, and he'd just received his dose from the nurse. She must have fancied him, since she'd doubled up with ibuprofen. They'd been small and grey and unfamiliar – prison issue she'd said - and he relaxed into the mattress in a semi-fog. He hardly felt the springs where they pushed at his back, or the pull on his stiches when his leg sunk flat to the surface of the bed.

Joel stood quietly at the door as Capo pushed past him. He didn't enjoy his role, but this one was a mouthy cunt. He may even have *been* a skinner.

He still turned his back as Capo pulled the hatchet from his jacket and stepped forward.

Chapter 51

Home

How many dogs make a pack? Three? Four? Ten?

At least a dozen dogs formed a lazy semi-circle at the foot of Filippo's cabinet. A host of angels - predominantly gaudy trinkets from the tourist markets - were placed inside, but far from being 'displayed', the angels were dispersed about the central box in a haphazard scattering. Some angels were chipped, and one was absent a wing. They displayed like a boxer's grin.

Father Connor Calleary sat beside me on the bunk below Ginger.

'Why *do* they do that?' he asked, lilting his Galway dialect into questions.

'God lives there.' answered Ginger from above, seeing no particular need to explain further.

The dogs were not alone. Interspersed between them was an assembly of cats, rabbits, mice and a finger count of other furries, each content to loaf in the company of the others. If there'd been a donkey, the scene could have played like a nativity.

Father Connor had been sent by Leonardo. The old bishop had taken to the young ordinand, just as he'd taken to Filippo several decades earlier. He even had a beard, 'though Connor's was black and trimmed tightly to a narrow jaw. The day I met him, he'd told me that he'd grown it to balance his nose. I didn't tell him, of course, but it hadn't worked. Fuck, no.

I'd thought that my dreams may have ended with Gamma on that staircase, but last night I'd REM'd right through Gingers best efforts. They *had* changed, though - my adventures no longer occurred in the past. In fact, I didn't seem to *do* much at all. Each night I'd sit on that seat in Retiro Park and talk. A gentle conversation with Jesus Christ – my grown-up version - who'd tell me His thoughts like I'd usurped John as his favourite apostle. His thoughts. His wishes, and His plans, and the things that He wanted me to tell the world.

Tomorrow I was going to see Hettie and His baby alter-ego. She'd promised to catch up with me and Ginger despite her fledgling relationship with a culinary gourmet. It made for an interesting proposition.

The daylight throbbed with grunts and footsteps and the whispering howl of a cafetiere, just as it always had. Now, though, people stepped between paws and tails on their way to queue for their morning shits. In between ablutions, most sat or knelt or otherwise meshed with their animal brothers and sisters. They all seemed to like it.

'Heavens, it's a circus in here.' Connor blurted as a large Newfoundland plonked itself across his feet. It must have weighed seven stones and fur puffed from its tail as it sat.

'I wonder what Filippo would say?'

Connor watched as man and beast radiated from the slovenly angels. A man in a patched-up Harrington and unmatched shoes sat with a tiny tabby on his lap. A lady in her seventies cried as an ancient ginger tom rubbed against her legs, and the Newfoundland moved between people shedding hair and slaver over everything.

'I don't think he'd say anything.' I said, 'I think he'd just watch.'

Connor looked down as a puppy with a hollow belly stole his croissant. He didn't say anything either.

'I don't believe this man is just twenty-four.' I thought, before wondering how big his nose would be once he'd reached Leonardo's age.

I'd rung Sara as soon as I arrived home. 'Sara, it's for you.' shouted Gabriel, who'd picked up. I knew better than to ask about *that* situation.

Filippo was still in hospital, from what she knew. She'd snuck in the day after I left and viewed him sleeping through the ward's windows. The same ward clerk slipped her covert updates until her manager shifted her to Emergency Admissions.

Ginger was stirring. He was the same Ginger as he'd always been. He was still unkempt, with lank hair and dirty feet, and his flatulence would have shamed a herd of heifers. He still barely spoke, but now, when he did, I listened.

His animals followed him into the kitchen, and the clank of food bowls saw tails wag and a snake of drool enter the room behind him. Once they were done, they trotted back to Filippo's cabinet and their adulation. All of them, except one. A long-haired collie, slightly squat and slightly scruffy, eyed me with a questioning look that my indignant self believed was quite unwarranted.

'What's your name?' I asked, and she pursed her lips in an 'Elvis' curl. It spread to both sides until she looked like she'd lost her dentures, and her head cocked in curious suspicion. When she was ready, she relaxed her face and dropped behind my ankles with a thud and a 'humph'. Within minutes, she was snoring like a miniature Ginger.

'That's Duma.' he said.

When I looked around, I realised that the circle of animals had grown, and that Duma had taken me within it.

That night, as I slept, I asked Jesus to look after Angus.

Chapter 52

The beginning

Three became four. Hettie, Connor, Ginger and I sat around the tiny table in Filippo's vestry. It was still bedecked in blankets. Ginger kept them in place as a medley of creatures swept through its comforting induction. Most of them now milled clumsily around our feet, and Hettie appeared in her element. She literally squealed as a skinny kitten rubbed across her jeans and she picked the mewling fuzz onto her lap. It purred its joy and clawed happily at her dreadlocks where they tumbled down her smock. Ginger nodded his approval, silently thinking what a D'artagnan she was going to make.

Duma demonstrated no respect for Hettie's position as newcomer, let alone her status as mother to a deity. She adopted her - as she had with me - and had followed her entry through the building with the vigour of a puppy. When Hettie sat, she stretched herself as far as she could under the table, attempting to lay across all eight feet.

Gamma held court on a blanket on the floor. He had proven even more appealing than a cupboard of angels and giggled as the procession of creatures gave reverence, licking and bunting against him as he dribbled his reciprocated love upon them.

Connor had provided refreshments. I'd become used to Filippo's choice of cannoli and olives, and Connor's more Anglican selection was an uncommon delight. I was accosted by a malteser which he launched with some force as I reached for the last of the swiss roll. It popped off my cheek as he swept in to steal the jammy sponge before shovelling it into his hole in one go, spraying me with crumbs as he laughed them out of his mouth and over my face.

'Forgive me Lord, my need was greater' he said and smiled hopefully, awaiting my response. I picked jam from my eyebrow.

'What should we do?' I asked.

'Cards?' replied Connor, 'I'm sure I could find a pack in the sacristy.' He grinned again. Another attempt to entreat a retort. I must have disappointed him.

'That's not what I meant.'

I felt a wrapper bounce off my face where he flicked it across the table.

'Maybe, Loman, we don't need to *do* anything.'

Faith is weird. You'd think that someone like me, who – in their dreams at least - had experienced God's will first hand, would be relaxed in the face of this mortal life, but it's stark realities still frightened me. We each have our ragged mile to walk, but where exactly does it lead? I believed that there was *something* after - but I still didn't know what. Perhaps it was a conversation for later. For the moment, I just felt impotent.

Connor was far more relaxed about the whole thing. In his comparatively short life he'd developed a languid comfort with his inevitable demise. He'd already stated his delight at being able to tell Saint Peter that he'd met Gamma and His mother - and looked forward to engaging him in a long and detailed conversation. I still had questions for the present.

'What about the seals?'

'Seals? Where am I supposed to put *them*?' Ginger piped up.

'Not those seals. The seals in Revelations. The ones that need to be broken before Christ's second coming.'

And there you go. I'd broken a seal of my own. For all that had happened, and despite our residence in His house, none of us had actually mentioned the potential of Gamma's birth directly. I think we were *all* relieved once I'd actually broached the topic. It certainly enlivened Connor. He swallowed his chocolate and clasped his hands together like he was going to pee. His excitement hit pause as Gamma did pee, and Hettie rose to attend his needs.

'Ok, Loman. What's your theory?' Connor waited.

But I didn't have a theory, just questions. I felt fortunate that Father Connor Calleary had the empathy to see through my silence, and he piped up with a theory of his own. Or at least the questions that may lead to one.

'Right. The verses in the bible are clear that when He returns, the whole world will know. That all nations will see Him descend to earth on the clouds in the sky. Have we actually seen that, or anything at all that could fit that description?'

He looked around the table. No-one answered.

'So, in that case, have we seen any evidence of the breaking of the seals at all?'

Still nothing. Hettie dropped a clean Gamma back to the floor and looked uncomfortable. I just felt confused. Connor pushed on.

'Right then, let's get back to basics. I'll lose the flowery language within the book of Revelations and try to keep things simple.

The world is due an apocalypse. This apocalypse is to be held back by seven seals, until a time that has been pre-determined by God.

Christ's return to earth is preceded by the breaking of these seven seals. Now, we should remember that His return will ultimately lead to a 'New Jerusalem', a new world of paradise for everyone, but before that can happen the old world must be wiped away. That happens *through* the apocalypse – the spread of pestilence and disease and famine across the earth, delivered by four horsemen. The four horsemen are released by the breaking of the first four seals. Keeping up?'

'No.'

'Good. Seal five signals the lament of the good people of the earth, pleading with God for His judgement on evildoers and that He prevents them from continuing with their crimes.

Number six handles the physical destruction of the earth. The wiping away of the past to make way for something new.

The breaking of the seventh signals a silence in Heaven. Now, this bit frightened the bejesus out of me as a child – I thought that it represented an emptiness in God's home - but it's actually a celebration. Heaven is silent because the angels are gone. But they've gone because they're all at Jesus's side, praising him as he rebuilds the world in accordance with God's plan.'

Gamma lay on the floor on his blanket. A great slobbery bulldog lay next to him, as grim and jowly as Winston Churchill, rolling on its back exhorting a gurgling speech which was half bark and half wheeze. The infant listened intently until the dog had finished before breaking into a grin, rolling onto his front and grasping at the old mutt's face with tiny fingers.

'The thing is' finished Conner, 'it's Jesus who breaks the seals. Doesn't look like that little one could break wind.'

'You're wrong there.' Hettie interjected, and Gamma raised a brow. It must have been co-incidence.

'Still, is there actually any evidence of anything like this happening? Regardless of who opened what?'

Finally, I had something to offer.

'Yes, of course there is. The evidence is everywhere. Plagues and storms and all manner of cataclysm. It's getting worse every year. *We've* made it worse every year. Just because we've gotten used to it doesn't mean that it isn't apocalyptic. Factory farming, cosmetics testing, global warming, overcrowding. People have been fucking the world over since the first time Christ was on it. Why *wouldn't* He want to start over?'

Gamma stopped his chortling. If it had been one of us, I'd have guessed I'd touched a nerve, but His distraction lasted a millisecond before Churchill woofed and their conversation began over.

Hettie was frowning. 'Just to remind everyone, Gamma *is* just a baby. Look at Him. He's *my* baby. I don't think I want Him saddled with a crown of thorns. And for Christ's sake, all this DNA - it's only *blood,* isn't it? He can't actually *do* anything except shit himself and puke down my back.'

A long pause was followed by 'Maybe we should just wait.'

Ultimately, what did any of us know? Me, Ginger, Connor and Hettie. Not even an experienced priest among us. We were just people, jabbering away like we could understand God's will. I think we all felt embarrassed.

'We can't do *nothing*, can we?'

'Waiting isn't doing nothing. It's waiting.'

***

The next morning, Ginger had added to our numbers. A box of black kittens that had been left at the side of the Via del Giubbonari. The animals were spilling from the church. They covered the alter, the nave and the sanctuary. They lazed in the aisle and lounged in the vestibule.

Ginger opened the door to the vestry. Several spilled on into the churchyard, sniffing or scratching or gamboling or whatever else animals do when they're happy. The hostel visitors had mostly gone for the day, but we knew that they'd be back at sundown, to find solace from the harshness of the world.

Duma shifted. Not unusual – she'd fidget like an old man on a hard seat. Her head appeared on my lap from under the table - a smiling, bright eyed, pointy eared joy. She barked.

'What is it girl?' I asked, and was answered by a round of woofs and meows and squeaks and whatever noise it is that rabbits make. Someone was coming.

Maybe it was la polizia. We *had* slipped from their questioning with half the case left hanging. Maybe they'd found Enzo. Maybe they'd lost Santo. Maybe they'd sacked Perez.

Connor pushed back from the table as the door frame filled.

'Can I help you?'

'I fucking hope so.'

It wasn't the police. That may still come, but for now it seemed as though their authority had been replaced by a greater one.

Connor didn't know the face, but I did, and so did Hettie. Ginger did too, but shrugged it off like the most natural thing in the world, and returned to his animals.

Hettie's face crinkled. I saw her squint, before her eyes grew wide. The face *was* the same, but this man looked young - his stance solid and strong, as it must have been twenty years ago. He glowed with vitality and stood straighter than the colonnades which supported his church. He didn't even have shit in his beard.

'*Filippo*?' I asked, and as if to confirm it, Filippo replied.

'Ok, you fuckers. Let's get the fuck started' he said.

Chapter 53

Epilogue

'Watch therefore, for ye know not what hour your Lord doth come....be ye also ready, for in such an hour as ye think not, the son of man cometh.' (Matthew 24.42:44).

The morning sun pushed the shadows from my eyes, and I emerged onto that familiar park bench with the Palacio de Cristal at my back and the soothing splash of a crested fountain in my ears. A crumb of seasoned pork still sat beside the bench, and my empty sandwich wrapper twitched with the breeze on the seat to my left.

He sat to my right.

'You know, Loman, the last time I entered this world the love of God's creatures filled a stable. This time it's going to fill the planet.'

'What? I don't get it. You're not supposed to be here yet, are you? What about the seals?'

'Ah, don't get hooked into what you've read, Loman. All books are authored by people.'

'What, even that one?'

'Yep, even that one.'

'But it's supposed to be the word of God. I read it.'

'Yes, you probably did. People wrote that bit too.'

He gestured at the seat. The sandwich pack was full again. I passed one to him.

'Pork? You're kidding me, right?.' He grinned.

A cloud passed overhead, and the sky moved behind it. When the cloud had gone, the evening sun cast light on the horizon - a golden crown for the earth - while a crescent moon hung like a sickle.

'What do you remember?'

'Just my dreams.'

'Good.'

'Good? Is it? But where did I come from?'

'Does it matter, Loman? Do you care, really? Surely it's what you've become that's important. You've got a big role coming, you know. John says good things about you. He said that you should have his gift. We're going to need it, while I grow.'

'What? What gift?'

He laughed again.

'Don't worry, Loman. You have work to do, but for now, there's someone who's been waiting to see you.'

My Lord moved aside, and there he was. He'd been sitting with a grin broader than seas, and rose to greet me with a helicopter wag and a puppy yip. He padded on the spot for an instant until leaping upon me in a flash of pink tongued rapture. I held his face and kissed his fuzzy snout, and saw that his eyes were framed in black, a little like a panda. Otherwise, he was all white, except for the dots on his paws and a thin saddle of black across his back.

Some time later I awoke to the sounds of Filippo brewing the morning's coffee. Duma stretched and Ginger coughed up something which gurgled, and the first light of summer shone upon me from a room without windows.

The end

Printed in Great Britain
by Amazon

57489407R00169